D1106620

SIR GIBBIE

GEORGE MACDONALD

SIR GIBBIE

EDITED AND WITH A FOREWORD BY

ELIZABETH YATES

E. P. DUTTON & CO., INC. NEW YORK

First Printing August 1963
Second Printing January 1964

Published simultaneously in Canada by Clarke, Irwin & Company Limited, Toronto and Vancouver

Library of Congress Catalog Card Number: 63-15762

ACKNOWLEDGMENT

Quotations in Foreword are from *George MacDonald and His Wife* by Greville MacDonald, Copyright, 1924, Allen & Unwin, Ltd.

FOREWORD

Some years ago a friend asked, "Have you ever read *Sir Gibbie?*"

"No," I answered, wondering what I had missed.

"Oh, but you must."

And I meant to read *Sir Gibbie,* but the book had long been out of print and there seemed no copy easily available in either bookstore or library.

Then, one day, my friend quietly took down *Sir Gibbie* from her shelf and put it into my hands. It was an old copy, small of print, and worn. She did not say, even then, why I should read it or what it was about; but, now, reading it became inescapable.

"You'll like it," she said patiently, "and don't be put off by the Scotch dialect. It's more readable than it looks."

But I was put off by it and found myself during the first fifty pages setting the book down many times. Then, suddenly it seemed, I reached the point where Gibbie—the ragged little baronet, "the foundling of the universe," the waif with shaggy golden hair under which "looked out two eyes of heaven's own blue, and through the eyes looked out something that dwells behind the sky and every blue thing"—became real and imperative. He took me by the hand, as I read, and led me through the streets of the old gray Scottish city and up the slopes of Glashgar where he ran through the heather with the sheep.

The book defied hasty reading but it implored constant reading, and from the moment it caught me up I was conscious of a breadth and depth and height of feeling such as I had not known for a long time. It moved me the way books did when, as a child, the great gates of literature began to open and first encounters with noble thoughts and utterances were unspeakably thrilling. But this was different, too. It was as if a wind blew over me, coming from heights even higher than that of Glashgar. I wanted not to put the book down until it was finished, and yet I could not bear to come to its end. Once at its last page, I felt I would have to do what I had often done as a child—turn back to the first page and begin reading all over again. I longed to tell everyone I knew to read it. Just that, to read it. It would not do to tell them anything about it. This was not only a book, it was an experience.

Sir Gibbie is George MacDonald at his deep-hearted best, the man whose Curdie stories, *Light Princess* and *At the Back of the North Wind* have been read by generations of children and are sought after today as they were nearly a century ago when they were first written. But why had *Sir Gibbie* been lost? Why had it been out of print and well-nigh unobtainable for more than thirty years? Could it be that the same thing that had held me off held others off, too—the witty-wise-and-beautiful-to-those-familiar-with-it Scotch dialect and to those who were not familiar with it awkward-and-incomprehensible? *Sir Gibbie,* too, was enormously long, and not always with the story. MacDonald, like one of his mountain burns in its spring spate, thought prodigiously and could not resist putting into the book he was writing all that he was thinking, some of which had already found its way into lectures and sermons.

Now here and now there, I discovered among my friends those who had read *Sir Gibbie* and loved it as I did, but their copies of the book—some dating from its publication in 1878—though cherished were very, very worn. There was need for a new edition of *Sir Gibbie,* an edition that would make a new appeal.

This is what I have done: I have cut the original *Sir Gibbie* almost by half, taking out the pages that were a digression from the story; and I have "translated" the Scotch dialect into English, except for certain flavorful words which have long been familiar. Often as I did this I found myself inwardly exclaiming, "So, that's what was really meant!" The core of the story—the shining wonder which is the ministrant character of Gibbie—is untouched. What seemed important to me was that the book be made available to readers today, not continue to remain on a few bookshelves as a dusty, however charming, relic of another day.

George MacDonald's long life (1824–1905) spanned the greater part of the nineteenth century. He was a true exponent of his age, but with a prophetic flair. Coming from a race of pipers and bards, he inherited Celtic tradition with its blend of sympathy, romance, vision, and sense of community with Nature. One of a large family, his childhood was rich in hard work, religious teaching, and sturdy oatmeal porridge. Of a distinctly scholarly bent, he entered King's College, Aberdeen, at sixteen. He was drawn to the ministry, but his warmly human and imaginative ideas were unorthodox according to the standards of his day. "I well remember feeling as a child," he wrote, "that I did not care for God to love me if He did not love everybody: the kind of love I needed was the love that all men needed, the love that belonged to their nature as the children of the Father, a love He could not give me except He gave it to all men."

A few years later he was a theological student at Highbury College, London, and deeply in love with Louisa Powell. A pastorate of his own and marriage to Louisa followed in 1851. From then on life was to be a continuing struggle, but with such a widening of his powers and such an outreach to his love that there was never any line for him between faith and practice. Those were days of narrow-bound doctrine and he was soon accused of heresy—heresy for his teaching in regard to the Sabbath, heresy because he expressed the hope that animals might share in the life to come, heresy because he believed there was provision made for the heathen after death. A deputation of the deacons in his church called upon him to reduce his salary; soon after, in 1853, they demanded his resignation. George MacDonald's spirit was untouched, as he wrote to a friend, "I do not myself believe in misfortune; anything to which men give the name is merely the shadow-side of a good."

The years that followed held a full share of difficult times. Family ties increased as one after another child, up to eleven, came to George and Louisa; and then, because eleven seemed the wrong side of a dozen, they adopted two more. He could teach, and he did, but he was a preacher at heart though he could not conform to the dogma of his day. He had no church of his own but he continued to preach wherever he was called, and he was increasingly in demand throughout England and Scotland, and later in the United States. People listened to him hungrily and opened their hearts to him, warmed by his gentleness and humanity, drawn by his strength. But preaching and teaching were not enough to support his family so he took to writing. In 1855 the first book was published and for nearly fifty years words were to flow from his pen as unstintingly as they did from his lips. "I can see more and more," he said, "that nothing will do for anybody but an absolute enthusiastic confidence in God."

Recognition began to come to him and with it a little more ease in living. When one of his children exclaimed, "It all seems too good to be true!" he was ready with his reply. "Nay, it is just so good it must be true." His novels were immensely popular in his day and they served their purpose well, as support for his family and in making him a vocal influence for his generation, but few are read now. Of the fifty-two volumes of novels, stories, and poems, it is the stories told for children that continue to live.

When Greville, the eldest son, became a practicing man of medicine in London, he asked his father one day if he could tell him that the God who Jesus proclaimed did exist. "Can you tell it me with the same certainty that I can vouch for this table I am touching?" It was said that a look of spiritual indignation flashed over the father's face. "Of course not!" MacDonald exclaimed. "Do you think I could believe in a God demonstrated, proved by weight, resistance, inevitability?" No, the God in whom George MacDonald had always rested his faith was the "live heart at the center of the lovely order of the universe." "All my life," he wrote in a letter,

"I have been trying to find that one Being, and to know him consciously present; hope grows and grows with the years that lead me nearer to the end of my earthly life; and in my best moods it seems ever that the only thing worth desiring is that His will be done; that there lies before me a fullness of life, sufficient to content the giving of a perfect Father, and that the part of His child is to yield all and see that he does not himself stand in the way of the mighty design."

He was to outlive his beloved Louisa by a few years, and even some of the children, but his faith became ever stronger. Near the end of his long life his prayer was, "God be with us here and there —that is all."

Greville, who wrote of that life in an immensely readable book, *George MacDonald and His Wife,* wrote the Foreword to the Everyman's Library edition of *Sir Gibbie* in 1914. In it he said, "*Sir Gibbie* is, I think, the most direct and most beautiful of all George MacDonald's novels. It is so simple and stirring in its narrative, so invigorating in its mountain air and running waters, so happy, humorous, and pathetic, that children as much delight in its magic as they cherish the enchantment of his fairy tales. It teaches, too, everything it was his mission to teach; yet, less than any of his other finest novels, is it didactic. His life's warfare . . . marches through the pages of this book with bagpipes and bonnet and broadsword, making young and old feel a heroic joy in the eternal fight."

Now and then a book is read as a friend is made and after it life is not the same, nor will it ever be the same, for it has become richer, more meaningful, more challenging. *Sir Gibbie* did this to me. *Sir Gibbie* holds that within its covers to do something to all who read it.

ELIZABETH YATES

Peterborough
New Hampshire
February 1963

CONTENTS

SIR GIBBIE

1: *Up Daurside*

IT WAS A gray morning toward the close of autumn. The days began and ended with a fog; but often between, as golden a sunshine glorified the streets of the gray city as any that ripened purple grapes. Today the mist had lasted longer than usual—had risen instead of dispersing; but now it was thinning, and at length, like a slow blossoming of the sky flower, the sun came melting through the cloud.

In the part of the city called the Widdiehill stood an old house around which yet clung a musty fame of departed grandeur and ancient note. From a shed in the courtyard came a tapping sound as a man bent over a bench cobbling boots and shoes. The man, as well as the house in which he lodged in two garret rooms, had once seen better days. George Galbraith, addressed as Sir George by his friends, accepted the title; for, if it was not universally known in the city, it was known to the best lawyers in it that he was a baronet by direct derivation from the hand of King James the Sixth. Once a man of wealth and property, Sir George's only wealth now was in his son Gibbie, whose lovely mother had died soon after he was born. Gibbie was now eight years old, though he looked no more than six, and when he was not helping his father he trotted about the streets of the city.

It was a hard, severe city; its streets were paved with granite blocks and its houses were massive and strong. At one side the sea lapped against the wharves where ships tied up; on the other the hills rose distantly.

The sun was hot for an hour or two in the middle of the day, but even then in the shadow dwelt a cold breath. To Gibbie, however, barelegged, barefooted, almost barebodied as he was, sun or shadow made small difference, except as one of the musical intervals of life that makes the melody of existence. His bare feet knew the difference on the flags, and his heart recognized unconsciously the secret as it were of a meaning and a symbol, in the change from the one to the other, but he was almost as happy in the dull as in the bright day. Hardy through hardship, he knew nothing better than a constant good-humored sparring with nature and circumstance for the privilege of being, enjoyed what came to him thoroughly, never mourned over what he had not, and, like the animals, was at peace.

Hopping about in the gutters like the town sparrow he was, Gibbie often found treasures. On this morning, a shaft of sunlight coming between the gables of two houses revealed to Gibbie something he had been looking for—a little earring of amethyst-colored glass which Mysie, the baker's daughter, had lost. Gibbie sprang to his feet and bounded with it into the sun, rubbing it as he ran upon what he had for trousers, of which there was nothing below the knees but a few streamers, and nothing above the knees but the body of the garment, which had been last worn by a boy three times his size.

Gibbie was in an ecstasy over his find. He rubbed it on his sleeve, sucked it to clear it from the last of the gutter, and held it up once more in the sun, where, for a few blissful moments, he contemplated it speechless. He then caused it to disappear somewhere about his garments and ran off, his little bare feet sounding *thud, thud, thud* on the pavement, and the collar of his jacket sticking halfway up the back of his head, and threatening to rub it bare as he ran.

At the door of the baker's shop, he met Mysie and presented her with her earring.

"That's real good of you, wee Gibbie!" she cried. "Where did you get it?"

He pointed to the gutter and drew back from the door.

"I thank you," she said heartily, and, pressing down the thumbstall of the latch, went in.

"Who's that you're talking with, Mysie?" asked her mother.

"It's only wee Gibbie, Mother."

"What had you to say to him? He's not fit company for the likes of you that has a father and a mother and a shop. You must have little to say to such a rintheroot laddie.

"Gibbie has a father, though they say he never had a mother," said the child.

"A fine father!" rejoined the mother, with a small scornful laugh. "Such a father, lassie, as it would be telling him he had none! What said you to wee Gibbie?"

"I thanked him because I lost my drop as I went to school this morning and he found it for me. They say he's always finding things."

"He's a goodhearted creature!" said the mother, "—for one, that is, that's been so ill brought up."

She rose, took from the shelf a large piece of bread, composed of many adhering penny loaves, detached one, and went to the door.

"Here, Gibbie!" she cried as she opened it; "here's a fine piece for you."

But no Gibbie was there. Up and down the street not a child was to be seen. A sandboy with a donkey cart was the sole human arrangement in it. The baker's wife drew back, shut the door, and resumed her knitting.

The day went on, and went out, its short autumnal brightness quenched in a chilly fog. All along the Widdiehill, the gas was alight in the low-browed dingy shops. In his shed under the stair it had been dark for some time—too dark for work, that is, and George Galbraith had lighted a candle: he never felt at liberty to leave off so long as a man was recognizable in the street by daylight. But now at last, with a sigh of relief, he rose. His hand trembled with expectation as he laid from it the awl, took from between his knees the great boot on the toe of which he had been stitching a patch, lifted the yoke of his leather apron over his head, and threw it aside. With one hasty glance around, as if he feared some enemy lurking near to prevent his escape, he caught up a hat which looked as if it had been brushed with grease, pulled it on his head with both hands, stepped out quickly, closed the door behind him, turned the key, left it in the lock, and made straight for Mistress Croale's. Above the door was a small board, nearly square, upon which was painted in lead-color on a black ground the words LICENSED TO SELL BEER, SPIRITS, AND TOBACCO TO BE DRUNK ON THE PREMISES. There was no other sign.

George was a tall man, of good figure, loosened and bowed. His face was well favored, but not a little wronged by the beard and dirt of a week, through which it gloomed haggard and white. Beneath his projecting black brows, his eyes gleamed doubtful, as a wood fire where white ash dims the glow. He looked neither to right nor left, but walked on with moveless dull gaze, noting nothing.

"He's his own worst enemy," said the kindly grocer-wife, as he passed her door.

"Ay," responded her customer—"ay, I daresay. But eh! to see that poor neglected bairn of his running about the town with little of a jacket and less of the trousers! Eh, woman, it makes a mother's heart sore to look on it."

Many a person, including the Reverend Clement Sclater in whose parish Sir George and wee Gibbie lived, shook their heads in shame and sorrow over the Galbraiths, but there seemed little that anyone could do.

Through the city streets Gibbie had been roaming happily enough all day, unaware of the concern he caused people. When he was not looking in at a shopwindow, or turning on one heel to take in all at a sweep, he was oftenest seen trotting. Seldom he walked. A gentle trot was one of his natural modes of being. And though this day he had been on the trot all the sunshine through, nevertheless, when the sun was going down there was wee Gibbie upon the trot in the chilling and darkening streets. He had not had much to eat. He had been very near having a penny loaf. Half a cookie, which a stormy child had thrown away to ease his temper, had done further and perhaps better service in easing Gibbie's hunger. The green-grocer woman at the entrance of the court where his father lived, a good way down the same street in which he had found the lost earring, had given him a small yellow turnip—to Gibbie nearly as welcome as an apple. A fishwife from Finstone with a creel on her back had given him all his hands could hold of the seaweed called "dulse." She had added to the gift a small crab, but that he had carried to the seashore and set free, because it was alive. These, the half-cookie, the turnip, and the dulse, with the smell of the baker's bread, was all he had had. It had been rather one of his meager days.

Now that the lamps were being lit and the frosty dark of the autumn night was coming down over the city, Gibbie was drawn to Mistress Croale's as surely as ever Sir George had been. Under the window of the parlor where the light of revel shone radiant through a red curtain, he would stand listening for a moment, then, darting off a few yards suddenly and swiftly like a scared bird, fall at once into his own steady trot—up the lane and down, till he reached the window again, where again he would stand and listen. Whether he made this departure and return twenty or a hundred times in a night, he nor any one else could have told. Sometimes he would for a change extend his trot along the Widdiehill, sometimes along the parallel Vennel, but never far from Jink Lane and its glowing window. Never moth haunted lamp so persistently. Ever as he ran, up this pavement and down that, on the soft-sounding soles of his bare feet, the smile on the boy's face grew more and more sleepy, but still he smiled and still he trotted, still paused at the window, and still started afresh.

He was not to be pitied. Never in his life had he yet pitied himself. The thought of hardship or wrong had not occurred to him. It would have been difficult to get the idea into his head that existence bore to him any other shape than it ought. Things were with him as they had always been, and whence was he to take a fresh start and question what had been from the beginning?

It was now late, and those streets were empty; neither carriage nor cart, wheelbarrow nor truck, went anymore bumping and clattering over their stones. They were well lighted with gas, but most of the bordering houses were dark. Now and then a single foot-farer passed with loud, hollow-sounding boots along the pavement; or two girls would come laughing along, their merriment echoing rude in the wide stillness. A cold wind, a small, forsaken, solitary wind, moist with a thin fog, seemed, as well as wee Gibbie, to be roaming the night, for it met him at various corners, and from all directions. But it had nothing to do and nowhere to go, and there it was not like Gibbie, the business of whose life was even now upon him, the mightiest hope of whose conscious being was now awake.

All he expected, or even desired to discover, by listening at the window, was simply whether there were yet signs of the company's breaking up. Seldom had he there heard the voice of his father, still seldomer anything beyond its tone. This night, however, as the time drew near when they must go, and

Gibbie stood once more on tiptoe, with his head just on the level of the window sill, he heard his father utter two words: "Up Daurside" came to him through the window, in the voice he loved, plain and distinct. The words conveyed to him nothing at all; the mere hearing of them made them memorable. For the time, however, he forgot them, for he perceived that the company was on the point of separating, and from that moment did not take his eyes off the door until he heard the first sounds of its opening. As, however, it was always hard for Gibbie to stand still, and especially hard on a midnight so cold that his feet threatened to grow indistinguishable from the slabs of the pavement, he was driven, in order not to lose sight of it, to practice the art, already cultivated by him to a crab-like perfection, of running first backward, then forward with scarcely superior speed. But it was not long ere the much-expected sound of Mistress Croale's voice heralded the hour for patience to blossom into possession.

Gibbie bounded up and stood still as a statue at the very doorcheek, until he heard Mistress Croale's hand upon the lock, when he bolted, trembling with eagerness, into the entry of a court a few houses nearer to the Widdiehill.

One after one the pitiable company issued from its paradise, and each stumbled away, too far gone for leave-taking. Most of them passed Gibbie where he stood, but he took no heed; his father was always the last—and the least capable. But often as he left her door, never did it close behind him until with her own eyes Mistress Croale had seen Gibbie dart like an imp out of the court—to take him in charge, and, all the weary way home, hover, not very like a guardian angel, but not the less one in truth, around the unstable equilibrium of his father's tall and swaying form.

Home the big one staggered, reeled, gyrated, and tumbled; round and round him went the little one, now behind, now before, now on this side, now on that, his feet never more than touching the ground but dancing about like those of a prize fighter, his little arms up and his hands well forward, like flying buttresses. And such indeed they were—buttresses which flew and flew all about a universally leaning tower. They propped it here, they propped it there; with wonderful judgment and skill and graduation of force they applied themselves, and with perfect success.

The first special difficulty, that of turning the corner of Jink Lane and the Widdiehill, successfully overcome, the twain went reeling and revolving along the street, much like a whirlwind that had half forgotten the laws of gyration, until at length it spun into the court and up to the foot of the outside stair over the baronet's workshop. Then commenced the real struggle of the evening for Gibbie—and for his father too, all up the outside and the two inside stairs. Gibbie stuck to his business like a man, and his resolution and perseverance were at length, as always, crowned with victory.

The house in which lords and ladies had often reposed was now filled with very humble folk, who were all asleep when Gibbie and his father entered; but the noise they made in ascending caused no great disturbance of their rest; for, if any of them were roused for a moment, it was but to recognize at once the cause of the tumult, and with the remark, "It's only wee Gibbie luggin' home Sir George," to turn on the other side and fall asleep again.

Arrived at last at the garret door, which stood wide open, Gibbie had small need of light in the nearly pitch darkness of the place, for there was positively nothing to stumble over or against between the door and the ancient fourpost bed, which was all of his father's house that remained to Sir George. With heavy shuffling feet the drunkard lumbered laboriously bedward; and the bare posts and crazy frame groaned and creaked as he fell upon the oat chaff that lay waiting him in place of the vanished luxury of feathers. Wee Gibbie flew at his legs, nor rested until, the one after the other, he had got them on the bed; if then they were not very comfortably deposited, he knew that, in his first turn, the owner would get them all right.

And now rose the *culmen* of Gibbie's day! In triumph he spread over his sleeping father his dead mother's old plaid of Gordon tartan, all the bedding they had, and without a moment's further delay—no shoes even to put off—crept under it, and nestled close upon the bosom of his unconscious parent. A victory more! another day ended with success! his father safe, and all his own! the canopy of the darkness and the plaid over them, as if they were the one and only two in the universe! his father unable to leave him—his for whole dark hours to come! It was Gibbie's paradise now! His heaven was his father's bosom, to which he clung. He never thought to pity himself that the embrace was all on his side, that no answering pressure came back from the prostrate form. He never said to himself, "My father is a drunkard, but I must make the best of it; he is all I have!" He clung to his one possession—only clung: this was his father—all in all to him.

Sir George was a man of few words and Gibbie of none. A sharp cry, a radiant smile, blue eyes were Gibbie's means of communication, for he had been born without the ability to speak. They were notable eyes out of which he looked—of such a deep blue were they, and having such long lashes; but more notable far from their expression, the nature of which, although a certain witchery of confidence was at once discoverable, was not to be determined without the help of the whole face, whose diffused meaning seemed in them to deepen almost to speech. Whatever was at the heart of that expression, it was something that enticed question and might want investigation. The face as well as the eyes was lovely—not very clean, and not too regular for hope of a fine development, but chiefly remarkable from a general effect of luminosity. The hair, which stuck out from his head in every direction, like a round fur cap, would have been of the red-gold kind, had it not been sunburned into a sort of human hay.

One evening, sitting in their garret with a penny candle burning in a stone blacking bottle on the chimney piece, Sir George's words were to be ever memorable.

"Gibbie, do you know what folk will call you when I'm dead?"

Gibbie shook his head.

"They'll call you Sir Gibbie Galbraith, my man," said his father, "and rightly, for it will be no nickname, though some may laugh because your father was a cobbler and you never had a pair of shoes to your feet. Poor fellow! Never mind what they say, Gibbie. Remember that you're Sir Gibbie and have the honor of the family to hold up. And remember, my man, that you *cannot* do and drink, for it's drink that's been the ruin of all the Galbraiths."

Gibbie nodded solemnly.

Sir George sighed and went on with his sorry tale. "My grandfather was a big bonny man, Gibbie, but he drank most everything there was—lands and lordship, till there was hardly an acre left upon all Daurside to come to him and nothing but one small house. My father was a good man but he early learned to drink and because of it got no schooling. If a kind neighbor had not taught me my trade, I do not know what would have become of you and me, Gibbie. Ah well, it's a weary world! Go to your bed now and leave me to my own thoughts, not that they're always the best company, laddie."

Gibbie obeyed, and getting under the Gordon tartan, lay and looked out, like a weasel from its hole, at his father's back.

Gibbie slept some time. When he awoke, it was pitch dark, and he was not lying on his father's bosom. He felt about with his hands till he found his father's head. Then he got up and tried to rouse him, and, failing, to get him onto the bed. But in that too he was sadly unsuccessful; what with the darkness and the weight of him, the result of the boy's best endeavor was that Sir George half slipped, half rolled down upon the box and from that to the floor. Assured then of his own helplessness, wee Gibbie dragged the miserable bolster from the bed, and got it under his father's head; then covered him with the plaid, and, creeping under it, laid himself on his father's bosom, where soon he slept again.

He awoke very cold, and, getting up, turned heels over head several times to warm himself, but quietly, for his father was still asleep. The room was no longer dark, for the moon was shining through the skylight. When he had got himself a little warmer, he turned to have a look at his father. The pale light shone full upon his face, and it was that, Gibbie thought, which made him look so strange. He darted to him, and stared aghast. He threw himself upon him. He pulled and shook him, but he would not wake.

Gibbie did not know anything about death, and went on trying to wake him. At last he observed that, although his mouth was wide open, the breath did not come from it. His heart began to fail him: father-worshiping as that heart was, Gibbie knew that he had lost his idol. Then the house rang with the despairing shriek of the little orphan.

Two years passed. Gibbie's agony passed, too, and life became again life, and he ran about the streets as before. Some may think that wee Sir Gibbie—as many now called him, some knowing the truth, and others in kindly mockery—would get on all the better for the loss of such a father; but it was not so. In his father he had lost his paradise and was now a creature expelled.

He was not so much to be pitied as many a child dismissed by sudden decree from a home to a school; but the streets and the people and the shops, the horses and the dogs, even the penny loaves though he was hungry, had lost half their precious delight when his father was no longer in the accessible background, the heart of the blissful city. As to food and clothing, he did neither much better nor any worse than before; people were kind as usual, and kindness was to Gibbie the very milk of Mother Nature. Whose the hand that proffered it, or what the form it took, he cared no more than a stray kitten cares whether the milk set down to it be in a blue saucer or a white. But he always made the right return. The first thing a kindness deserves is acceptance, the next is transmission; Gibbie gave both, without thinking much about either.

He roamed the streets, as all his life before, the whole of the day, and part of the night; he took what was given him and picked up what he found. There were some who would gladly have brought him within the bounds of an ordered life; he soon drove them to despair, however, for the streets had been his nursery, and nothing could keep him out of them.

However Gibbie's habits might shock the ladies of Mr. Sclater's congregation who sought to civilize him, the boy was no more about mischief in the streets at midnight than they were in their beds. They collected enough for his behoof to board him for a year with an old woman who kept a school, and they did get him to sleep one night in her house. But in the morning, when she would not let him run out, brought him into the schoolroom, her kitchen, and began to teach him to write, Gibbie failed to see the good of it. He must have space, change, adventure, air, or life was not worth the name to him. Above all he must see friendly faces, and that of the old dame was not such.

Like a shell from a mortar, he departed from the house. She hobbled to the door after him, but his diminutive figure many yards away, his little bare legs misty with swiftness as he ran, was the last she ever saw of him, and her pupils had a bad time of it the rest of the day. He never even entered the street again in which she lived. Thus, after one night's brief interval of respectability, he was again a rover of the city, a flitting insect that lighted here and there, and spread wings of departure the moment a fresh desire awoke.

It would be difficult to say where he slept. In summer anywhere; in winter where he could find warmth. Like animals better clad than he, yet like him able to endure cold, he reveled in mere heat when he could come by it. Sometimes he stood at the back of a baker's oven, for he knew all the haunts of heat about the city; sometimes he buried himself in the husks of oats lying ready to feed the kiln of a meal mill; sometimes he lay by the furnace of the steam engine of the waterworks. One man employed there, when his time was at night, always made a bed for Gibbie; he had lost his own only child, and this one of nobody's was a comfort to him.

The merits the police recognized in him were mainly two—the first, the negative yet more important one, that of utter harmlessness; the second, and positive one, a passion and power for rendering help, taking notable shape chiefly in two ways. The first was the peculiar faculty now pretty generally known—his great gift, some, his great luck, others called it—for finding things lost. It was no wonder the town crier had sought his acquaintance, and when secured, had cultivated it—neither a difficult task; for the boy, ever since he could remember, had been in the habit, as often as he saw the crier, or heard his tuck of drum in the distance, of joining him and following, until he had acquainted himself with all particulars concerning everything proclaimed as missing. The moment he had mastered the facts announced, he would dart away to search, and not infrequently to return with the thing sought. The crier spoke kindly to Gibbie, as well he might, and now and then gave him a penny.

The second of the positive merits by which Gibbie found acceptance in the eyes of the police, was a yet more peculiar one, growing out of his love for his father, and his experience in the exercise of that love. It was indeed the main cause of his being, like themselves, so much in the street at night. If the finding of things was a gift, this other peculiarity was a passion: it was to play the guardian angel to drunk folk. If such a distressed human craft heaved in sight, he would instantly bear down upon and hover about him, until resolved as to his real condition. If he was in such distress as to require assistance, he never left him till he saw him safe within his own door.

He was least known to those to whom he rendered most assistance. Rarely had he thanks for it, never halfpence, but not infrequently blows and abuse. For the last he cared nothing; the former, owing to his great agility, seldom visited him with any directness. Though almost nothing could now have induced him to go down Jink Lane, yet about the time the company at Mistress Croale's would be breaking up, he would on most nights be lying in wait a short distance down the Widdiehill, ready to minister to that one of his father's old comrades who might prove most in need of his assistance; and if he showed him no gratitude, Gibbie had not been trained in a school where he was taught to expect or even to wish for any.

He was not shocked by the things he saw, even when he liked them least. He regarded the doing of them much as he had looked upon his father's drunkenness—as a pitiful necessity that overtook men—one from which there was no escape, and which caused a great need for Gibbies. Evil language and coarse behavior alike passed over him, without leaving the smallest stain upon heart or conscience, desire or will. No one could doubt it who considered the clarity of his face and eyes, in which the occasional but not frequent expression of keenness and promptitude scarcely even ruffled the prevailing look of unclouded heavenly babyhood.

When Mistress Croale moved to a new abode near the docks, Gibbie haunted it. He grew fond of the sailors with their jolly manners and openhearted ways, particularly of Black Sambo who showed special kindness to him. But, one night, when Black Sambo was killed as the result of a drunken brawl, the light went out again for Gibbie. The boy never could recall what came next. When he knew himself again, he was in the street, running like the wind, he knew not whither. It was not that he dreaded any hurt to himself; horror, not fear, was behind him.

His next recollection of himself was in the first of the morning, on the lofty chain bridge over the River Daur. Before him lay he knew not what, only escape from what was behind. His faith in men seemed ruined. The city, his home, was frightful to him. Quarrels and curses and blows he had been used to, and amid them life could be lived. If he did not consciously weave them into his theories, he unconsciously wrapped them up in his confidence, and was at peace. But the last night had revealed something unknown before. It was as if the darkness had been cloven, and through the cleft he saw into hell. A thing had been done that could not be undone, and he thought it must be what people called *murder.*

Brooding thus, he fell into a dreamy state, in which, brokenly, from here and there, pictures of his former life grew out upon his memory. Suddenly, plainer than all the rest, came the last time he stood under Mistress Croale's window, waiting to help his father home. The same instant, back to the ear of his mind came his father's two words, as he had heard them through the window—*"Up Daurside."*

"Up Daurside!"—Here he was upon Daurside: he would go farther up. He rose and went on, while the great river kept flowing the other way.

As far as the city was concerned, the urchin that had run about its streets like a town sparrow had disappeared. Before he was forgotten, there was some talk of who he might be, but only the Reverend Mr. Sclater set himself to discover and verify the facts. For this purpose he burrowed about in the neighborhoods Gibbie had chiefly frequented, and was so far successful as to satisfy himself that Gibbie, if he was alive, was Sir Gilbert Galbraith, Baronet; but his own lawyer was able to assure him that not an inch of property remained anywhere attached to the title. There were indeed relations of the boy's mother, who were of some small consequence in a neighboring county, also one in business in Glasgow, or its neighborhood, reported wealthy; but these had entirely disowned her because of her marriage. All Mr. Sclater discovered besides was, in a lumber room next the garret in which Sir George died, a box of papers —a glance at whose contents showed that they must at least prove a great deal of which he was already certain from other sources. A few of them had to do with the house in which they were found, still known as the Auld Hoose o' Galbraith; but most of them referred to property in land, and many were of ancient date. If the property were in the hands of descendants of the original stock, the papers would be of value in their eyes; and, in any case, it would be well to see to their safety. Mr. Sclater therefore had the chest removed to the garret of the manse, where it stood thereafter, little regarded, but able to answer for more than itself.

2: *To Glashgar*

IT WAS A cold, fresh morning, cloudy and changeful, toward the end of April. It had rained and would rain again; it might snow. Heavy undefined clouds, with saffron breaks and borders, hung about the east. To Gibbie, city-creature as he was, it was plain *something* was going to happen there. And happen it did presently, and that with a splendor that for a moment blinded Gibbie. For just at the horizon there was a long horizontal slip of blue sky, and through that crack the top-most arc of the rising sun shot suddenly a thousand arrows of radiance into the brain of the boy.

To no traveler could one land well be so different from another, as to Gibbie the country was from the town. The sun seemed but to have looked up to mock him and go down again, for he had crossed the crack, and was behind a thick mass of cloud; a cold damp wind, spotted with sparkles of rain, blew fitfully from the east; the low bushes among which he sat, sent forth a chill sighing all about him, as they sifted the wind into sound; the smell of the damp earth was strange to him; below him the gloomy river, here deep, smooth, moody, sullen, there puckered with the gray ripples of a shallow laughter under the cold breeze, went flowing heedless to the city. There only was, or had been, friendliness, comfort, home! This was emptiness—the abode of things, not beings. Yet never once did Gibbie think of returning to the city.

He rose and wandered up the wide road along the river bank, farther and farther from it—his only guide the words of his father, *"Up Daurside"*; his sole comfort the feeling of having once more to do with his father so long departed, some relation still with the paradise of his old world. Along cultivated fields and copses on the one side, and on the other a steep descent to the river, covered here and there with trees, but mostly with rough grass and bushes and stones, he followed the king's highway. There were buttercups and plenty of daisies within his sight—primroses, too, on the slopes beneath; but he did not know flowers, and his was not now the mood for discovering what they were. The exercise revived him, and he began to be hungry. Hunger, however, was far less enfeebling to Gibbie than to one accustomed to regular meals, and he was in no anxiety about either when or what he should eat.

The morning advanced, and by and by he began to meet a fellow creature now and then upon the road; but he was so uncomfortable from the way the people he met scrutinized him that, when he saw anyone coming, he would instantly turn aside and take to the covert of thicket or hedge or stone wall, until the bearer of eyes had passed.

Up Daurside was the one vague notion he had of his calling, his destiny, and with his short, quick step, his progress was considerable; he passed house after house, farm after farm; but, never in the way of asking for anything, he went nearer none of them than the road led him. He came at length to a field, sloping to the road, which was covered with leaves like some he had often seen in the market. They drew him; and as there was but a low and imperfect hedge between, he got over, and found it was a crop of small yellow turnips. He gathered as many as he could carry and ate them as he went along. In the city he would never have dreamed of touching anything that was not given him, except it lay plainly a lost thing. But here, where everything was so different, and he saw none of the signs of ownership to which he was accustomed, the idea of property did not come to him; here everything looked lost, or in the same category with the chips and parings and crusts that were thrown out in the city, and became common property.

He came upon a little girl feeding a cow by the roadside. She saw how he ate the turnips and offered him a bit of oatmeal bannock. He received it gladly, and with beaming eyes offered her a turnip. She refused it with some indignation. Gibbie, disappointed, but not ungrateful, resumed his tramp, eating his bannock. He came soon after to a little stream that ran into the great river. For a few moments he eyed it very doubtfully, thinking it must, like the kennels along the sides of the streets, be far too dirty to drink of; but the way it sparkled and sang soon satisfied him, and he drank and was refreshed. He had still two turnips left, but, after the bannock, he did not seem to want them, and stowed them in the ends of the sleeves of his jacket, folded back into great cuffs.

All day the cold spring weather continued, with more of the past winter in it than of the coming summer. The sun would shine out for a few moments, with a gray, weary, old light, then retreat as if he had tried, but really could not. Once came a slight fall of snow, which, however, melted the moment it touched the earth. The wind kept blowing cheerlessly by fits, and the world seemed growing tired of the same thing over again so often. At length the air began to grow dusk: then, first, fears of the darkness, to Gibbie utterly unknown before, began to make him aware of their existence in the human world. They seemed to rise up from his lonely heart; they seemed to descend upon him out of the thickening air; they seemed to catch at his breath and gather behind him as he went.

But, happily, before it was quite dark, and while yet he

could distinguish between objects, he came to the gate of a farmyard; it waked in him the hope of finding some place where he could sleep warmer than in the road, and he clambered over it. Nearest of the buildings to the gate stood an open shed, and he could see the shafts of carts projecting from it; perhaps in one of those carts, or under it, he might find a place that would serve him to sleep in. But just as he entered the shed, he spied at the farther corner of it, outside, a wooden structure, like a small house, and through the arched door of it saw the floor covered with nice-looking straw. He suspected it to be a dog's kennel; and presently the chain lying beside it, with a collar at the end, satisfied him it was. The dog was absent, and it looked altogether enticing! He crept in, got under as much of the straw as he could heap over him, and fell fast asleep.

In a few minutes, as it seemed to him, he was roused by the great voice of a dog in conversation with a boy; the boy seemed, by the sound of the chain, to be fastening the collar on the dog's neck and presently left him. The dog, which had been on the rampage the whole afternoon, immediately turned to creep in and rest till supper time, presenting to Gibbie, who had drawn himself up at the back of the kennel, the intelligent countenance of a large Newfoundland. Now Gibbie had been honored with the acquaintance of many dogs, and the friendship of most of them. Even among dogs, however, there are ungracious individuals. Hence, with the sight of the owner of the dwelling, it dawned upon him that he must be startled to find a stranger in his house, and might, regarding him as an intruder rather than a guest, worry him before he had time to explain himself. He darted forward therefore to get out, but had scarcely reached the door, when the dog put in his nose, ready to follow with all he was and had.

Gibbie, thereupon, began a loud barking. The dog started back in extreme astonishment, his ears erect. Gibbie, amused at the dog's fright, and assured by his looks that he was both a good-natured and reasonable animal, burst into a fit of merry laughter as loud as his previous barking, and a good deal more musical. The dog evidently liked it better and took it as a challenge to play; after a series of sharp bursts of barking, his eyes flashing straight in at the door, and his ears lifted up like two plumes on the top of them, he darted into the kennel, and began poking his nose into his visitor. Gibbie fell to patting and kissing and hugging him as if he had been a human; and they were friends at once. Both were tired, however, for both had been active that day, and a few minutes of mingled wrestling and endearment, to which, perhaps, the narrowness of their playground gave a speedier conclusion, contented both, after which they lay side by side in peace, Gibbie with his head on the dog's back, and the dog every now and then turning his head over his shoulder to lick Gibbie's face.

Again he was waked by approaching steps, and the same moment the dog darted from under him, and with much rattle out of the kennel, in front of which he stood and whined expectantly. It was not quite dark, for the clouds had drifted away, and the stars were shining, so that, when he put out his head, he was able to see the dim form of a woman setting down something before the dog—into which he instantly plunged his nose and began gobbling. The sound stirred up all the latent hunger in Gibbie, and he leaped out, eager to have a share. A large wooden bowl was on the ground, and the half of its contents of porridge and milk was already gone; it was plain that, if Gibbie was to have any, he must lose no time in considering the means.

Had he had a long nose and mouth all in one like him, he would have plunged them in beside the dog's; but the flatness of his mouth causing the necessity, in the case of such an attempt, of bringing the whole of his face into contact with the food, there was not room in the dish for the two to feed together after the same fashion, so that he was driven to the sole other possible expedient, that of making a spoon of his hand. The dog neither growled nor pushed away the spoon, but instantly began to gobble twice as fast as before, and presently was licking the bottom of the dish. Gibbie's hand, therefore, made but few journeys to his mouth, but what it carried him was good food—better than any he had had that day. When all was gone he crept again into the kennel; the dog followed, and soon they were both fast asleep in each other's arms and legs.

Gibbie woke at sunrise and went out. His host came after him, and stood wagging his tail and looking wistfully up in his face. Gibbie understood him, and, as the sole return he could make for his hospitality, undid his collar. Instantly he rushed off, his back going like a serpent, cleared the gate at a bound, and scouring madly across a field, vanished from his sight; whereupon Gibbie too set out to continue his journey up Daurside.

This day was warmer; the spring had come a step nearer; the dog had been a comforter to him, and the horror had begun to assuage; he began to grow aware of the things about him and to open his eyes to them. Upon his right hand was the great river, flowing down toward the home he had left; now through low meadows, now through upshouldered fields of wheat and oats, now through rocky heights covered with the graceful silver-barked birch, the mountain ash, and the fir.

That second day he fared better than the first. Now from this quarter, now from that, he got all that was needful for one of God's birds. Once he found in a hedge the nest of an errant and secretive hen, and, recognizing the eggs as food authorized by the shopwindows and market of the city, soon qualified himself to have an opinion of their worth. Another time he came upon a girl milking a cow in a shed, and his astonishment at the marvels of the process was such that he forgot even the hunger that was rendering him faint. He had often seen cows in the city, but had never suspected what they were capable of.

When the girl caught sight of him, staring with open mouth, she was taken with such a fit of laughter, that the cow, which was ill-tempered, kicked out, and overturned the pail. Now because of her troublesomeness this cow was not milked beside the rest, and the shed where she stood was used for farm implements only. The floor of it was the earth, beaten hard, and worn into hollows. When the milk settled in one of these, Gibbie saw that it was lost to the girl and found to him; undeterred by the astounding nature of the spring from which he had just seen it flow, he threw himself down and drank like a calf. Her laughter ended, the girl was troubled; she would be scolded for her clumsiness in allowing Hawkie to kick over the pail, but the eagerness of the boy after the milk troubled her more. She told him to wait, and running to the house, returned with two large pieces of oatcake, which she gave him.

Thus, one way and another, food came to Gibbie. Drink was to be had in almost any hollow. Sleep was scattered everywhere over the world. For warmth, only motion and a seasoned skin were necessary; the latter Gibbie had; the former, already a habit learned in the streets, had now become almost a passion.

By this time Gibbie had got well up toward the roots of the hills of Gormgarnet, and the river had dwindled greatly. He was no longer afraid of it, but would lie for hours listening to its murmurs over its pebbly bed, and sometimes even sleep in the hollows of its banks, or below the willows that overhung it. Every here and there, a brown rivulet from some peat bog on a hill—brown and clear, like smoke crystals molten together—flowed into it, and when he had lost it, guided him back to his guide. Farm after farm he passed, here one widely bordering a valley stream, there another stretching its skirts up the hillsides till they were lost in mere heather, where the sheep wandered about, cropping what stray grass blades and other eatables they could find. Lower down he had passed through small towns and large villages: here farms and cottages, with an occasional countryseat and little village of low, thatched houses, made up the abodes of men. By this time he had become greatly reconciled to the loneliness of Nature, and no more was afraid in her solitary presence.

At the same time his heart had begun to ache and long after the communion of his kind. For not once since he set out—and that seemed months where it was only weeks, had he had an opportunity of doing anything for anybody—except, indeed, unfastening the dog's collar; and not to be able to help was to Gibbie like being dead.

May had now set in. The green crops were growing darker, and the trees were all getting out their nets to catch carbon. The lambs were frolicking, and in sheltered places the flowers were turning the earth into a firmament. And now a mere daisy was enough to delight the heart of Gibbie. His joy in humanity so suddenly checked, and his thirst for it left unslaked, he had begun to see the human look in the face of the commonest flowers, to love the trusting stare of the daisy, that goldhearted boy, and the gentle despondency of the girl harebell, dreaming of her mother, the azure. The wind, of which he had scarcely thought as he met it roaming the streets like himself, was now a friend of his solitude, bringing him sweet odors, alive with the souls of bees, and cooling with bliss the heat of the long walk. Even when it blew cold along the waste moss, waving the heads of the cotton grass, the only live thing visible, it was a lover, and kissed him on the forehead.

One evening his path vanished between twilight and moonrise, and just as it became dark he found himself at a rough gate, through which he saw a field. There was a pretty tall hedge on each side of the gate, and he was now a sufficiently experienced traveler to conclude that he was not far from some human abode. He climbed the gate and found himself in a field of clover. It was a splendid big bed, and even had the night not been warm, he would not have hesitated to sleep in it. So down he lay in the clover and was at once unconscious.

When he awoke, the moon was high in the heavens and had melted the veil of the darkness from the scene of still, well-ordered comfort. A short distance from his couch stood a little army of ricks, between twenty and thirty of them, constructed perfectly—smooth and upright and round and large, each with its conical top netted in with straw rope, and finished off with what the herdboy called a "toupican"—a neatly tied and trim tuft of the straw with which it was thatched, answering to the stoneball on the top of a gable. Like triangles their summits stood out against the pale blue moon-diluted air. While he stood gazing, a wind arose behind the hills and came blowing down some glen that opened northward; Gibbie felt it cold, and sought the shelter of the ricks.

He wandered about them, now in a dusky yellow gloom, and now in the cold blue moonlight, which they seemed to warm. At length he discovered that the huge things were flanked on one side by a long low house, in which there was a door, horizontally divided into two parts. Gibbie would fain have got in, to try whether the place was good for sleep; but he found both halves fast. In the lower half, however, he spied a hole, which, though not so large, reminded him of the entrance to the kennel of his dog host. It was, in fact, the cat's door, specially constructed for her convenience of entrance and exit.

The hole was a small one, but tempting to the wee baronet; he might perhaps be able to squeeze himself through. He tried and succeeded, though with some little difficulty. The moon was there before him, shining through a pane or two of glass over the door, and by her light on the hard brown clay floor, Gibbie saw where he was, though if he had been told he was in the barn, he would neither have felt nor been at all the wiser. It was a very old-fashioned barn. About a third of it was floored with wood—dark with age—almost as brown as the clay—for threshing upon with flails. At that labor two men had been busy during the most of the preceding day, and that was how, in the same end of the barn, rose a great heap of oat straw, showing in the light of the moon like a mound of pale gold.

What he saw in the other corner was still more like gold, and was indeed greater than gold, for it was life—the heap, namely, of corn threshed from the straw: Gibbie recognized this as what he had seen given to horses. But now the temptation to sleep, with such facilities presented, was overpowering, and took from him all desire to examine further; he shot into the middle of the loose heap of straw and vanished from the glimpses of the moon, burrowing like a mole. In the heart of the golden warmth, he lay so dry and comfortable that, notwithstanding his hunger had awakened with him, he was presently in a faster sleep than before.

When at length Gibbie became once more aware of existence, it was through a stormy invasion of the still realm of sleep; the blows of two flails fell persistent and quick-following, first on the thick head of the sheaf of oats untied and cast down before them, then grew louder and more deafening as the oats flew and the chaff fluttered, and the straw flattened and broke and thinned and spread—until at last they thundered in great hard blows on the wooden floor. It was the first of these last blows that shook Gibbie awake. What they were or indicated he could not tell. He wormed himself softly around in the straw to look out and see.

It was well that the man with the pitchfork did not spy his eyes peering out from the midst of the straw: he might have taken him for some wild creature, and driven the prongs into him. The men at length swept up the corn and tossed up the straw for the last time and went out. Gibbie crept out and began to look about him—first of all for something he could eat. The oats looked the most likely, and he took a mouthful for a trial. He ground at them severely, but, hungry as he was, he failed to find oats good for food.

Looking around him afresh, he saw an open loft, and climbing on the heap in which he had slept, managed to reach it. It was at the height of the walls, and the couples of the roof rose immediately from it. At the farther end was a heap of hay, which he took for another kind of straw. Then he spied something he knew: a row of cheeses lay on a shelf suspended from the rafters, ripening. Gibbie knew them well from the shopwindows—knew they were cheeses, and good to eat, though whence and how they came he did not know, his impression being that they grew in the fields like the turnips. He pounced upon a cheese and lifted it between his two hands; it smelled good, but felt very hard. That was no matter: what else were teeth made strong and sharp for? He tried them on one of the round edges, and, nibbling actively, soon got through to the softer body of the cheese.

At length he crept softly toward the other end of the loft to see what was to be seen there. He found that the heap of hay was not in the loft at all. It filled a small chamber in the stable, in fact; and when Gibbie clambered upon it, what should he see below him on the other side but a beautiful white horse, eating some of the same sort of stuff he was now lying upon! Beyond he could see the backs of more horses, but they were very different—big and clumsy, and not white. They were all eating, and this was their food on which he lay! He wished he too could eat it—and tried, but found it even less satisfactory than the oats.

A door opened beyond, and a man came in and led two of the horses out, leaving the door open. Gibbie clambered down from the top of the hay into the stall beside the white horse and ran out. He was almost in the fields, had not even a fence to cross.

He cast a glance around and went straight for a neighboring hollow, where, taught by experience, he hoped to find water.

Once away, Gibbie had no thought of returning. *Up Daurside* was the sole propulsive force whose existence he recognized. When he lifted his head from drinking at the stream, which was one of some size, and, greatly refreshed, looked up its channel, a longing seized him to know whence came the water of life which had thus restored him to bliss. So away he went, yielding at once, as was his wont, to the first desire that came. He had not trotted far along the bank, however, before, at a sharp turn it took, he saw that its course was a much longer one than he had imagined, for it turned from the mountain and led up among the roots of other hills; while here in front of him, direct from the mountain, as it seemed, came down a smaller stream and tumbled noisily into this. The larger burn would lead him too far from the Daur; he would follow the smaller one. He found a wide shallow place, crossed the larger, and went up the side of the smaller.

A little way up the stream, he came to a bridge over it, closed at the farther end by iron gates between pillars, each surmounted by a wolf's head in stone. Over the gate on each side leaned a rowan tree, with trunk and branches aged and gnarled amid their fresh foliage. He crossed the burn to look through the gate and pressed his face between the bars to get a better sight of a tame rabbit that had got out of its hutch. Suddenly from the wood a large spaniel came bounding upon the rabbit. Gibbie gave a shriek, and the rabbit made one white flash into the wood, with the dog after him. He turned away sad at heart.

Resuming his journey of investigation, he trotted along the bank of the burn, farther and farther up, until he could trot no more but must go clambering over great stones, or sinking to the knees in bog, patches of it red with iron. Sometimes he walked in the water, along the bed of the burn itself; sometimes he had to scramble up its steep side to pass one of the many little cataracts of its descent. Here and there a small silver birch, or a mountain ash, or a stunted fir tree hung over the stream. Its banks were mainly of rock and heather, but now and then a small patch of cultivation intervened. Gibbie had no thought that he was gradually leaving the abodes of men behind him; he knew no reason why in ascending things should change and be no longer as in plainer ways. For what he knew, there might be farm after farm, up and up forever, to the gates of heaven.

After so long wandering, Gibbie had hardly enough dress left to carry the name. Shoes he had none. Of the shape of trousers there remained nothing, except the division before and behind in the short petticoat to which they were reduced; and those rudimentary divisions were lost in the multitude of rents of equal apparent significance. He had never, so far as he knew, had a shirt upon his body; and his sole other garment was a jacket, so much too large for him, that to retain the use of his hands he had folded back the sleeves quite to his elbows. Thus reversed they became pockets, the only ones he had, and in them he stowed whatever provisions were given him of which he could not make immediate use.

His head had plentiful protection in his own natural crop. That would have been of the gold order, had not a great part of its color been sunburned, rained, and frozen out of it. All ways it pointed, as if surcharged with electric fluid, crowning him with a wildness which was in amusing contrast with the placidity of his countenance. A sort of live peace resided in that weather-beaten little face under its wild crown of human herbage. The features of it were well shaped, and not smaller than proportioned to the small whole of his person. His eyes—partly, perhaps, because there was so little flesh upon his bones—were large, and in repose had much of a soft animal expression. Frequently, too, when occasion roused the needful instinct, they had a sharp expression of outlook and readiness, which, without a trace of fierceness or greed, was yet equally animal. Only all the time there was present something else, beyond characterization; behind them something seemed to lie asleep. His hands and feet were small and childishly dainty, his whole body well shaped and well put together.

Such was Gibbie to the eye, as he rose from Daurside to the last cultivated ground on the borders of the burn, and the highest dwelling on the mountain. It was the abode of a cotter and was a dependency of the farm he had just left. The cotter was an old man of seventy; his wife was nearly sixty. They had reared stalwart sons and shapely daughters, now at service here and there in the valleys below—all ready to see God in nature and recognize Him in Providence.

It was a very humble dwelling, built of turf upon a foundation of stones, and roofed with turf and straw—warm, and nearly impervious to the searching airs of the mountainside. One little window of a foot and a half square looked out on the universe. At one end stood a stack of peat, half as big as the cottage itself. All around it were huge rocks. Here and there a thin crop was growing in patches among them, the red-gray stone lifting its baldness in spots numberless through the soft waving green. A few of the commonest flowers grew about the door, but there was no garden. The doorstep was live rock, and a huge projecting rock behind formed the back and a portion of one of the end walls. This latter rock had been the attraction to the site, because of a hollow in it, which now served as a dairy. For up there with them lived the last cow of the valley—the cow that breathed the loftiest air on all Daurside—a good cow, and gifted in feeding well upon little.

Facing the broad south and leaning against the hill, as against the bosom of God, sheltering it from the north and east, the cottage looked so high-humble, so still, so confident, that it drew Gibbie with the spell of heart-likeness. He knocked at the old weather-beaten, shrunk and rent but well-patched door. A voice, alive with the soft vibrations of thought and feeling, answered, "Come in, whoever you are."

Gibbie pulled the string that came through a hole in the door, so lifting the latch, and entered.

A woman sat on a creepie, her face turned over her shoulder to see who came. It was a gray face, with good simple features and clear gray eyes. The plentiful hair that grew low on her forehead was half gray, mostly covered by a white cap with frills. A clean wrapper and apron, both of blue print, over a blue winsey petticoat, blue stockings, and strong shoes completed her dress. A book lay on her lap; always when she had finished her morning's work and made her house tidy, she sat down to have her comfort, as she called it.

The moment she saw Gibbie she rose. Had he been the angel Gabriel, come to tell her she was wanted at the throne, her attention could not have been more immediate or thorough. She was rather a little woman and carried herself straight and light.

"Eh, you poor outcast!" she said, in the pitying voice of a mother, "how came you up here? Creature, you've left the world behind you. What would you here? I have nothing."

Receiving no answer but one of the child's bewitching smiles, she stood for a moment regarding him, not in mere silence, but with a look of dumbness.

Now the very moment before Gibbie entered, she had been reading the words of the Lord: "Inasmuch as ye have done it unto one of the least of these my brethren, ye have done it unto me"; and with her heart full of them, she lifted her eyes and saw Gibbie. For one moment, with the quick flashing response of the childlike imagination of the Celt, she fancied she saw the Lord Himself. Often had Janet pondered, as she sat alone on the great mountain, while Robert was with the sheep, or she lay awake by his side at night, with the wind howling about the cottage, whether the Lord might not sometimes take a lonely walk to look after such solitary sheep of His flock as they, and let them know He had not lost sight of them, for all the ups and downs of the hills.

In the meantime Gibbie stood motionless in the middle of the floor, smiling his innocent smile, asking for nothing, hinting at nothing, but resting his wild calm eyes, with a sense of safety and mother-presence, upon the gray thoughtful face of the gazing woman.

Her awe deepened; it seemed to descend upon her and fold her in as with a mantle. Involuntarily she bowed her head, and stepping to him took him by the hand and led him to the stool she had left. There she made him sit, while she brought forward her table, white with scrubbing, took from a hole in the wall and set upon it a platter of oatcakes, carried a wooden bowl to her dairy in the rock through a whitewashed door, and bringing it back filled, half with cream half with milk, set that also on the table. Then she placed a chair before it and said—

"Sit down and help yourself. If you were the Lord Himself, my bonny man, and you might be for all I know, for you look poor and despised enough, I could give you nothing better, for it's all I have to offer—except it might be an egg," she added, correcting herself, and turned and went out.

Presently she came back with a look of success, carrying two eggs, which, having raked out a quantity, she buried in the hot ashes of the peats, and left in front of the hearth to roast, while Gibbie went on eating the thick oatcake, sweet and substantial, and drinking such milk as the wildest imagination of town boy could never suggest.

Janet resumed her seat on the low three-legged stool and took her knitting that he might feel neither that he was watched as he ate nor that she was waiting for him to finish.

Every other moment she gave a glance at the stranger she had taken in; but never a word he spoke, and the sense of mystery grew upon her.

Presently came a great bounce and scramble; the latch jumped up, the door flew open, and after a moment's pause, in came a sheep dog carrying in his mouth a tiny, long-legged lamb, which he dropped half dead in the woman's lap. It was a late lamb, born of a mother which had been sold from the hill, but had found her way back from a great distance, in order that her coming young one might have the privilege of being yeaned on the same spot where she had herself awoke to existence. Another moment, and her *mba-a* was heard approaching the door. She trotted in and went up to Janet. Her udder was full, but the lamb was too weak to suck. Janet rose, and going to the side of the room, opened the door of what might have seemed an old press, but was a bed. Folding back the counterpane, she laid the lamb in the bed, and covered it over. Then she got a caup, a wooden dish like a large saucer, and into it milked the ewe. Next she carried the caup to the bed.

In the meantime the collie, having done his duty by the lamb, and perhaps forgotten it, sat on his tail and stared with his two brave trusting eyes at the little beggar that sat in the master's chair and ate of the fat of the land. Oscar was a gentleman. Gibbie was a stranger, and therefore as a stranger Oscar gave him welcome—now and then stooping to lick the little brown feet that had wandered so far.

Like all wild creatures, Gibbie ate fast, and had finished everything set before him ere the woman had done feeding the lamb. Without a notion of the rudeness of it, his heart full of gentle gratitude, he rose and left the cottage. When Janet turned from her shepherding, there sat Oscar looking up at the empty chair.

"What's become of the laddie?" she said to the dog, who answered with a low whine, half-regretful, half-interrogative.

Janet hastened to the door, but already Gibbie's nimble feet, refreshed to the point of every toe with the food he had just swallowed, had borne him far up the hill, behind the cottage, so that she could not get a glimpse of him. Thoughtfully she returned, and thoughtfully removed the remnants of the meal. She would then have resumed her Bible, but her hospitality had rendered it necessary that she should put on her griddle—a disk of iron on the fire, to bake thereon cakes ere her husband's return. It was a simple enough process, for the oatmeal wanted nothing but water and fire; but her joints had not yet got rid of the winter's rheumatism, and the labor of the baking was the hardest part of the sacrifice of her hospitality.

When at last she had done, and put the things away, and swept up the hearth, she milked the ewe, sent her out to nibble, took her Bible, and sat down once more to read. The lamb lay at her feet, with his little head projecting from the folds of her new flannel petticoat; and every time her eye fell from the book upon the lamb, she felt as if somehow the lamb was the boy that had eaten of her bread and drunk of her milk.

Not for years and years had Janet been to church; she had long been unable to walk so far; and having no book but the best, and no help to understand it but the highest, her faith was simple, strong, real, all-pervading. Day by day she pored over the great gospel until she had grown to be one of the noble ladies of the kingdom of heaven—one of those who inherit the earth and are ripening to see God. For the Master, and His mind in hers, was her teacher. To Janet, Jesus Christ was a living man, who somehow or other heard her when she called to him, and sent her the help she needed.

Up and up the hill went Gibbie. The mountain grew steeper and barer as he went, and he became absorbed in his climbing. Not once while he ascended had the idea come to him that by and by he should be able to climb no farther. For aught he knew there were oatcakes and milk and sheep and collie dogs ever higher and higher still.

The sun was about two hours toward the west, when Gibbie, his little legs almost as active as ever, surmounted the final slope. Running up like a child that would scale heaven, he stood on the bare round, the head of the mountain, and saw, with an invading shock of amazement, and at first of disappointment, that there was no going higher: in every direction the slope was downward. He had never been on the top of anything before. He had always been in the hollows of things. Now the whole world lay beneath him. It was cold; but Gibbie felt no cold. In a glow with the climb, which at the last had been hard, his lungs filled with the heavenly air and his soul with the feeling that he was above everything that was; uplifted on the very crown of the earth, he stood in his rags, a fluttering scarecrow, the conqueror of height, the discoverer of immensity, the monarch of space. Nobody knew of such marvel but him!

Gibbie gazed and dreamed and gazed. The mighty city that had been to him the universe was dropped and lost, like a thing that was now nobody's, in far indistinguishable distance; and he who had lost it had climbed upon the throne of the world. The air was still; when a breath awoke, it but touched his cheek like the down of a feather, and the stillness was there again. The stillness grew great and slowly descended upon him. It deepened and deepened. Surely it would deepen to a voice!—it was about to speak! It was as if a great single thought was the substance of the silence and was all over and around him, and closer to him than his clothes, than his body, than his hands. In after years, when Gibbie had the idea of God, when he had learned to think about Him, to desire His presence, to believe that a will of love enveloped His will, as the brooding hen spreads her wings over her eggs—as often as the thought of God came to him, it came in the shape of the silence on the top of Glashgar.

As he sat, with his eyes on the peak he had just chosen from the rest as the loftiest of all within his sight, he saw a cloud begin to grow upon it. The cloud grew and gathered and descended, covering its sides as it went, until the whole was hidden. Then swiftly, as he gazed, the cloud opened as it were a round window in the heart of it, and through that he saw the peak again. The next moment a flash of blue lightning darted across the opening. The clouds swept together, and the window closed. Then again burst forth the lightning. He saw no flash, but an intense cloud illumination, accompanied by the deafening crack and followed by the appalling roar and roll of the thunder. Nor was it noise alone that surrounded him, for, as if he were in the heart and nest of the storm, the very wind waves that made the thunder rushed in driven bellowing over him; and had nearly swept him away. He clung to the rock with hands and feet.

To him there was no wrath in the thunder any more than in the greeting of the dog that found him in his kennel. Gibbie sat calm, awful, but, with a clear forehead and smile-haunted mouth, while the storm roared and beat and flashed and ran about him. The tumult at last seized Gibbie like an intoxication; he jumped to his feet and danced and flung his arms about, as if he himself were the storm. But the uproar did not last long. Almost suddenly it was gone, as if, like a bird that had been flapping the ground in agony, it had at last recovered itself, and taken to its great wings and flown. The sun shone out clear, and in all the blue abyss not a cloud was to be seen, except far away to leeward, where one was spread like a banner in the lonely air, fleeting away, the ensign of the charging storm—bearing for its device a segment of the many-colored bow.

Gibbie, wet and cold, began to think of the cottage where he had been so kindly received, of the friendly face of its mistress and her care of the lamb. So he rose and set out. But he lost his way; came upon one precipice after another, down which only a creeping thing could have gone; was repeatedly turned aside by torrents and swampy places; and when the twilight came was still wandering upon the mountain.

It was not the friendly cottage he found, at last, but the farm, and he recognized it by the shape of the ricks that stood between him and the sky. Creeping through the cathole, he felt about in the dark barn. Happily the heap of straw was not yet removed. Gibbie shot into it like a mole and burrowed to the very center, there coiled himself up and slept.

3: *Gibbie Wins a Friend*

WHEN GIBBIE AWOKE, he clambered up to the loft, found the cheese he had already gnawed on, and satisfied his hunger by gnawing further. Then he went stealthily about the business of reconnoitering and soon discovered the farm dairy. Creeping again along the ceiling, he discovered himself to be over the kitchen. He saw below him that a woman was sweeping the room toward the hearth, where the peat fire was already burning, with a great pot hanging over it, covered with a wooden dish, in which she began to wash other dishes, thus giving the observant Gibbie his first notion of housekeeping. Then she scoured the deal table, dusted the bench and the chairs, arranged the dishes on shelves and rack, except a few which she placed on the table, put more water on the fire, and disappeared in the dairy.

Presently she returned, carrying a great jar, which, to Gibbie's astonishment, having lifted a lid in the top of the churn, she emptied into it, and began to turn the handle vigorously. Then Gibbie had another astonishment, when he saw a great mass of something half solid tumble out where he had seen a liquid poured in—nor that alone, for the liquid came out again too! But when at length he saw the mass, after being well washed, molded into certain shapes, he recognized it as butter, such as he had seen in the shops, and had now and then tasted on the "piece" given him by some more than usually generous housekeeper.

The butter-making brought to a successful close, the woman proceeded to make porridge for the men's breakfast, and with hungry eyes Gibbie watched that process next.

Prostrate on the ceiling Gibbie lay and watched the splendid spoonfuls tumble out of sight into the capacious throats of four men; all took their spoonfuls from the same dish, but each dipped his spoonful into his private caup of milk, ere he carried it to his mouth. A little apart sat a boy, whom the woman seemed to favor, having provided him with a plateful of porridge by himself. The boy's countenance greatly attracted Gibbie. It was a long, solemn face, and when he smiled, which was not very often, it was a good and meaningful smile.

When the meal was over, and Gibbie saw the little that was left, with all the drops of milk from the caups tumbled into a common receptacle, he felt very empty and forsaken. He crawled away sad at heart, with nothing before him except a drink of water at the burn. Carefully he crept across the ceiling, his head hanging like a dog scolded by his master, carefully along the shelf of the dairy and through the opening in the wall, quickly down the ladder and through the cathole in the barn door.

There was no one in the cornyard now, and he wandered about among the ricks looking, with little hope, for something to eat. Turning a corner he came upon a henhouse—and there was a crowd of hens and half-grown chickens about the very dish into which he had seen the remnants of the breakfast thrown, all pecking billfuls out of it. He always felt a liberty to share with the animals, so he dipped his hand into the dish. Greatly refreshed, he got up from among the hens, scrambled over the dry stone wall, and trotted away to the burn.

Passing through a fine meadow where a number of cattle were grazing, Gibbie saw a boy whom he instantly recognized. The boy was reading a book, but he glanced up from it every now and then to make sure that none of the cows wandered beyond their pasture of rye grass and clover. As soon as he seemed thoroughly occupied, a certain black cow, with short sharp horns and a wicked look, which had been gradually edging nearer and nearer to the corn, turned suddenly and ran for it, jumped the dike, and plunging into a mad revelry of greed, tore and devoured with all the haste not merely of one insecure, but of one that knew she was stealing.

Now Gibbie had been observant enough during his travels to learn that this was against the law and custom of the country and like a shot he was after the black marauder. The same instant the herdboy too, lifting his eyes from his book, saw her, and springing to his feet, caught up his great stick, and ran also; he had more than one reason to run, for he understood only too well the dangerous temper of the cow, and saw that Gibbie was a mere child and unarmed. The boy as he ran full speed to the rescue kept shouting to warn Gibbie from his purpose, but Gibbie was too intent to understand the sounds he uttered and supposed them addressed to the cow. With the fearless service that belonged to his very being, he ran straight at Hornie, and, having nothing to strike her with, flung himself against her with a great shove toward the dike. The next moment the herdboy came up, and with a storm of fiercest blows, delivered with the full might of his arm, drove her in absolute rout back into the meadow. Drawing himself up in the unconscious majesty of success, Donal Grant looked down upon Gibbie, but with eyes of admiration.

"Ho, creature!" he said, "you're more of a man than you look! What made you run down the devil's very horns that way?"

Gibbie stood smiling.

"If it hadn't been for my club we would both have been over the moon. What's your name, man?"

Still Gibbie only smiled.

"Where do you come from? Who's your folk? Where do you live? Haven't you a tongue in your head, you rascal?"

Gibbie burst out laughing.

"The creature's foolish!" concluded Donal to himself pityingly. "Poor thing! poor thing!" he added aloud, and laid his hand on Gibbie's head.

It was but the second touch of kindness Gibbie had received since he was the dog's guest. His emotion was one of unmingled delight and embodied itself in a perfect smile.

"Come, creature, and I'll give you a piece; you'll understand that all right!" said Donal, as he turned to leave the corn for the grass, where Hornie was eating with the rest like the most innocent of hum'le (hornless) animals. Gibbie obeyed and followed.

"I hope none of them's swallowed my napkin!" Donal said musingly. "I'm not sure where I was sitting. I have my place in the book, but I've lost my place in the field."

Long before he had ended, for he spoke with utter deliberation, Gibbie was yards away, flitting hither and thither like a butterfly. A minute more and Donal saw him pounce upon his bundle, which he brought to him in triumph.

"Fegs! You're not the gowk I took you for," said Donal.

Whether Gibbie took the remark for a compliment, or merely was gratified that Donal was pleased, the result was a merry laugh.

The bundle had in it a piece of hard cheese such as Gibbie had already made acquaintance with and a few quarters of cakes. One of these Donal broke in two, gave Gibbie the half, replaced the other, and sat down again to his book—this time with his back against the fell-dike dividing the grass from the corn. Gibbie seated himself like a Turk, with his bare legs crossed under him, a few yards off, where, in silence and absolute content, he ate his piece and gravely regarded him.

Never since his father's death had he looked on a face that drew him as Donal's. It was fair of complexion by nature, but the sun had burned it brown, and it was covered with freckles. Its forehead was high, with a mass of foxy hair over it, and under it two keen hazel eyes in which the green predominated over the brown. Its nose was long and solemn over his well-made mouth, which rarely smiled, but not unfrequently trembled with emotion over his book. For age, Donal was getting toward fifteen and was strongly built and well grown. A general look of honesty and an attractive expression of reposeful friendliness pervaded his whole appearance. Conscientious in regard to his work, he was yet in danger of forgetting his duty for minutes together in his book. He knew his master would threaten him with dismissal if he came upon him reading in the field, but he knew also his master was well aware that he did read, and that it was possible to read and yet herd well.

It was Fergus Duff, second son of the master of the Mains at Glashruach who lent Donal books. He had a store of them for he had been two years at college. Donal, son of a poor shepherd, might never get to college but he had a great hunger for what was in the books. Donal now had an ally, for Gibbie had begun to comprehend the situation. He could not comprehend why or how anyone should be absorbed in a book, for all he knew of books was from his one morning of dame-schooling; but he could comprehend that, if one's attention were so occupied, it must be a great vex to be interrupted continually. Therefore, as Donal watched his book, Gibbie for Donal's sake watched the herd, and, as he did so, gently possessed himself of Donal's club. Nor had many minutes passed before Donal, raising his head to look, saw the curst cow again in the green corn, and Gibbie manfully encountering her with the club, hitting her hard upon the head and horns, and deftly avoiding every rush she made at him.

"Give her it upon the nose." Donal shouted.

Gibbie heard and obeyed, and the next moment Hornie had turned tail and was fleeing back to the safety of the lawful meadow.

"Hech, creature! but you must come of fighting folk!" said Donal, regarding him with fresh admiration. He then resumed his book, while Gibbie again sat down nearby and watched both Donal and his charge.

By and by Donal raised his head once more, but this time it was to regard Gibbie and not the nowt. It had gradually sunk into him that the appearance and character of the creature were peculiar. He had regarded him as a little tramp whose people were not far off, and who would soon get tired of herding and rejoin his companions; but while he read, a strange feeling of the presence of the boy had, in spite of the witchery of his book, been growing upon him. He seemed to feel his eyes without seeing them; and when Gibbie rose to look how the cattle were distributed, he became vaguely uneasy lest the boy should be going away. For already he had begun to feel him a humble kind of guardian angel. He had already that day, through him, enjoyed a longer spell of his book than any day since he had been herd at the Mains of Glashruach. And now the desire had come to regard him more closely.

For a minute or two he sat and gazed at him. Gibbie gazed at him in return, and in his eyes the herdboy looked the very type of power and gentleness. How he admired even his suit of small-ribbed, greenish-colored corduroy, the ribs much rubbed and obliterated! Then his jacket had round brass buttons! his trousers had patches instead of holes at the knees! their short legs revealed warm woolen stockings! and his shoes had their soles full of great broad-headed iron tacks! while on his head he had a small round blue bonnet with a red tuft!

The little outcast, on the other hand, with his loving face and pure clear eyes, bidding fair to be naked altogether before long, woke in Donal a divine pity, a tenderness like that nestling at the heart of womanhood. The neglected creature could surely have no mother to shield him from frost and wind and rain. Yet there he sat before Donal's eyes, full of service, of smiles, of contentment.

Donal took up his book but laid it down again and gazed at Gibbie. Several times he tried to return to his reading, but as often resumed his contemplation of the boy. At length it struck him as something more than shyness would account for, that he had not yet heard a word from the lips of the child, even when running after the cows. He must watch him more closely.

By this it was his dinnertime. Again he untied his handkerchief, and gave Gibbie what he judged a fair share for his bulk. What a day it had been for Gibbie! A whole human being, and some five-and-twenty four-legged creatures besides, to take care of!

After their dinner, Donal gravitated to his book, and Gibbie resumed the executive. Some time had passed when Donal, glancing up, saw Gibbie lying flat on his chest, staring at something in the grass. He slid himself quietly nearer and discovered it was a daisy—one by itself alone; there were not many in the field. Like a mother leaning over her child, he was gazing at it. The daisy was not a cold white one, neither was it a red one; it was just a perfect daisy: it looked as if some gentle hand had taken it while it slept and its star points were all folded together, and dipped them—just a tiny touchy dip, in a molten ruby, so that, when it opened again, there was its crown of silver, pointed with rubies all about its golden sun heart.

"He's been reading Burns!" said Donal. "Can you read, creature?"

Gibbie shook his head.

"Can't you speak, man?"

Again Gibbie shook his head.

"Can you hear?"

Gibbie burst out laughing. He knew that he heard better than other people.

"Hearken to this then," said Donal.

He took his book from the grass and read, in a chant, or rather in a lilt, the Danish ballad of Chyld Dyring, as translated by Sir Walter Scott. Gibbie's eyes grew wider and wider as he listened; their pupils dilated and his lips parted; it seemed as if his soul were looking out of door and windows at once —but a puzzled soul that understood nothing of what it saw.

When Donal ceased, he remained openmouthed and motionless for a time; then, drawing himself slidingly over the grass to Donal's feet, he raised his head and peeped above his knees at the book. A moment only he gazed and drew back with a hungry sigh; he had seen nothing in the book like what Donal had been drawing from it—as if one should look into the well of which he had just drunk and see there nothing but dry pebbles and sand! To his amazement, Donal saw the tears gathering in Gibbie's eyes. The child in whom neither cold nor hunger nor nakedness nor loneliness could move a throb of self-pity was moved to tears that a loveliness, to him strange and unintelligible, had passed away, and he had no power to call it back.

"Would you like to hear it again?" asked Donal.

Gibbie's face answered with a flash, and Donal read the poem again, and Gibbie's delight returned greater than before, for now something like a dawn began to appear among the cloudy words. Donal read it a third time and closed the book, for it was almost the hour for driving the cattle home.

Donal rose and Gibbie lay where he had again thrown himself upon the grass. When he lifted his head, Donal and the cows had vanished.

After Donal left him in the field, Gibbie lay on the grass, as happy as child could well be. A loving hand laid on his feet or legs would have found them like ice; but where was the matter so long as he never thought of them? The sun, however, was going down behind a great mountain, and its huge shadow, made of darkness and haunted with cold, came sliding across the river and over valley and field, nothing staying its silent wave, until it covered Gibbie with the blanket of the dark, under which he could not long forget that he was in a body to which cold is unfriendly. At the first breath of the night wind that came after the shadow, he shivered, and starting to his feet, began to trot, increasing his speed until he was scudding up and down the field like a wild thing of the night, whose time was at hand, waiting until the world should lie open to him. Suddenly he perceived that the daisies, which all day long had been full-facing the sun, had folded their petals together to points and held them like spearheads tipped with threatening crimson, against the onset of the night and her shadows, while within its white cone each folded in the golden heart of its life, until the great Father should return, and, shaking the wicked out of the folds of the night, render the world once more safe with another glorious day.

Gibbie gazed and wondered; and while he gazed—slowly, glidingly, back to his mind came the ghost-mother of the ballad, and in every daisy he saw her folding her neglected orphans to her bosom, while the darkness and the misery rolled by defeated. He wished he knew a ghost that would put her arms around him. He must have had a mother once, he supposed, but he could not remember her, and of course she must have forgotten him.

The stars came out, to Gibbie the heavenly herd, feeding at night, and gathering gold in the blue pastures. He saw them, looking up from the grass where he had thrown himself to gaze more closely at the daisies; and the sleep that pressed down his eyelids seemed to descend from the spaces between the stars. But it was too cold that night to sleep in the fields when he knew where to find warmth. Like a fox into his hole, the child would creep into the corner where God had stored sleep for him; back he went to the barn, gently trotting, and wormed himself through the cathole.

There stood the ladder against the loft. Up he went. He groped his way forward through the dark loft until he found the hay, when at once he burrowed into it like a sandfish into the wet sand. All night the white horse, a glory vanished in the dark, would be close to him, behind the thin partition of boards. He could hear his very breath as he slept, and to the music of it, audible sign of companionship, he fell fast asleep and slept until the waking horses woke him.

4: *The Broonie i' the Hoose*

WHEN LIGHT CAME again, Gibbie gazed down from the hay at the white horse, and for the first time in his life wondered if he was as clean as he ought to be. He did not know, but he would make an experiment for information when he got down to the burn. Meantime was there nothing he could do for the splendid creature? From above, leaning over, he filled his rack with hay. What should he do next? The thing he would like best would be to look through the ceiling again and watch the woman at her work. Then, too, he would again smell the boiling porridge and the burning of the little sprinkles of meal that fell into the fire. Carefully he crept to the ceiling, whence he peeped once more down into the kitchen. As yet it lay unvisited, as witnessed by its disorder.

Suddenly came to Gibbie the thought that here was a chance for him—here a path back to the world. Rendered daring by the eagerness of his hope, he got again upon the shelf, and with every precaution lest he should even touch a milkpan, descended by the lower shelves to the floor. There finding the door only latched, he entered the kitchen and proceeded to do everything he had seen the woman do, as nearly in her style as he could. He swept the floor and dusted the seats, the window sill, the table, with an apron he found left on a chair, then arranged everything tidily, roused the rested fire, and had just concluded that the only way to get the great pot full of water upon it would be to hang first the pot on the chain, and then fill it with the water, when his sharp ears caught sounds and then heard approaching feet. He darted into the dairy, and in a few seconds, had clambered upon the ceiling, and was lying flat across the joists, with his eyes to the most commanding crack he had discovered.

When Jean Mavor—the farmer's half-sister—opened the door, she stopped short and stared; the kitchen was not as she had left it the night before! The floor had been swept, the table wiped, the place "redd up," and the fire roused.

"Hoot! I must have been walking in my sleep," said Jean to herself aloud. "Or maybe that good laddie Donal Grant's been willing to give me a helping hand for his mother's sake, honest woman! The laddie's good enough for anything! Ay, even to be a minister!"

Eagerly, greedily, Gibbie now watched her every motion, and, bent upon learning, nothing escaped him; he would do much better next morning! At length the men came in to breakfast. Gibbie, as he could not eat, ran to the burn and drank—but had no heart that morning for his projected inquiry into the state of his person. He must go to Donal. The sight of him would help him to bear his hunger.

The first indication Donal had of his proximity was the rush of Hornie past him in flight out of the corn. Gibbie was pursuing her with stones for lack of a stick. Thoroughly ashamed of himself, Donal threw his book from him and ran to meet Gibbie.

"You mustn't fling stones, creature," he said. "Haith! It's not for me to find fault, though," he added, "sitting reading books like the gowk that I am and letting the beasts run wild in the corn! I'm clean affronted with myself, creature!"

Gibbie's response was to set off at full speed for the place where Donal had been sitting. He was back in a moment with the book, which he pressed into Donal's hand, while from the other he withdrew his club. This he brandished aloft once or twice, then starting at a steady trot, speedily circled the herd, and returned to his adopted master. Donal therefore left all to Gibbie and did not once look up for a whole hour.

At last, however, Donal laid down his book, called out to Gibbie, "Creature, it's dinnertime," and took his bundle.

Gibbie drew near with sparkling eyes. Donal, who himself knew nothing of want, perceived that he was ravenous, and made haste to undo the knots of the handkerchief, which Mistress Jean appeared that day to have tied with more than ordinary vigor. When the last knot yielded, he gazed with astonishment at the amount and variety of provision disclosed.

"Losh!" he exclaimed, "the mistress must have known there were two of us."

Before the day was over, Donal gave his helper more and other pay for his service. Choosing a fit time, when the cattle were well together and in good position, Hornie away at the stone dike, he took from his pocket a somewhat wasted volume of ballads and said, "Sit down, creature. Never mind the nowt. I'm going to read to you."

Gibbie dropped on his crossed legs like a lark to the ground and sat motionless. Donal, after deliberate search, began to read, and Gibbie to listen.

When the hour came for the cattle to go home, Gibbie again remained behind, waiting until all should be still at the farm. He lay on the dike, brooding over what he had heard and wondering how it was that Donal got all those strange beautiful words and sounds and stories out of the book.

Every morning, Gibbie got into the kitchen in good time; and not only did more and more of the work, but did it more and more to the satisfaction of Jean, until, short of the actual making of the porridge, he did everything antecedent to the men's breakfast. When Jean came in, she had but to take the lid from the pot, put in the salt, assume the spurtle, and, grasping the first handful of the meal, which stood ready waiting in the bossy on the stone cheek of the fire, throw it in, thus commencing the simple cookery of the best of all dishes to a truehearted and healthy Scotsman. Without further question she attributed all the aid she received to the goodness of Donal Grant and continued to make acknowledgement of the same in both sort and quantity of victuals, whence the real laborer received his due reward.

Until he had thoroughly mastered his work, Gibbie persisted in regarding matters economic "from his loophole in the ceiling"; and having at length learned the art of making butter, soon arrived at some degree of perfection in it. But when at last one morning he not only churned, but washed and made it up entirely to Jean's satisfaction, she did begin to wonder how a mere boy could both have such perseverance and be so clever at a woman's work. For now she entered the kitchen every morning without a question of finding the fire burning, the water boiling, the place clean and tidy, the supper dishes well washed and disposed on shelf and rack: her own part was merely to see that proper cloths were handy to so thorough a user of them. She took no one into her confidence on the matter; it was enough, she judged, that she and Donal understood each other.

And now if Gibbie had contented himself with rendering this house service in return for the shelter of the barn and its hay, he might have enjoyed both longer; but from the position of his night quarters, he came gradually to understand the work of the stable also; and before long, the men, who were quite ignorant of anything similar taking place in the house, began to observe, more to their wonder than satisfaction, that one or other of the horses were generally groomed before his man came to him; that often there was hay in their racks which they had not given them; and that the master's white horse every morning showed signs of having had some attention paid him that could not be accounted for.

The result was much talk and speculation, suspicion and offense; for all were jealous of their rights, their duty, and their dignity in relation to their horses; no man was at liberty to do a thing to or for any but his own pair. Even the brightening of the harness brass, in which Gibbie sometimes indulged, was an offense; for did it not imply a reproach? Many were the useless traps laid for the offender, many the futile attempts to surprise him; as Gibbie never did anything except for half an hour or so while the men were sound asleep or at breakfast, he escaped discovery.

But he could not hold continued intercourse with the splendor of the white horse and neglect carrying out the experiment on which he had resolved with regard to the effect of water upon his own skin; and having found the result a little surprising, he soon got into the habit of daily and thorough ablution. With his clothes he could do nothing, alas! but he bathed every night in the Lorrie as soon as Donal had gone home with the cattle. Once he got into a deep hole, but managed to get out again, and so learned that he could swim.

All day he was with Donal and took from him by much the greater part of his labor; Donal had never had such time for reading. In return he gave him his dinner, and Gibbie could do very well upon one meal a day. He paid him also in poetry. It never came into his head, seeing he never spoke, to teach him to read. He soon gave up attempting to learn anything from him as to his place or people or history, for to all questions in that direction Gibbie only looked grave and shook his head. As often, on the other hand, as he tried to learn where he spent the night, he received for answer only one of his merriest laughs.

Nor was larger time for reading the sole benefit Gibbie conferred upon Donal. Such was the avidity and growing intelligence with which the little naked town-savage listened to what Donal read to him that his presence was just so much added to Donal's own live soul of thought and feeling. From listening to his own lips through Gibbie's ears, he not only understood many things better, but, perceiving what things must puzzle Gibbie, came sometimes, rather to his astonishment, to see that in fact he did not understand them himself. Thus the bond between the boy and the child grew closer.

It was not all fine weather up there among the mountains in the beginning of summer. In the first week of June even, there was sleet and snow in the wind. Then would Donal's heart be sore for Gibbie, when he saw his poor rags blown about like streamers in the wind and the white spots melting on his bare skin. Once, in great pity, he pulled off his jacket and threw it on Gibbie's shoulders. But the shout of laughter that burst from the boy as he flung the jacket from him and rushed away into the middle of the feeding herd, a shout that came from no cave of rudeness but from the very depths of delight, stirred by the loving kindness of the act, startled Donal out of his pity into brief anger, and he rushed after him in indignation.

But Gibbie dived under the belly of a favorite cow and peering out sideways from under her neck and between her forelegs, his arms grasping each a leg while the cow went on twisting her long tongue around the grass and plucking it undisturbed, showed such an innocent countenance of holy merriment, that the pride of Donal's hurt benevolence melted away, and his laughter emulated Gibbie's.

Things had gone on in this way for several weeks when one

morning the men came in to breakfast all out of temper together, complaining loudly of the person unknown who would persist in interfering with their work. They were the louder that their suspicions fluttered about Fergus, who was rather overbearing with them, and therefore not a favorite. He carried himself high, they said, doing nothing but ride over the farm and pick out every fault he could find—they fancied that he carried their evil report to his father, and that this underhand work in the stable must be part of some sly scheme for bringing them into disgrace.

Gibbie had discovered the cornbin, and having no notion but that everything in the stable was for the delectation of the horses, had been feeding them largely with oats; and the consequences had begun to show themselves in the increased unruliness of the more wayward among them.

The same day brought things nearly to a crisis; for the overfed Snowball, proving too much for Fergus' horsemanship, came rushing home at a fierce gallop without him, having indeed left him in a ditch by the roadside. The remark thereupon made by the men in his hearing, that it was his own fault, led him to ask questions, when he came gradually to know what they attributed to him and was indignant at the imputation of such an employment of his mornings to one who had his studies to attend to.

In the evening, Jean sought a word with Donal and expressed her surprise that he should be able to do everybody's work about the place, warning him it would be said he did it at the expense of his own. But what could he mean, she said, by wasting the good corn to put devilry into the horses?

Donal stared in utter bewilderment. He knew perfectly that to the men suspicion of him was as impossible as of one of themselves. Did he not sleep in the same chamber with them? Could it be allusion to the way he spent his time when out with the cattle that Mistress Jean intended?

He was so confused, looked so guilty as well as astray, and answered so far from any point in Jean's mind, that she at last became altogether bewildered. Her first feeling was one of resentment—as if Donal, in not doing her the kindness her fancy had been attributing to him, had all the time been doing her an injury; but the boy's honest bearing and her own good sense made her almost at once dismiss the absurdity.

Then came anew the question, utterly unanswerable now—who could it be that did not only all her morning work but part of the men's also? She gazed with big eyes fixed on his face, and Donal, struck silent, gazed in return. At length, in a broken voice, low and solemn and fraught with mystery, she said,

"Donal, it's the broonie!"

Donal's mouth opened wide at the word, and his heart seemed to give a gape in his bosom, and it rushed back upon his memory how he had heard certain old people talk of the brownie that used, when their mothers and grandmothers were young, to haunt the Mains of Glashruach. His mother did not believe such things, but what if there should be something in them? To think that Mistress Jean, for whom everybody had such a respect, should speak of the creature in such a tone sent a thrill of horrific wonder and delight through the whole frame of the boy. Not once did the real brownie occur to him—the small, naked Gibbie, far more marvelous and admirable than any brownie of legendary fable or fact.

Jean Mavor came from a valley far withdrawn in the folds of the Gormgarnet Mountains, where in her youth she had heard yet stranger tales than had ever come to Donal's ears, of which some had perhaps kept their hold the more firmly that she had never heard them even alluded to since she left her home. Her brother, a hardheaded highlander, as canny as any lowland Scot, would have laughed to scorn the most passing reference to such an existence; and Fergus, who had

had a lowland mother, would have joined heartily in his mockery. For the cowherd, however, the idea had no small attraction, and his stare was the reflection of Mistress Jean's own.

"Do you really think it, ma'am?" said Donal at last.

"Think what?" retorted Jean, sharply, jealous instantly of being compromised, and perhaps not certain that she had spoken aloud.

"Do you really think that there are such creatures as broonies, Mistress Jean?"

"Who knows what there is and what there isn't?" returned Jean; she was not going to commit herself either way. Even had she imagined herself above believing such things, she would not have dared to say so. "You hold your tongue, laddie," she went on; "it's the least you can do after all that's happened; and least said is soonest mended. Go to your work."

But either Mistress Jean's influx of caution came too late, and someone had overheard her suggestion, or the idea was already abroad, for that very night it began to be reported upon the nearer farms that the Mains of Glashruach was haunted by a brownie who did all the work for both men and maids.

Quick at disappearing as Gibbie was, a very little cunning on the part of Jean might soon have entrapped the brownie; but a considerable touch of fear was now added to her other motives for continuing to spend a couple of hours longer in bed than had formerly been her custom. So that for yet a few days things went on much as usual; Gibbie saw no sign that his presence was suspected or that his doings were offensive; and life being to him a constant present, he never troubled himself about anything before it was there to answer for itself.

One morning the long thick mane of Snowball was found carefully plaited up in innumerable locks. This was properly elf-work, but no fairies had been heard of on Daurside for many a long year. The brownie, on the other hand, was already in everyone's mouth—only a stray one, probably, that had wandered from some old valley away in the mountains, where they were still believed in—but not the less a brownie; and if it was not the brownie who plaited Snowball's mane, who or what was it?

The rumor spread in long slow ripples, till it reached the laird in the House of Glashruach.

Thomas Galbraith was by birth Thomas Durrant but had married an heiress by whom he came into possession of Glashruach and had, according to previous agreement, taken her name. When she died he mourned her loss as well as he could, but was consoled by feeling himself now first master of both position and possession, when the ladder by which he had attained them was removed. Had he been a little more sensitive still, he would have felt that the property was then his daughter's, and his only through her; but this he failed to consider.

To his servants and tenants he was what he thought *just*. In general expression he looked displeased, but meant to look dignified. In person, he was very tall and very thin, with a head much too small for his height; a narrow forehead, above which the brown hair looked like a wig; pale-blue, ill-set eyes, that seemed too large for their sockets, consequently tumbled about a little, and were never at once brought to focus; a large but soft-looking nose, a loose-lipped mouth, and very little chin. He had no turn for farming, and therefore let all his land, yet liked to interfere, and as much as possible kept a personal jurisdiction.

There was one thing, however, which, if it did not throw the laird into a passion, brought him nearer to the outer verge of displeasure than any other, and that was, anything whatever to which he could affix the name of superstition.

Thomas Galbraith sat at luncheon with his daughter Ginevra, who was barely visible over the top of a game pie. The girl never sat nearer her father at meals than the whole length of the table, where she occupied her mother's place. She was a solemn-looking child, of eight or nine, dressed in a brown merino frock of the plainest description. Her hair, which was nearly of the same color as her frock, was done up in two triple plaits which hung down her back and were tied at the tips with black ribbons. To the first glance she did not look a very interesting or attractive child; but looked at twice, she was sure to draw the eyes a third time. She was undeniably like her father, and that was much against her at first sight; but it required only a little acquaintance with her face to remove the prejudice; for in its composed, almost resigned expression, every feature of her father's seemed comparatively finished and settled into harmony with the rest. The nose was firm, the mouth modeled, the chin larger, the eyes a little smaller and full of life and feeling. The longer it was regarded by any seeing eye, the child's countenance showed fuller of promise, or at least of hope. Gradually the look would appear in it of a latent sensitive anxiety—then would dawn a glimmer of longing question; and then, all at once, it would slip back into the original ordinary look, which, without seeming attractive, had yet attracted.

Her father was never harsh to her, yet she looked rather frightened at him; but then he was cold, very cold. It troubled Ginevra greatly that, when she asked herself whether she loved her father better than anybody else, as she believed she ought, she became immediately doubtful whether she loved him at all.

She was eating porridge and milk. With spoon arrested in mid-passage, she stopped suddenly, and said—

"Papa, what's a broonie?"

"I have told you, Jenny, that you are never to talk broad Scotch in my presence."

His words came out slowly and sounded as if each was a bullet wrapped around with cotton wool to make it fit the barrel. Ginevra looked perplexed for a moment.

"Should I say *brownie,* Papa?"

"How can I tell you what you should call a creature that has no existence?" rejoined her father.

"If it be a creature, Papa, it must have a name!"

"What foolish person has been insinuating such contemptible superstition into your silly head? Tell me, child, that I may put a stop to it at once."

"They say," said Ginevra, "there's a broonie—brownie—at the Mains who does all the work."

"What is the meaning of this, Joseph?" said Mr. Galbraith, turning from her to the butler with the air of rebuke which was almost habitual to him.

"The meaning of what, sir?"

"I ask you, Joseph," answered the laird, "what this—this outbreak of superstition imports? You must be aware that nothing in the world could annoy me more than that Miss Galbraith should learn folly in her father's house. That staid servants, such as I had supposed mine to be, should use their tongues as if their heads had no more in them than so many bells hung in a steeple, is to me a mortifying reflection."

"Tongues as well as clappers were made to wag, sir; and wag they will, sir, as long as the string hangs out at both ends," answered Joseph. "Besides, sir," he went on, "if tongues didn't wag how would you, who must set things right, know what was wrong?"

"That is not a bad remark, Joseph," replied the laird with woolly condescension. "Pray acquaint me with the whole matter."

"I have nothing to acquaint your honor with but the ting-a-ling of tongues," replied Joseph, "and you'll have to arrange it to your own satisfaction."

Therewith he proceeded to report what he had heard reported, which was in the main the truth, considerably exaggerated—that the work of the house was done overnight by invisible hands—and the work of the stables, too; but that in the latter, cantrips were played as well; that some of the men talked of leaving the place; and that Mr. Duff's own horse, Snowball, was nearly out of his mind with fear.

The laird clenched his teeth and for a whole minute said nothing.

"It is one of the men themselves," he said at last, with outward frigidity. "Or some ill-designed neighbor," he added. "But I shall soon be at the bottom of it. Go to the Mains at once, Joseph, and ask young Fergus Duff to be so good as step over, as soon as he conveniently can."

Fergus was pleased enough to be sent for by the laird, and soon told him all he knew from his aunt and the men, confessing that he had himself been too lazy of a morning to take any steps toward personal acquaintance with the facts, but adding that, as Mr. Galbraith took an interest in the matter, he would be only too happy to carry out any suggestion he might think proper to make on the subject.

"Fergus," returned the laird, "do you imagine things inanimate can of themselves change their relations in space? In other words, are the utensils in your kitchen endowed with powers of locomotion? Can they take to themselves wings and fly? Or to use a figure more to the point, are they provided with members necessary to the washing of their own—*persons,* shall I say? Answer me those points, Fergus."

"Certainly not, sir," answered Fergus solemnly, for the laird's face was solemn, and his speech was very solemn.

"Then, Fergus, let me assure you that to discover by what agency these apparent wonders are effected, you have merely to watch. If you fail, I will myself come to your assistance. Depend upon it, the thing when explained will prove simplicity itself."

Fergus at once undertook to watch, but went home not quite so comfortable as he had gone. Not even to himself did he confess that he felt frightened, for he was a youth of nearly eighteen; but he could not quite hide from himself the fact that he anticipated no pleasure in the duty which lay before him.

For more reasons than one, Fergus judged it prudent to tell not even Auntie Jean of his intention; but, waiting until the house was quiet, stole softly from his room and repaired to the kitchen, at the other end of the long straggling house, where he sat down, and, taking his book, began to read. He read and read, but no brownie came. His candle burned into the socket. He lighted another and read again. Still no brownie appeared, and, hard and straight as was the wooden chair on which he sat, he began to doze. Presently he started wide-awake, fancying he heard a noise; but nothing was there. He raised his book once more and read until he had finished.

When the gray of the dawn appeared, he said to himself he would lie down on the bench awhile, he was so tired of sitting; he would not sleep. He lay down and in a moment was asleep.

The light grew and grew, and the brownie came—with the daintiest-shaped hands and feet coming out of the midst of rags, and with no hair except roughly parted curls over the face of a cherub—for the combing of Snowball's mane and tail had taught Gibbie to use the same comb upon his own thatch. But as soon as he opened the door of the dairy, he was warned by the loud breathing of the sleeper, and looking about, espied him on the bench behind the table, and swiftly retreated.

The same instant Fergus woke, stretched himself, saw it was broad daylight, and, with his brain muddled by fatigue and sleep combined, crawled shivering to bed. Then in came the brownie again; and when Jean Mavor entered, there was her work done as usual.

Fergus was hours late for breakfast, and when he went into the common room, found his aunt alone there.

"Well, Auntie," he said, "I think I frightened your broonie!"

"Did you that, man? Ay! And then you set to and did the work yourself to save your Auntie Jean's old bones?"

"No, no, I was overtired for that. So would you have been yourself if you'd been sitting up all night."

"Who did it, then?"

"Ow, just yourself, I'm thinking, Auntie."

"Never a finger of mine was laid to it, Fergus. If you frightened one broonie, another came; for there's the work done, the same's ever!"

"Damn the creature!" cried Fergus.

"Whisht, whisht, laddie! he's maybe hearing you this minute. And if he isn't, there's One that is that doesn't like swearing."

"I beg your pardon, Auntie, but it's just provoking!" returned Fergus, and therewith recounted the tale of his night's watch.

As soon as he had had his breakfast, he went to carry his report to Glashruach.

The laird was vexed and told him he must sleep well before night and watch to better purpose.

The next night, Fergus' terror returned in full force; but he watched thoroughly notwithstanding, and when his aunt entered, she found him there, and her kitchen in a mess. He had caught no brownie, it was true, but neither had a stroke of her work been done. The floor was unswept; not a dish had been washed; it was churning day, but the cream stood in the jar in the dairy, not the butter in the pan on the kitchen dresser. Jean could not quite see the good or the gain of it. She had begun to feel like a lady, she said to herself, and now she must tuck up her sleeves and set to work as before. It was a comedown in the world, and she did not like it.

"You must add cunning to courage, my young friend," said Mr. Galbraith; and Fergus went home resolved on yet another attempt.

He felt much inclined to associate Donal with him in his watch this time, but was too desirous of proving his courage both to himself and to the world to yield to the suggestion of his fear. He went to bed with a book immediately after the noonday meal and rose in time for supper.

There was a large wooden press in the kitchen, standing out from the wall; this with the next wall made a little recess, in which there was just room for a chair; and in that recess Fergus seated himself in the easiest chair he could get into it. He then opened wide the door of the press, and it covered him entirely.

This night would have been the dreariest of all for him, the laird having insisted that he should watch in the dark, had he not speedily fallen fast asleep, and slept all night—so well that he awoke at the first noise Gibbie made.

It was broad clear morning, but his heart beat so loud and fast with apprehension and curiosity mingled, that for a few moments Fergus dare not stir, but sat listening breathless to the movement beside him, none the less appalling that it was so quiet. Recovering himself a little, he cautiously moved the door of the press, and peeped out.

The dread brownie of his idea shrunk to a tiny ragged urchin with a wonderful head of hair, azure eyes, and deft hands, noiselessly bustling about on bare feet. He watched him at his leisure, watched him keenly, assured that any moment he could spring upon him.

As he watched, his wonder sank, and an evil cloud of anger began to gather in his mental atmosphere. His chair gave a loud creak. Without even looking around, Gibbie darted into the dairy and shut the door.

Instantly Fergus was after him, but only in time to see the vanishing of his last heel through the hole in the wall, and that way Fergus was much too large to follow him. He rushed from the house and across the corner of the yard to the barn door. Gibbie, who did not believe he had been seen, stood laughing on the floor, when suddenly he heard the key entering the lock. He bolted through the cathole—but again just one moment too late. The key of the door to the rickyard was inside, and Fergus was after him in a moment, but the ricks came close to the barn door, and the next he saw of him was the fluttering of his rags in the wind, and the flashing of his white skin in the sun, as he fled across the clover field; and before Fergus was over the wall, Gibbie was a good way ahead toward the Lorrie.

Gibbie was a better runner for his size than Fergus, and in better training too; but, alas! Fergus' legs were nearly twice as long as Gibbie's. The little one reached the Lorrie first, and dashing across it, ran up the side of the Glashburn, with a vague idea of Glashgar in his head. Fergus behind him was growing more and more angry as he gained upon him but felt his breath failing him. Just at the bridge to the iron gate to Glashruach, he caught him at last, and sunk on the parapet exhausted. The smile with which Gibbie, too much out of breath to laugh, confessed himself vanquished, would have disarmed one harder-hearted than Fergus, had he not lost his temper in the dread of losing his labor; and the answer Gibbie received to his smile was a box on the ear that bewildered him. He looked pitifully in his captor's face, the smile not yet faded from his, only to receive a box on the other ear, and the water gathered in his eyes.

Fergus, a little eased in his temper by the infliction, and in his breath by the wall of the bridge, began to ply him with questions; but no answer following, his wrath rose again and again he boxed both his ears. He turned upon his prisoner and told him he was an impudent rascal. Gibbie had recovered again and was able once more to smile a little. He had been guilty of burglary, said Fergus; and Gibbie smiled. He could be sent to prison for it, said Fergus; and Gibbie smiled—but this time a very grave smile. Fergus took him by the collar, which amounted to nearly a third part of the jacket, and shook him till he had half torn that third from the other two; then opened the gate, and, holding him by the back of the neck, walked him up the drive, every now and then giving him a fierce shake that jarred his teeth.

Thus, over the old gravel, mossy and damp and grassy, and cool to his little bare feet, between rowan and birch and pine and larch, like a malefactor, and looking every inch the outcast he was, did Sir Gilbert Galbraith approach the house of his ancestors for the first time. His history was about him and in him, yet of it all he suspected nothing. It would have made little difference to him if he had known it all; he would none the less have accepted everything that came, just as part of the story in which he found himself.

The laird was talking to his gamekeeper, a heavy-browed man, by the coachhouse door, when Fergus appeared holding the dwindled brownie by the huge collar of his tatters.

"So this is your vaunted brownie, Mr. Duff!" the laird said.

"It's all the brownie I could lay hands on, sir," answered Fergus. "I took him in the act."

"Boy," said the laird, rolling his eyes, more unsteady than usual with indignation, in the direction of Gibbie, "what have you to say for yourself?"

Gibbie had no say.

"What is your name?" asked the laird, speaking yet more sternly.

Gibbie still smiled and was silent, looking straight in his questioner's eyes. He had no idea of his silence causing annoyance. Everybody in the city had known he could not answer; and now when Fergus and the laird persisted in questioning him, he thought they were making kindly game of him and smiled the more.

"I see the young vagabond is as impertinent as he is vicious," the laird said at last, finding that to no interrogation could he draw forth any other response than a smile. "Here, Angus" —and he turned to the gamekeeper—"take him into the coachhouse and teach him a little behavior. A touch or two of the whip will find his tongue for him."

Angus seized the little gentleman by the neck, as if he had been a polecat, and at arm's length walked him unresistingly into the coachhouse. There, with one vigorous tug, he tore the jacket from his back, and his only other garment, dependent thereupon by some device known only to Gibbie, fell from him, and he stood in helpless nakedness, smiling still. But when the scowling keeper, to whom poverty was first cousin to poaching and who hated tramps as he hated vermin, approached him with a heavy cart whip in his hand, he cast his eyes down at his white sides, very white between his brown arms and brown legs, and then lifted them in a mute appeal.

"You devil's child!" cried the fellow, "I'll let you know what comes of breaking into honest people's houses and taking things that are not your own!"

A vision of the gnawed cheese rose before Gibbie's mental eyes, and inwardly he bowed to the punishment. But the look he had fixed on Angus was not without effect, for the man was a father, though a severe one, and was not all a brute: he turned and changed the cart whip for a gig one with a broken shaft, which lay near.

When the blow fell the child shivered all over, his face turned white, and without uttering even a moan, he doubled up and dropped senseless. A swollen cincture, like a red snake, had risen all round his waist, and from one spot in it the blood was oozing.

"Up with you, or I'll hit you again," the gamekeeper said from between his teeth, lifting the whip for a second blow.

Just as the stroke fell, marking him from the nape all down the spine, so that he now bore upon his back in red the sign the ass carries in black, a piercing shriek assailed Angus' ears, and his arm, which had mechanically raised itself for a third blow, hung arrested.

The same moment, in at the coachhouse door shot Ginevra, as white as Gibbie. She darted to where he lay, and there stood over him, arms rigid and hands clenched hard, shivering as he had shivered, and sending from her body shriek after shriek, as if her very soul were the breath of which her cries were fashioned.

"Go away, missie," cried Angus, who had respect for this child, though he had not yet learned to respect childhood; "he's a coarse creature and must be whipped."

But Ginevra was deaf to his evil charming. She stopped her cries, however, to help Gibbie up and took one of his hands to raise him. But his arm hung limp and motionless; she let it go; it dropped like a stick and again she began to shriek.

Angus laid his hand on her shoulder. She turned on him, and opening her mouth wide, screamed at him like a wild animal, with all the hatred of mingled love and fear; then threw herself on the boy, and covered his body with her own. Angus, stooping to remove her, saw Gibbie's face and became uncomfortable.

"He's dead! he's dead! You've killed him, Angus! You're an evil man!" she cried fiercely. "I hate you. I'll tell on you. I'll tell my papa."

"Hoot! whisht, missie!" said Angus. "It was by your papa's own orders I gave him the whip, and he well deserved it besides. If you don't go away and be a good young lady, I'll give him more yet."

"I'll tell God," shrieked Ginevra with fresh energy of defensive love and wrath.

Again he sought to remove her, but she clung so with both legs and arms to the insensible Gibbie that he could but lift both together and had to leave her alone.

"If you dare to touch him again, Angus, I'll bite you—*bite you*—BITE YOU," she screamed, in a passage wildly crescendo.

The laird and Fergus had walked away together, perhaps neither of them quite comfortable at the orders given, but the one too self-sufficient to recall them, and the other too submissive to interfere. They heard the cries, nevertheless, and had they known them for Ginevra's, would have rushed to the spot; but they took them for Gibbie's and supposed the whip had had the desired effect and loosed his tongue.

Ginevra's shrieks brought Gibbie to himself. Faintly he opened his eyes, and stared, stupid with growing pain, at the tear-blurred face beside him. In the confusion of his thoughts he fancied the pain he felt was Ginevra's, not his, and sought to comfort her, stroking her cheek with feeble hand, and putting up his mouth to kiss her. But Angus, utterly scandalized at the proceeding, and restored to energy by seeing that the boy was alive, caught her up suddenly and carried her off—struggling, writhing, and scratching like a cat.

The moment she thus disappeared, Gibbie began to apprehend that she was suffering for him, not he for her. He started to spring to his feet but fell back almost powerless; then tried more cautiously and got up wearily, for the pain and the terrible shock seemed to have taken the strength out of every limb. Once on his feet, he could scarcely stoop to pick up his remnant of trousers without again falling, and the effort made him groan with distress. He was in the act of trying in vain to stand on one foot, so as to get the other into the garment, when he fancied he heard the step of his executioner, returning doubtless to resume his torture. He dropped the rag, and darted out of the door, forgetting aches and stiffness and agony. All naked as he was, he fled like the wind, unseen, of any eye.

He ran he knew not whither, feeling nothing but the desire

first to get into some covert, and then to run farther. His first rush was for the shubbery, his next across the little park to the wood beyond. He did not feel the wind of his running on his bare skin. He did not feel the hunger that had made him so unable to bear the lash. On and on he ran, fancying ever he heard the cruel Angus behind him. If a dry twig snapped, he thought it was the crack of the whip; and a small wind that rose suddenly in the top of a pine seemed the hiss with which it was about to descend upon him. He ran and ran, but still there seemed nothing between him and his persecutors. He felt no safety. At length he came where a high wall joining some water formed a boundary. The water was a brook from the mountain, here widened and deepened into a still pool. He threw himself in, and swam straight across.

Then first awoke a faint sense of safety; for on the other side he was knee deep in heather. He was on the wild hill, with miles on miles of cover! He would get right into the heather and lie with it all around and over him till the night came. Where he would go then, he did not know. But it was all one; he could go anywhere. Donal must mind his cows, and the men must mind the horses, and Mistress Jean must mind her kitchen, but Sir Gibbie could go where he pleased.

Thus he communed with himself as he went over the knoll. On the other side he chose a tall patch of heather and crept under. How nice and warm and kind the heather felt, though it did hurt the wales dreadfully.

And now Sir Gibbie, though not much poorer than he had been, really possessed nothing separable, except his hair and his nails—nothing therefore that he could call *his*, as distinguished from *him*. He was not nearly reduced to extremity yet though—this little heir of the world; in his body he had splendid health, in his heart a great courage, and in his soul an ever-throbbing love.

Poor Ginny was sent to bed for interfering with her father's orders; and what with rage and horror and pity, an inexplicable feeling of hopelessness took possession of her.

Fergus told his aunt what had taken place and made much game of her brownie. But the more Jean thought about the affair, the less she liked it. It was she upon whom it all came! What did it matter who or what her brownie was? And what had they whipped the creature for? What harm had he done? If indeed he was a little ragged urchin, the thing was only the more inexplicable! He had taken nothing! She had never missed so much as a barley scone! The cream had always brought her the right quantity of butter! Not even a bannock, so far as she knew, was ever gone from the press, or an egg from the bossy where they lay heaped! There was more in it than she could understand! Her nephew's mighty feat, so far from explaining anything, had only sealed up the mystery. She could not help cherishing a shadowy hope that, when things had grown quiet, he would again reveal his presence by his work, if not by his visible person. It was mortifying to think that he had gone as he came, and she had never set eyes upon him.

Donal Grant, missing his "creature" that day for the first time, heard enough when he came home to satisfy him that he had been acting the brownie in the house and the stable as well as in the field. Then first also, after he had thus lost him, he began to understand his worth, and to see how much he owed him.

5: *Refuge*

IT WAS A lovely Saturday evening on Glashgar. The few flowers about the small turf cottage scented the air in the hot western sun. The heather was not in bloom yet, and there were no trees; but there were rocks and stones and a brawling burn that half surrounded a little field of oats, one of potatoes, and a small spot with a few stocks of cabbage and kale, on the borders of which grew some bushes of double daisies and primroses and carnations. These Janet tended as part of her household, while her husband saw to the oats and potatoes.

Robert had charge of the few sheep on the mountain which belonged to the farmer at the Mains, and for his trouble had the cottage and the land, most of which he had himself reclaimed. They were never in any want, and never had any money, except what their children brought them out of their small wages. But that was plenty for their every need.

It was very cold up there in winter, and they both suffered from rheumatism; but they had no debt, no fear, much love, and between them, this being mostly Janet's, a large hope for what lay on the other side of death; as to the rheumatism, that was necessary, Janet said, to teach them patience, for they had no other trouble. They were indeed growing old, but neither had begun to feel age a burden yet, and when it should prove such, they had a daughter prepared to give up service and go home to help them. Their thoughts about themselves were nearly lost in their thoughts about each other, their children, and their friends. Janet's main care was her old man, and Robert turned to Janet as the one stay of his life, next to the God in whom he trusted. He did not think so much about God as she; he was not able; nor did he read so much of his Bible; but she often read to him; and when any of his children were there of an evening, he always "took the book."

While Janet prayed at home, his closet was the mountain-side, where he would kneel in the heather, and pray to Him who saw unseen. The sheep took no heed of him, but sometimes when he rose from his knees and saw Oscar gazing at him with deepest regard, he would feel a little as if he had not quite entered enough into his closet and would wonder what the dog was thinking. All day, from the mountain and sky and preaching burns, from the sheep and his dog, from winter storms, spring sun and winds, or summer warmth and glow, but more than all, when he went home, from the presence and influence of his wife, came to him somehow spiritual nourishment and vital growth. He loved life, but if he had been asked why, he might not have found a ready answer. He loved his wife—just because she was Janet.

To Robert, Janet was one who knew—one who was far "ben" with the Father of Lights. She perceived His intentions, understood His words, did His will, dwelt in the secret place of the Most High. When Janet entered into the kingdom of her Father, she would see that he was not left outside. His sole anxiety, on the other hand, was neither about life nor death, about this world nor the next, but that his children should be honest and honorable, fear God and keep His commandments. Around them, all and each, the thoughts of father and mother were constantly hovering, as if to watch them and ward off evil.

When Janet found herself in this remote spot, where she could see so little of her kind, she began to turn her study upon the story of our Lord's life. Nor was it long before it possessed her utterly, so that she concentrated upon it all the light and power of vision she had gathered from her experience of humanity. It followed naturally that the thought of Him, and the hope of one day seeing Him, became her one informing idea.

A certain gentle indifference she showed to things considered important, the neighbors attributed to weakness of character and called *softness;* while the honesty, energy, and directness with which she acted upon insights they did not possess, they attributed to intellectual derangement. She was "overeasy," they said, when the talk had been of prudence or worldly prospect; she was "overhard," they said, when the question had been of right and wrong.

The same afternoon, a neighbor, on her way over the shoulder of the hill to the next village, had called upon her and found her brushing the rafters of her cottage with a broom at the end of a long stick.

"Save us, Janet! What are you after? I never saw such a thing!" she exclaimed.

"I don't know as I ever thought of such a thing before myself," answered Janet, leaning her broom against the wall and dusting a chair for her visitor; "but this morning, when my man and me were sitting at our breakfast, there came such a clap of thunder as made the wee hoose tremble; and down fell a snot of soot into the very spoon that my man was carrying to his honest mouth. That could not be as things were intended, you know; so what was to be said but set them right?"

"Oh, well! but you might have waited till Donal came home;

he would have done it in half the time and not raxed his joints."

"I could not put it off," answered Janet. "Who knows when the Lord might come? He can't come at cock-crowing today, but He may be here before night."

"Well, I'll be away," said her visitor, rising. "I'm going over to the town to buy a few hanks of worsted to weave a pair of stockings for my man. Good day to you, Janet. What next, I wonder?" she added to herself as she left the house. "The woman's clean demented!"

The moment she was gone, Janet caught up her broom again, and went spying about over the roof—ceiling there was none—after long tangles of agglomerated cobweb and smoke.

"Ay!" she said to herself, "who knows when He may be at the door? And I would not like to hear Him say—'Janet, you might have had your wee hoose a bit cleaner, when you knew I might be at hand!' "

Having finished at last, she took her besom to the door and beat it against a stone. That done, she stood looking along the path down the hill. It was that by which her sons and daughters, every Saturday, came climbing, one after the other, to her bosom, from their various labors in the valley below, through the sunset, through the long twilight, through the moonlight, each urged by a heart eager to look again upon father and mother.

The sun was now far down his western arc, and nearly on a level with her eyes; and as she gazed into the darkness of the too much light, suddenly emerged from it, rose upward, staggered toward her—was it an angel? was it a specter? Did her old eyes deceive her? Or was the second sight born in her now first in her old age? It seemed a child—reeling and spreading out hands that groped. She covered her eyes for a moment, for it might be a vision in the sun, not on the earth, and looked again. It was indeed a naked child! And—was she still so dazzled by the red sun as to see red where red was none? Or were those indeed blood-red streaks on his white skin? Straight now, though slow, he came toward her. It was the same child who had come and gone so strangely before! He held out his hands to her and fell on his face at her feet like one dead.

Then, with a horror of pitiful amazement, she saw a great cross marked in two cruel stripes on his back. Could it be that the Lord was still, child and man, suffering for his race, to deliver his brothers and sisters from their sin?—wandering, enduring, beaten, blessing still?

Vaguely shadowed were thoughts like these in Janet's mind, as she stood half-stunned, regarding for one moment motionless the prostrate child and his wrongs. The next she lifted him in her arms and holding him tenderly to her mother-heart, carried him into the house, murmuring over him dovelike sounds of pity and endearment mingled with indignation. There she laid him on his side in her bed, covered him gently over, and hastened to the little byre at the end of the cottage to get him some warm milk.

When she returned, he had already lifted his heavy eyelids and was looking wearily about the place. But when he saw her, did ever so bright a sun shine as that smile of his! Eyes and mouth and whole face flashed upon Janet! She set down the milk and went to the bedside. Gibbie put up his arms, threw them around her neck, and clung to her as if she had been his mother. And from that moment she was his mother.

"What have they done to you, my bairn?" she said, in tones pitiful with the pity of the Shepherd of the Sheep Himself.

No reply came back—only another heavenly smile, a smile of absolute content.

She raised him with one arm and held the bowl to his mouth, and he drank; but all the time he drank, his eyes were fixed upon hers. When she laid him down again, he turned on his side, off his scored back, and in a moment was fast asleep. She stood gazing at him. So still was he that she began to fear he was dead and laid her hand on his heart. It was beating steadily, and she left him to make some gruel for him against his waking. Gruel, as such a one makes it, is no common fare, but delicate enough for a queen. She set it down by the fire and proceeded to lay the supper for her expected children. The clean yellow-white table of soft smooth fir needed no cloth—only horn spoons and wooden caups.

At length a hand came to the latch, and mother and daughter greeted as mother and daughter only can; then came a son, and mother and son greeted as mother and son only can. They kept on arriving singly to the number of six—two daughters and four sons, the youngest some little time after the rest. Each, as he or she came, Janet took to the bed and showed her seventh child where he slept. Each time she showed him, to secure like pity with her own, she turned down the bedclothes, and revealed the little back. The women wept. The young men were furious, each after his fashion.

"God damn the rascal that did that!" cried one of them, clenching his teeth, and forgetting himself quite in the rage of the moment.

"Laddie, take back that word," said his mother calmly. "Unless you forgive your enemies, you'll not be forgiven yourself."

"Well, but he's not my enemy," said the youth.

"Not your enemy!" returned his mother; "not your enemy and treat a bairn like that! My certy! but he's the enemy of the whole race of mankind!"

The sixth of the family now entered and his mother led him up to the bed.

"The Lord preserve us!" cried Donal Grant, "it's the creature! And is that the way they have treated him! The quietest creature and the willingest." Donal began to choke.

"You know him then, laddie?" said his mother.

"Well that," answered Donal. "He's been with me and the nowt every day for weeks till today." He hurried into the story of his acquaintance with Gibbie. When he finished and turned toward the bed, there were Gibbie's azure eyes wide open and fixed upon him.

"Eh, creature!" he cried. Bending over he took Gibbie's face between his hands and said, in a voice to which pity and sympathy gave a tone like his mother's, "What devil was it that beat you like that? Eh! I wish I had the trimming of him!"

Gibbie smiled.

"Has the ill-guideship taken the tongue from him, do you think?" asked the mother.

"No, no," answered Donal, "he's been like that since I knew him. I've never heard a word from his mouth."

"He must be one of the deaf and dumb," said Janet.

"He's not deaf, Mother, that I know well; but dumb he must be, I'm thinking. Creature," he continued, stooping over the boy, "if you hear what I'm saying, take hold of my nose."

Thereupon, with a laugh like that of an amused infant, Gibbie raised his hand, and with thumb and forefinger gently pinched Donal's large nose, at which they all burst out laughing with joy. It was as if they had found an angel's baby in the bushes and been afraid he was an idiot, but were now relieved.

Away went Janet and brought him his gruel. It was with no small difficulty and not without a moan or two that Gibbie sat up in the bed to take it. There was something very pathetic in the full content with which he sat there in his nakedness and looked smiling at them all. It was more than content—it was bliss that shone in his countenance. He took the wooden bowl and began to eat; and the look he cast on Janet seemed to say he had never tasted such delicious food.

Janet went to her "kist," whence she brought out a garment of her own, and aired it at the fire. It had no lace at the neck or cuffs, no embroidery down the front; but when she put it on him, amid the tearful laughter of the women, and had tied it around his waist with a piece of list that had served as a garter, it made a dress most becoming in their eyes, and gave Gibbie indescribable pleasure from its whiteness and its coolness to his inflamed skin.

They had just finished clothing him thus, when the good man came home, and the mother's narration had to be given afresh, with Donal's notes explanatory and completive. As the latter reported the doings of the imagined brownie, and the commotion they had caused at the Mains and along Daurside, Gibbie's countenance flashed with pleasure and fun; and at last he broke into such a peal of laughter as had never, for pure merriment, been heard before so high on Glashgar.

All joined involuntarily in the laugh—even the old man, who had been listening with his gray eyebrows knit, and hanging like bosky precipices over the tarns of his deepset eyes, taking in every word, but uttering not one. When at last his wife showed him the child's back, he lifted his two hands and moved them slowly up and down, as in pitiful appeal for man against man to the sire of the race. But still he said not a word. As to utterance of what lay in the deep soul of him, the old man, except sometimes to his wife, was nearly as dumb as Gibbie himself.

They sat down to their homely meal. Of Janet's supper it is enough to say that it was such as became her heart. In the judgment of all her guests, the porridge was such as none could make but Mother, the milk such as none but Mother's cow could yield, the cakes such as she only could bake.

Gibbie sat in the bed like a king on his throne, gazing on his kingdom. For he that loves has, as no one else has. It is the divine possession. Gibbie could not have invented a heaven more to his mind, and as often as one of them turned eyes toward the bed, his face shone up with love and merry gratitude.

It was now almost time for the sons and daughters to go down the hill again and leave the cottage and the blessed old parents and the harbored child to the night, the mountain-silence, and the living God. The sun had long been down; but far away in the north, the faint thin fringe of his light-garment was still visible, moving with the unseen body of his glory softly eastward, dreaming along the horizon, growing fainter and fainter as it went, but at the faintest then beginning to revive and grow.

"Now, lads and lasses, before we have worship, run each one of you," said the mother, "and put heather to make a bed for the wee man—in the nook there, at the head of ours. He'll sleep there bonny, and no ill-will come near him."

She was obeyed instantly. The heather was pulled and set together upright as it grew, only much closer, so that the tops made a dense surface, and the many stalks, each weak, a strong upbearing whole. They boxed them in below with a board or two for the purpose and bound them together above with a blanket over the top and a white sheet over that—a linen sheet it was, and large enough to be doubled and receive Gibbie between its folds. Then another blanket was added, and the bed, a perfect one, was ready. The eldest of the daughters took Gibbie in her arms, and, tenderly careful over his hurts, lifted him from the old folks' bed, and placed him in his own and Gibbie sank into it with a sigh that was but a smile grown vocal.

Then Donal, as the youngest, got down the big Bible, and having laid it before his father, lighted the rush-pith-wick projecting from the beak of the little iron lamp that hung against the wall, its shape descended from Roman times. The old man put on his spectacles, took the book, and found the passage that fell, in continuous process, to that evening.

Now he was not a very good reader, and, what with blindness and spectacles, and poor light, would sometimes lose his place. But it never troubled him, for he always knew the sense of what was coming, and being no idolater of the letter, used the word that first suggested itself, and so recovered his place without pausing. It reminded his sons and daughters of the time when he used to tell them Bible stories as they crowded about his knees.

On this occasion he was reading of our Lord's cure of the leper; and having read *put forth his hand,* lost his place, and went straight on without it, from his memory of the facts.

"He put forth his hand and gripped him, and said, I will, be clean."

After the reading followed a prayer, very solemn and devout. It was then only, when before God, with his wife by his side, and his family around him, that the old man became articulate.

By the time the prayer was over, Gibbie was fast asleep again. What it all meant he had not an idea; and the sound lulled him. When he woke next, from the aching of his stripes, the cottage was dark. The old people were fast asleep. A hairy thing lay by his side, which, without the least fear, he examined by palpation, and found to be a dog, whereupon he fell fast asleep again, if possible happier than ever.

While the cottage was thus quiet, the brothers and sisters were still tramping along the moonlight paths of Daurside. They had all set out together, but at one point after another there had been a parting, and now they were on six different roads, each drawing nearer to the labor of the new week.

6: *Gibbie Takes to Learning*

THE FIRST opportunity Donal had, he questioned Fergus as to his share in the ill-usage of Gibbie. Fergus treated the inquiry as an impertinent interference and mounted his high horse at once. What right had his father's herdboy to question him as to his conduct? He put it so to him and in nearly just as many words. Thereupon answered Donal—

"It's this, you see, Fergus: you have been very good to me and I'm more obliged than I can say. But it would be a scunnerful thing for me to take books from you and ask you questions that I can't make out myself, and then go away despising you in my heart for cruelty and wrong. What was the creature punished for? Tell me that. According to your aunt's own account, he had taken nothing, and had done nothing but good."

"Why didn't he speak up then, and defend himself, and not be so damned obstinate?" returned Fergus. "He wouldn't open his mouth to tell his name or where he came from even. I couldn't get him to utter a single word. As for his punishment, it was by the laird's orders that Angus MacPholp took the whip to him. I had nothing to do with it."

"Well, I'll be a man some day, and Angus will have to settle with me!" said Donal through his clenched teeth. "Man, Fergus! the creature's as dumb as a worm. I don't believe that he ever spoke a word in his life."

This cut Fergus to the heart, for he was far from being without generosity or pity.

Ginevra was hardly the same child after the experience of that terrible morning. At no time very much at home with her father, something had now come between them, to remove which all her struggles to love him as before were unavailing.

Fergus went back to college, Donal went on herding the cattle, cudgeling Hornie and reading what books he could lay his hands on.

In the meantime Gibbie slept and waked and slept again, night after night—with the loveliest days between, at the cottage on Glashgar. The morning after his arrival, the first thing he was aware of was Janet's face beaming over him, with a look in its eyes more like worship than benevolence. Her husband was gone, and she was about to milk the cow, and was anxious lest, while she was away, he should disappear as before. But the light that rushed into his eyes was in full response to that which kindled the light in hers, and her misgiving vanished; he could not love her like that and leave her. She gave him his breakfast of porridge and milk and went to her cow.

When she came back, she found everything tidy in the cottage, the floor swept, every dish washed and set aside; and Gibbie was examining an old shoe of Robert's to see whether he could not mend it. Janet, having therefore leisure, proceeded at once with joy to the construction of a garment she had been devising for him. The design was simple and its execution easy. Taking a blue winsey petticoat of her own, drawing it in around his waist, and tying it over the chemise which was his only garment, she found, as she had expected, that its hem reached his feet; she partly divided it up the middle, before and behind, and had but to backstitch two short seams, and there was a pair of sailorlike trousers, as tidy as comfortable. Gibbie was delighted with them. True, they had no pockets, but then he had nothing to put in pockets.

Then Janet thought about a cap; but considering him a moment critically and seeing how his hair stood out like thatch eaves around his head, she concluded with herself, "There must be some men as well as women folk, I'm thinking, whose hair has been given them for a covering," and betook herself instead to her New Testament.

Gibbie stood by as she read in silence, gazing with delight, for he thought it must be a book of ballads like Donal's that she was reading.

"Can you read, laddie?"

Gibbie shook his head.

"Sit down then and I'll read to you."

Gibbie obeyed more than willingly, expecting to hear some ancient Scots tale of love or chivalry. Instead, it was one of those love-awful, glory-sad chapters in the end of the Gospel of John, over which hangs the darkest cloud of human sorrow, shot through and through with the radiance of light.

Whether it was the uncertain response to Janet's tone merely, or to truth too loud to be heard, save as a thrill, of some chord in his own spirit, having its one end indeed twisted around an earthly peg but the other looped to a tailpiece far in the unknown—anyhow, when Janet looked up, she saw the tears rolling down the child's face. At the same time, from the expression of his countenance, she judged that his understanding had grasped nothing. She turned therefore to the parable of the prodigal son and read it. Janet saw the expression of the boy's face alter with every tone of the tale, through all the gamut between the swine's trough and the arms of the father. Then at last he burst into a laugh of loud triumph. He clapped his hands, and in a shiver of ecstasy, stood like a stork upon one leg, as if so much of him was all that could be spared for this lower world and screwed himself together.

Janet was well satisfied with her experiment. Thus had Gibbie his first lesson in the only thing worth learning, in that which, to be learned at all, demands the united energy of heart and soul and strength and mind; and from that day he went on learning it. I cannot tell how, or what were the slow stages by which his mind budded and swelled until it burst into the flower of humanity, the knowledge of God. I cannot tell the shape of the door by which the Lord entered into that house and took everlasting possession of it. I cannot even tell in what shape He appeared Himself in Gibbie's thoughts.

Happily Janet never suspected how utter was Gibbie's ignorance. She never dreamed that he did not know what was generally said about Jesus Christ. She thought he must know as well as she the outlines of His story and the purpose of His life and death, as commonly taught, and therefore never attempted explanations.

So, teaching him only that which she loved, Janet read to Gibbie of Jesus, talked to him of Jesus, dreamed to him about Jesus; until at length—Gibbie did not think to watch, and knew nothing of the process by which it came about—his whole soul was full of the man, of His doings, of His words, of His thoughts, of His life. Jesus Christ was in him—he was possessed by Him. Almost before he knew, he was trying to fashion his life after that of his Master.

Between the two, it was a sweet teaching, a sweet learning. Janet studied only Jesus, and as a man knows his friend, so she, only infinitely better, knew her more than friend—her Lord and her God. Being in the light she understood the light and had no need of system, either true or false, to explain it to her. She lived by the word proceeding out of the mouth of God. And seldom has there been a fitter soul, one clearer from evil, from folly, from human device—a purer cistern for such water of life as rose in the heart of Janet Grant to pour itself into than the soul of Sir Gibbie.

From that very next day, then, after he was received into the cottage on Glashgar, Gibbie, as a matter of course, took upon him the work his hand could find to do, and Janet averred to her husband that never had any of her daughters been more useful to her. At the same time, however, she insisted that Robert should take the boy out with him. She would not have him do woman's work, especially work for which she was herself perfectly able. She had not come to her years, she said, to learn idleset; and the boy would save Robert many a weary step among the hills.

"He can't speak to the dog," objected Robert, giving utterance to the first difficulty that suggested itself.

"The dog can't speak himself," returned Janet, "and the wonder is he can understand; who knows but he may come closer to one that's speechless like himself! Give the creature the chance, and I'll warrant he'll make himself plain to the dog. You just try him. Tell him to tell the dog so and so, and see what'll come of it."

Robert made the experiment, and it proved satisfactory. As soon as he had received Robert's orders, Gibbie claimed Oscar's attention. The dog looked up in his face, noted every glance and gesture, and partly from sympathetic instinct, that gift lying so near the very essence of life, partly from observation of the state of affairs in respect of the sheep, divined with certainty what the duty required of him was and was off like a shot.

"The two dumb creatures understand one another better than I understand either of them," said Robert to his wife when they came home.

And now indeed it was a blessed time for Gibbie. It had been pleasant down in the valley, with the cattle and Donal, and foul weather sometimes; but now it was the full glow of summer; the sweet keen air of the mountain bathed him as he ran, entered into him, filled him with life like the new wine of the kingdom of God, and the whole world rose in its glory around him.

Gibbie was one of the meek and inherited the earth. Throned on the mountain, he beheld the multiform "goings on of life," and in love possessed the whole. He was of the poet-kind also, and now that he was a shepherd, saw everything with shepherd eyes. One moment, to his fancy, the great sun above played the shepherd to the world, the winds were the dogs, and the men and women the sheep. The next, in higher mood, he would remember the good shepherd of whom Janet had read to him and pat the head of the collie that lay beside him; Oscar too was a shepherd and no hireling; he fed the sheep, he turned them from danger and barrenness, and he barked well.

Then what a joy it was to the heaven-born obedience of the child to hearken to every word, watch every look, divine every wish of the old man!

"I just love the bairn as the very apple of my eye," said Robert. "I can scarce conceive a wish, but there's the creature with a grip on it! He seems to know what's rising in my mind, and in a moment he's up like the dog to be ready, and looks at me waiting."

Nor was it long before the town-bred child grew to love the heavens almost as dearly as the earth. He would gaze and gaze at the clouds as they came and went, and watching them and the wind, weighing the heat and the cold, and marking many indications, known some of them perhaps only to himself, understood the signs of the earthly times at length nearly as well as an insect or a swallow, and far better than long-experienced old Robert. The mountain was Gibbie's very home. Often, when the two old people were in bed and asleep, Gibbie would be out watching the moon rise—seated, islanded in space, nothing alive and visible near him, perhaps not even a solitary night wind blowing and ceasing, and the awfully silent moon sliding up from the hollow of a valley below.

Then there was the delight, fresh every week, of the Saturday gathering of the brothers and sisters, whom Gibbie could hardly have loved more, had they been of his own immediate kin. Dearest of all was Donal, whose greeting—"Well, creature," was heavenly in Gibbie's ears. Donal would have had him go down and spend a day, every now and then, with him and the nowt, as in old times, but Janet would not hear of it, until the foolish tale of the brownie should have quite blown over.

"Eh, but I wish," she added, as she said so, "I could find out something about his folk, or even where he came from, or what they called him! Never a word has the creature spoken!"

"You should teach him to read, Mother," said Donal.

"How would I do that, laddie? I would have to teach him to speak first," returned Janet.

"Let him come down to me, and I'll try my hand," said Donal.

Janet, notwithstanding, persisted in her refusal—for the present. By Donal's words set thinking of the matter, however, she now pondered the question day after day—how she might teach him to read; and at last the idea dawned upon her to substitute writing for speech.

She took the Shorter Catechism, which, in those days, had always an alphabet as janitor to the gates of its mysteries and showed Gibbie the letters, naming each several times and going over them repeatedly. Then she gave him Donal's school slate, with a "sklet-pike," and said, "Now, make a muckle *A*, creature."

Gibbie did so, and well too: she found that already he knew about half the letters.

"He's no fool!" she said to herself in triumph.

The other half soon followed; and she then began to show him words—not in the Catechism, but in the New Testament. Having told him what any word was and led him to consider the letters composing it, she would desire him to make it on the slate, and he would do so with tolerable accuracy: she was not very severe about the spelling, if only it was plain he knew the word. Ere long he began to devise short ways of making the letters and soon wrote with remarkable facility in a character modified from the printed letters.

When at length Janet saw him take the book by himself and sit pondering over it, she had not a doubt he was understanding it, and her heart leaped for joy. He had to ask her a good many words at first and often the meaning of one and another; but he seldom asked a question twice; and as his understanding was far ahead of his reading, he was able to test a conjectured meaning by the sense or nonsense it made of the passage. He found the same delight which Donal used to divide to him from the book of ballads. His joy was unbounded. He jumped from his seat; he danced and laughed and finally stood upon one leg: no other mode of expression but this, the expression of utter failure to express, was of avail to the relief of his feeling.

One day, a few weeks after Gibbie had begun to read by himself, Janet became aware that he was sitting on his stool in what had come to be called "the creature's corner," more than usually absorbed in some attempt with slate and pencil—now ceasing, lost in thought, and now commencing anew. She went near and peeped over his shoulder. At the top of the slate he had written the word *give,* then the word *giving,* and below them, *gib,* then *gibing;* upon these followed *gib* again, and he was now plainly meditating something further. Suddenly he seemed to find what he wanted, for in haste, almost as if he feared it might escape him, he added a *y,* making the word *giby*

—then first lifted his head, and looked around, evidently seeking her. She laid her hand on his head.

He jumped up with one of his most radiant smiles, and holding out the slate to her, pointed with his pencil to the word he had just completed. She did not know it for a word, but sounded it as it seemed to stand, making the *g* soft. He shook his head sharply and laid the point of his pencil upon the *g* of the *give* written above. Janet had been his teacher too long not to see what he meant, and immediately pronounced the word as he would have it. Upon this he began a wild dance, but sobering suddenly, sat down, and was instantly again absorbed in further attempt. It lasted so long that Janet resumed her previous household occupation.

At length he rose, and with thoughtful, doubtful contemplation of what he had done, brought her the slate. There, under the foregone success, he had written the word *galatians,* and *breath,* and under them, *galbreath.* She read them all, and at the last, which, witnessing to his success, she pronounced to his satisfaction, he began another dance, which again he ended abruptly, to draw her attention once more to the slate. He pointed to the *giby* first, and the *galbreath* next, and she read them together. This time he did not dance, but seemed waiting some result.

Upon Janet the idea was dawning that he meant himself, but she was thrown out by the cognomen's correspondence with that of the laird, which suggested that the boy had been merely attempting the name of the great man of the district. With this in her mind, and doubtfully feeling her way, she essayed the tentative of setting him right in the Christian name, and said: "*Thomas—Thomas* Galbraith."

Gibbie shook his head as before and again resumed his seat. Presently he brought her the slate, with all the rest rubbed out, and these words standing alone—*sir giby galbreath.*

Janet read them aloud, whereupon Gibbie began stabbing his forehead with the point of his slate pencil, and dancing once more in triumph; he had, he hoped, for the first time in his life, conveyed a fact through words.

"That's what they call you, is it?" said Janet, looking motherly at him—"Sir Gibbie Galbraith?"

Gibbie nodded vehemently.

"It'll be some nickname the bairns have given him," said Janet to herself, but continued to gaze at him, in questioning doubt of her own solution. She could not recall having ever heard of a *sir* in the family; but ghosts of things forgotten kept rising formless and thin in the sky of her memory: *had* she never heard of a Sir Somebody Galbraith somewhere? And still she stared at the child, trying to grasp what she could not even see. But this time Gibbie was standing quite still, staring at her in return; he could not think what made her stare so at him.

"Who called you that?" said Janet at length, pointing to the slate.

Gibbie took the slate, dropped upon his seat, and after considerable cogitation and effort, brought her the words, *gibyse fapher*. Janet for a moment was puzzled, but when she thought of correcting the *p* with a *t,* Gibbie entirely approved.

"What was your father, creature?" she asked.

Gibbie, after a long pause, and more evident labor than hitherto, brought her the enigmatical word, a *cobbler,* which, the *sir* running about in her head, quite defeated Janet.

Perceiving his failure, he jumped upon a chair, and reaching after one of Robert's Sunday shoes on the "crap o' the wa'," the natural shelf running all around the cottage, formed by the top of the wall where the rafters rested, caught hold of it, tumbled with it upon his creepie, took it between his knees, and began a pantomime of the making or mending of the same with such verisimilitude of imitation that it was clear to Janet he must have been familiar with the processes collectively called shoemaking; and therewith she recognized the word on the slate—a *cobbler*.

She smiled to herself at the association of name and trade, and concluded that the *sir* at least was a nickname. And yet—and yet—whether from the presence of some rudiment of an old memory, or from something about the boy that belonged to a higher style than his present showing, her mind kept swaying in an uncertainty whose very object eluded her.

"What would you like us to call you, creature?" she asked, anxious to meet the child's own idea of himself.

He pointed to the *giby*.

"Well, Gibbie," responded Janet—and at the word, now for the first time addressed by her to himself, he began dancing more wildly than ever and ended with standing motionless on one leg. "Well, Gibbie, I shall call you what you think fit," said Janet. "And now go your way, Gibbie, and see that Crummie's not over far out of sight."

From that hour Gibbie had his name from the whole family—his Christian name only, however, Robert and Janet having agreed it would be wise to avoid whatever might possibly bring the boy again under the notice of the laird. The latter half of his name they laid aside for him, as parents do a dangerous or overvaluable gift to a child.

7: *Gibbie Takes to Growing*

ALMOST FROM THE first moment of his being domiciled on Glashgar, what with the good food, the fine exercise, the exquisite air, and his great happiness, Gibbie began to grow; and he took to growing so fast that his legs soon shot far out of his winsey garment. But that was a small matter in Gormgarnet, where the kilt was as common as trousers. His wiry limbs grew larger without losing their firmness or elasticity; his chest, the effort in running uphill constantly alternated with the relief of running down, rapidly expanded, and his lungs grew hardy as well as powerful; till he became at length such in wind and muscle that he could run down a wayward sheep almost as well as Oscar. And his nerve grew also with his body and strength, till his coolness and courage were splendid.

One afternoon, Donal, having got a half-holiday, came home to see his mother and having greeted her, set out to find Gibbie. He had gone a long way, looking and calling without success, and had come in sight of a certain tiny loch, or tarn, that filled a hollow of the mountain. It was called the Deid Pot; and the old awe, amounting nearly to terror, with which in his childhood he had regarded it, returned upon him, the moment he saw the dark gleam of it. While he stood gazing at it, almost afraid to go nearer, a great splash that echoed from the steep rocks surrounding it brought his heart into his mouth, and immediately followed a loud barking, in which he recognized the voice of Oscar.

Before he had well begun to think what it could mean, Gibbie appeared on the opposite side of the loch, high above its level, on the top of the rocks forming its basin. He began instantly a rapid descent toward the water, where the rocks were so steep, and the footing so precarious, that Oscar wisely remained at the top nor attempted to follow him. Presently the dog caught sight of Donal, where he stood on a lower level whence the water was comparatively easy of access, and starting off at full speed, joined him, with much demonstration of welcome. But he received little notice from Donal, whose gaze was fixed with much wonder and more fear on the descending Gibbie. Some twenty feet from the surface of the loch, he reached a point whence clearly, in Donal's judgment, there was no possibility of farther descent. But Donal was never more mistaken; for that instant Gibbie flashed from the face of the rock head foremost, like a fishing bird, into the lake. Donal gave a cry, and ran to the edge of the water, accompanied by Oscar, who, all the time, had showed no anxiety, but had stood wagging his tail, and uttering now and then a little half-disappointed whine; neither now were his motions as he ran other than those of frolic and expectancy.

When they reached the loch, there was Gibbie already but a few yards from the only possible landing place, swimming with one hand, while in the other arm he held a baby lamb, its head lying quite still on his shoulder; it had been stunned by the fall, but might come around again. Then first Donal began to perceive that "the creature" was growing an athlete. When he landed, he gave Donal a merry laugh of welcome, but without stopping flew up the hill to take the lamb to its mother. Fresh from the icy water, he ran so fast that it was all Donal could do to keep up with him.

The Deid Pot taught Gibbie what swimming it could and what diving it could, but the nights of the following summer, when everybody on mountain and valley were asleep, and the moon shone, he would often go down to the Daur, and throwing himself into its deepest reaches, spend hours in lonely sport with water and wind and moon. He had by that time learned things, knowing which a man can never be lonesome.

The few goats on the mountain were for a time very inimical to him. So often did they butt him over, causing him sometimes severe bruises, that at last he resolved to try conclusions with them; and when next a goat made a rush at him, he seized him by the horns and wrestled with him mightily. This exercise once begun, he provoked engagements, until his strength and aptitude were such and so well known, that not a billygoat on Glashgar would have to do with him. But when he saw that every one of them ran at his approach, Gibbie, who could not bear to be in discord with any creature, changed his behavior toward them, and took equal pains to reconcile them to him—nor rested before he had entirely succeeded.

Every time Donal came home, he would bring some book of verse with him, and, leading Gibbie to some hollow, shady or sheltered as the time required, would there read to him ballads or songs or verse more stately, as mood or provision might suggest. The music, the melody, and the cadence and the harmony, the tone and the rhythm, and the time and the rhyme, instead of growing common to him, rejoiced Gibbie more and more every feast, and with ever-growing reverence he looked up to Donal as a mighty master-magician.

While Donal read, rejoicing in the music both of sound and sense, Gibbie was doing something besides; he was listening with the same ears and trying to see with the same eyes which he brought to bear upon the things Janet taught him out of the book. He was always placing what he heard by the side, as it were, of what he knew; asking himself, in this case and that, what Jesus Christ would have done, or what He would require of a disciple. Whether successful or not in the individual inquiry, the boy's mind and heart and spirit, in this silent, unembarrassed brooding as energetic as it was peaceful, expanded upward when it failed to widen, and the widening would come after.

Gifted from the first of his being with such a rare drawing to his kind, he saw his utmost affection dwarfed by the words and deeds of Jesus. When he sank foiled from any endeavor to understand how a man was to behave in certain circumstances, these or those, he always took refuge in *doing* something—and doing it better than before; leaped the more eagerly if Robert called him, spoke the more gently to Oscar, turned the sheep more careful not to scare them—as if by instinct he perceived that the only hope of understanding lies in doing. He would cleave to the skirt when the hand seemed withdrawn; he would run to do the thing he had learned yesterday, when as yet he could find no answer to the question of today.

Thus, as the weeks of solitude and love and thought and obedience glided by, the reality of Christ grew upon him, till he saw the very rocks and heather and the faces of the sheep like him, and felt his presence everywhere, and ever coming nearer. Nor did his imagination aid only a little in the growth of his being. He would dream waking dreams about Jesus, gloriously childlike. He fancied He came down every now and then to see how things were going in the lower part of His kingdom; and that when He did so, He made use of Glashgar and its rocks for His stair, coming down its granite scale in the morning, and again, when He had ended His visit, going up in the evening by the same steps. Then high and fast would his heart beat at the thought that someday he might come upon His path just when He had passed, see the heather lifting its head from the trail of His garment, or more slowly out of the prints left by His feet, as He walked up the stairs of heaven, going back to His Father. Sometimes, when a sheep stopped feeding and looked up suddenly, he would fancy that Jesus had laid His hand on its head and was now telling it that it must not mind being killed; for He had been killed and it was all right.

Although he could read the New Testament for himself now, he always preferred making acquaintance with any new portion of it first from the mouth of Janet. Her voice made the word more a word to him. But the next time he read, it was sure to be what she had then read. She was his priestess; the opening of her Bible was the opening of a window in heaven; her cottage was the porter's lodge to the temple; his very sheep were feeding on the temple stairs.

When the winter came, with its frost and snow, Gibbie saved Robert much suffering. At first Robert was unwilling to let him go out alone in stormy weather; but Janet believed that the child doing the old man's work would be specially protected. All through the hard time, therefore, Gibbie went and came, and no evil befell him. Neither did he suffer from the cold; for, a sheep having died toward the end of the first autumn, Robert, in view of Gibbie's coming necessity, had begged of his master the skin and dressed it with the wool upon it; and of this, between the three of them, they made a coat for him; so that he roamed the hill like a savage, in a garment of skin.

It became, of course, before very long, well known about the country that Mr. Duff's crofters upon Glashgar had taken in and were bringing up a foundling—some said an innocent, some said a wild boy—who helped Robert with his sheep and Janet with her cow, but could not speak a word of either Gaelic or English. By and by, strange stories came to be told of his exploits. The rumor concerning him swelled as well as spread, until, toward the end of his second year on Glashgar, the notion of Gibbie in the imaginations of the children of Daurside was that of an almost supernatural being, who had dwelt upon, or rather who had haunted, Glashgar from time immemorial, and of whom they had been hearing all their lives; and, although they had never heard anything bad of him—that he was *wild*, that he wore a hairy skin, that he could do more than any other boy dared attempt, that he was dumb, and that sheep and dogs and cattle, and even the wild creatures of the mountain, could understand him perfectly—these statements were more than enough, acting on the suspicion and fear belonging to the savage in their own bosoms, to envelop the idea of him in a mist of dread, deepening to such horror in the case of the more timid and imaginative of them, that when the twilight began to gather about the cottages and farmhouses, the very mention of "the beast-loon o' Glashgar" was enough to send many of the children scouring like startled hares into the house.

Gibbie, in his atmosphere of human grace and tenderness, little thought what clouds of foolish fancies, rising from the valleys below, had made of him an object of terror to those whom at the very first sight he would have loved and served. Among these, perhaps the most afraid of him were the children of the gamekeeper, for they lived on the very foot of the haunted hill, near the bridge and gate of Glashruach; and the laird himself happened one day to be witness of their fear. He inquired the cause and was vexed by the persistency with which the shadows of superstition still hung about his lands.

He held therefore immediate communication with his gamekeeper on the subject. The expression of the man's face as he listened to the laird's complaint would not have been a pleasant sight to any lover of Gibbie; but it had not occurred either to master or man that the offensive being whose doubtful existence caused the scandal was the same toward whom they had once been guilty of such brutality.

The same afternoon, the laird questioned his tenant of the

Mains concerning his cotters, and was assured that better or more respectable people were not in all the region of Gormgarnet.

When Robert became aware of Gibbie's gifts of other kinds than those revealed to himself by his good shepherding, he began to turn it over in his mind, and by and by referred the question to his wife whether they ought not to send the boy to school, that he might learn the things he was so much more than ordinarily capable of learning.

Janet would give no immediate opinion. She must think, she said; and she took three days to turn the matter over in her mind.

"Ay, Robert," she answered, without preface, the third day. "It would be a sin not to let the laddie learn. But who will take the trouble needful to the learning of a poor dummie?"

"Let him go down to the Mains and herd with Donal," answered Robert. "He knows more than you or me or Gibbie either; and when he's learned all that Donal can show him it'll be time to think what next."

"Well," answered Janet, "none can say but that's sense, Robert; and though I'm loath, for your sake more than my own, to let the laddie go, let him go to Donal. I hope, between the two, they won't let the nowt into the corn."

"The corn's 'most all cut now," replied Robert; "and for the matter of that, two good consciences won't blow one another out. But he needn't go every day. He can give one day to the learning and the next to thinking about it among the sheep. And any day that you want to keep him, you can keep him; for it won't be as if he went to the school."

Gibbie was delighted with the proposal.

"Only," said Robert, in final warning, "don't let them take you, Gibbie, and score your back again, my creature; and don't answer anybody, when they ask what you're called, anything more than just *Gibbie*."

The boy laughed and nodded, and, as Janet said, the bairn's nick was good as the best man's word.

Now came a happy time for the two boys. Donal began at once to teach Gibbie Euclid and arithmetic. When they had had enough of that for a day, he read Scottish history to him; and when they had done what seemed their duty by that, then came the best of the feast—whatever tales or poetry Donal had laid his hands upon.

Somewhere about this time it was that he first got hold of a copy of *Paradise Lost*. He found that he could not make much of it. But he found also that, as before with the ballads, when he read from it aloud to Gibbie, his mere listening presence sent back a spiritual echo that helped him to the meaning; and when neither of them understood it, the grand organ roll of it, losing nothing in the Scotch voweling, delighted them both.

Once they were startled by seeing the gamekeeper enter the field. The moment he saw him, Gibbie laid himself flat on the ground, but ready to spring to his feet and run. The man, however, did not come near them.

8: *The Beast-Loon o' Glashgar*

THE SECOND winter came, and with the first frost Gibbie resumed his sheepskin coat and the brogues and leggings which he had made for himself of deer hide tanned with the hair. It pleased the two old people to see him so warmly clad. But very soon the stories about him were all stirred up afresh, and new rumors added. This one and that of the children declared they had caught sight of the beast-loon, running about the rocks like a goat; and one day a boy of Angus' own, who had been a good way up the mountain, came home nearly dead with terror, saying the beast-loon had chased him a long way. He did not add that he had been throwing stones at the sheep, not perceiving anyone in charge of them.

So, one fine morning in December, having nothing particular to attend to, Angus shouldered his double-barreled gun, and set out for a walk over Glashgar, in the hope of coming upon the savage that terrified the children. The sun shone bright, and a keen wind was blowing.

About noon he came in sight of a few sheep, in a sheltered spot, where were little patches of coarse grass among the heather. On a stone, a few yards above them, sat Gibbie, not reading, as he would be half the time now, but busied with a Panpipe—which, under Donal's direction, he had made for himself—drawing from it experimental sounds and feeling after the possibility of a melody. He was so much occupied that he did not see Angus approach, who now stood for a moment or two regarding him. He was hirsute as Esau, his head crowned with its own plentiful crop, his body covered with the wool of the sheep, and his legs and feet with the hide of the deer. The deerskin Angus knew for what it was from afar, and concluding it the spoil of the only crime of which he recognized the enormity, whereas it was in truth part of a skin he had himself sold to a saddler in the next village to make sporrans of, boiled over with wrath, and strode nearer, grinding his teeth.

Gibbie looked up, knew him, and starting to his feet, turned to the hill. Angus, leveling his gun, shouted to him to stop, but Gibbie only ran the harder, nor once looked around. Idiotic with rage, Angus fired. One of his barrels was loaded with shot, the other with ball: meaning to use the shot barrel, he pulled the wrong trigger, and liberated the bullet. It went through the calf of Gibbie's right leg, and he fell. It had, however, passed between two muscles without injuring either greatly and had severed no artery. The next moment he was on his feet again and running, nor did he yet feel pain. Happily he was not very far from home, and he made for it as fast as he could—preceded by Oscar, who, having once by accident been shot himself, had a mortal terror of guns.

Maimed as Gibbie was, he could yet run a good deal faster uphill than the rascal who followed him. But long before he reached the cottage, the pain had arrived, and the nearer he got to it the worse it grew. In spite of the anguish, however, he held on with determination; to be seized by Angus and dragged down to Glashruach would be far worse.

Robert Grant was at home that day, suffering from rheumatism. He was seated in the inglenook, with his pipe in his mouth, and Janet was just taking the potatoes for their dinner off the fire, when the door flew open, and in stumbled Gibbie and fell on the floor. The old man threw his pipe from him, and rose trembling, but Janet was before him. She dropped down on her knees beside the boy and put her arm under his head. He was white and motionless.

"Eh, Robert Grant!" she cried, "he's bleeding."

The same moment they heard quick yet heavy steps approaching. At once Robert divined the truth, and a great wrath banished rheumatism and age together. Like a boy he sprang to the "crap o' the wa'," whence his yet powerful hand came back armed with a huge rusty old broadsword that had seen service in its day. Two or three fierce tugs at the hilt proving the blade immovable in the sheath, and the steps being now almost at the door, he clubbed the weapon, grasping it by the sheathed blade, and holding it with the edge downward, so that the blow he meant to deal should fall from the round of the basket hilt. As he heaved it aloft, the gray old shepherd seemed inspired by the god of battles; the rage of a hundred ancestors was swelling up in his peaceful breast. His red eye flashed, and the few hairs that were left him stood erect on his head like the mane of a roused lion. Ere Angus had his second foot over the threshold, down came the helmetlike hilt with a dull crash on his head, and he staggered against the wall.

"Take that, Angus MacPholp!" panted Robert through his clenched teeth, following the blow with another from his fist that prostrated the enemy. Again he heaved his weapon, and, standing over him where he lay more than half-stunned, said in a hoarse voice—

"By the great God my maker, Angus MacPholp, if you try to get up I'll come down on you again. Here, Oscar! Watch him and take him by the throat if he moves a finger."

The gun had dropped from Angus' hand, and Robert, keeping his eye on him, secured it.

"She's loaded," muttered Angus.

"Lie still then," returned Robert, pointing the weapon at his head.

"It'll be murder," said Angus and made a movement to lay hold of the barrel.

"Hold him down, Oscar," cried Robert. The dog's paws were instantly on his chest, and his teeth grinning within an inch of his face. "It would be but blood for blood, Angus MacPholp," he went on. "Your hour's come, my man. That bairn's is not the first blood of man you've shed, and it's time the Scripture was fulfilled, and the hand of man shed yours."

"You're not going to kill me, Rob Grant?" growled the fellow in growing fright.

"I'm going to see whether the sheriff won't be persuaded to hang you," answered the shepherd. "This must be put a stop to. Quiet! or I'll brain you and save him the trouble. Here, Janet, bring your pot of potatoes. I'm going to empty the gun. If he dares to move, just give him the whole boiling lot in the face. Only take care and hold off the dog, poor fellow."

So saying, he carried the weapon to the door, and, in terror lest he might, through wrath or the pressure of dire necessity, use it against his foe, emptied its second barrel into the earth and leaned it up against the wall outside.

Janet obeyed her husband so far as to stand over Angus with the potato pot. When Robert returned and relieved her guard, Janet went back to Gibbie, whom she had drawn toward the fire. In a minute or two he was able to crawl to his bed in the corner, and then Janet proceeded to examine his wound.

By this time his leg was much swollen, but the wound had almost stopped bleeding, and it was plain there was no bullet in it, for there were the two orifices. She washed it carefully and bound it up. Then Gibbie raised his head and looked somewhat anxiously around the room.

"You're looking for Angus?" said Janet. "He's yonder upon

the floor. Don't be frightened. Your father and Oscar have him safe enough, I'll warrant."

"Here, Janet!" cried her husband; "if you're through with the bairn, I must be going."

"Hoot, Robert! You're not going to leave me and poor Gibbie in the house by ourselves with the murdering man!" returned Janet.

" 'Deed am I, lass! Just run and bring the bit tow that you hang your duds upon at the washing, and we'll bind the feet and the hands of him."

Janet obeyed and went. Angus, who had been quiet enough for the last ten minutes, meditating and watching, began to swear furiously, but Robert paid no more heed than if he had not heard him—stood calm and grim at his head, with the clubbed sword heaved over his shoulder.

When she came back, by her husband's directions, she passed the rope repeatedly round the keeper's ankles, then several times between them, drawing the bouts tightly together, so that, instead of the two sharing one ring, each ankle had now, as it were, a close-fitting one for itself. When they began to bind his hands, he turned desperate, and struck at both, cursing and raging.

"If you're not quiet, you'll taste the dog's teeth," said Robert.

Angus reflected that he would have a better chance when he was left alone with Janet, and yielded.

"Troth!" Robert went on, as he continued his task, "I have no pity left for you, Angus MacPholp. Now, Janet, bring a bundle of brackens from the byre and lay it beneath his head, and then I'll be away and get word to the sheriff. Scotland's come to a pretty pass when they shoot men with guns, as if they were wild creatures to be skinned and eaten. He may well be a keeper of game, for he's as ill a keeper of his brother as old Cain himself. But," he concluded, tying the last knot hard, "we'll do what we can to keep the keeper."

It was seldom Robert spoke at such length, but the provocation, the wrath, the conflict, and the victory had sent the blood rushing through his brain, and loosed his tongue like strong drink.

"You'll have your dinner before you go, Robert," said his wife.

"No, I can eat nothing; I'll take a bannock in my pocket. You can give my dinner to Angus: he'll want heartening."

So saying he put the bannock in his pocket, flung his broad blue bonnet upon his head, took his stick, and ordering Oscar to remain at home and watch the prisoner, set out for a walk of five miles, as if he had never known such a thing as rheumatism. He must find another magistrate than the laird; he would not trust him where his own gamekeeper, Angus MacPholp, was concerned.

"Keep your eye on him, Janet," he said, turning in the doorway. "Don't lose sight of him before I come back with the constable. Don't weaken. I'll be back in three hours likely."

With these words he turned finally and disappeared.

The mortification of Angus as he lay thus trapped in the den of the beast-loon, at being taken and bound by an old man, a woman, and a collie dog, was extreme.

Janet set out the dinner, peeled some potatoes, and approaching Angus, would have fed him. In place of accepting her ministration, he fell to abusing her with the worst language he could find. She withdrew without a word and sat down to her own dinner; but, finding the torrent of vituperation kept flowing, rose again, and going to the door, fetched a great jug of cold water from the pail that always stood there, and coming behind her prisoner, emptied it over his face. He gave a horrid yell taking the douche for a boiling one.

"You needn't cry out like that at good cold water," said Janet. "But you'll just abstain from any more such words in my hearing, or you shall get the like every time you break out." As she spoke, she knelt and wiped his face and head with her apron.

A fresh oath rushed to Angus' lips, but the fear of a second jugful made him suppress it, and Janet sat down again to her dinner. While she sat thus, she caught a swift investigation look he cast on the cords that bound his hands and then at the fire. She perceived at once what was passing in his mind. Rising, she went quickly to the byre and returned immediately with a chain they used for tethering the cow. The end of it she slipped deftly around his neck, and made it fast, putting the little bar through a link.

"Are you going to hang me, you she-devil?" he cried, making a futile attempt to grasp the chain with his bound hands.

"You'll be wanting a drop more of cold water, I'm thinking," said Janet.

She stretched the chain to its length, and with a great stone drove the sharp iron stake at the other end of it into the clay floor. Fearing next that, bound as his hands were, he might get a hold of the chain and drag out the stake, or might even contrive to remove the rope from his feet with them, or that he might indeed with his teeth undo the knot that confined his hands themselves, she got a piece of rope, and made a loop at the end of it; then, watching her opportunity, passed the loop between his hands, noosed the other end through it, and drew the noose tight. The free end of the rope she put through the staple that received the bolt of the cottage door, and gradually, as he grew weary in pulling against her, tightened the rope until she had his arms at their stretch beyond his head. Not quite satisfied yet, she lastly contrived, in part by setting Oscar to occupy his attention, to do the same with his feet, securing them to a heavy chest in the corner opposite the door, upon which chest she heaped a pile of stones. And now at last she believed she had him safe.

Gibbie had fallen asleep, but he now awoke and she gave

him his dinner; then "redd up," and took her Bible. Gibbie had lain down again, and she thought he was asleep.

Angus grew more and more uncomfortable, both in body and in mind. He knew he was hated throughout the country and had hitherto rather enjoyed the knowledge; but now he judged that the popular feeling would tell against him committed for trial. He knew also that the magistrate to whom Robert had betaken himself was not overfriendly with his master, and certainly would not listen to any intercession from him. At length, what with pain, hunger, and fear, his pride began to yield, and, after an hour had passed in utter silence, he condescended to parley.

"Janet Grant," he said, "let me go, and I'll trouble you or yours no more."

"Wouldn't you think me some fool to hearken to you?" suggested Janet.

"I'll swear any lawful oath that you like to lay upon me," protested Angus, "that I'll do whatever you please to require of me."

"I don't doubt you would swear, but what next?" said Janet.

"What next but you'll loose my hands?" rejoined Angus.

"It's no use mentioning it," replied Janet; "for, as you know, I'm under authority, and yourself heard my man tell me to take every precaution not to let you go."

"Was ever man," protested Angus, "made such a fool of by a pair of old cotters like you and Robert Grant!"

"With the help of the Lord, by means of the dog," supplemented Janet.

"Let me go, woman. I'll harm nobody. The poor idiot's no muckle the worse, and I'll take more care when I fire another time."

"Wiser folk than me must see to that," answered Janet.

"Hoots, woman! It was nothing but an accident."

"I know; but it'll be seen what Gibbie says."

"Awva! His word's good for nothing."

"For a penny, or a thousand pounds."

"My wife will be out of her wits," pleaded Angus.

"Would you like a drink of milk?" asked Janet, rising.

"I would that," he answered.

She filled her little teapot with milk, and he drank it from the spout, hoping she was on the point of giving way.

"Now," she said, when he had finished his draught, "you must just make the best of it, Angus. Anyway, it's a good lesson in patience to you, and that you have not had over often, I'm thinking. Robert'll be here before long."

With these words she set down the teapot and went out; it was time to milk her cow.

In a little while Gibbie rose, tried to walk, but failed, and getting down on his hands and knees, crawled out after her. Angus caught a glimpse of his face as he crept past him, and then first recognized the boy he had lashed. Not compunction, but an occasional pang of dread lest he should have been the cause of his death and might come upon his body in one of his walks, had served so to fix his face in his memory that, now he had a near view of him, pale with suffering and loss of blood and therefore more like his former self, he knew him beyond a doubt. With a great shoot of terror he concluded that the idiot had been lying there silently gloating over his revenge, waiting only till Janet should be out of sight, and was now gone after some instrument wherewith to take it. He pulled and tugged at his bonds, but only to find escape absolutely hopeless. In gathering horror, he lay moveless at last, but strained his hearing toward every sound.

Now the byre was just on the other side of the turf wall against which was the head of Gibbie's bed, and through the wall Gibbie had heard her voice, with that something in the tone of it which let him understand she was not talking to

Crummie, but to Crummie's Maker; and it was therefore he had got up and gone after her. For there was no reason, so far as he knew or imagined, why he should not hear, as so many times before, what she was saying to the Master. He supposed that as she could not well speak to Him in the presence of a man like Angus, she had gone out to the byre to have her talk with Him there. He crawled to the end of the cottage so silently that she heard no sound of his approach. He would not go into the byre, for that might disturb her, for she would have to look up to know that it was only Gibbie; he would listen at the door. He found it wide open, and peeping in, saw Crummie chewing away, and Janet on her knees with her forehead leaning against the cow and her hands thrown up over her shoulder. What she said was nearly this:

"O Lord, if You would but say what You would have me do! When a body doesn't know Your will, she's just driven to distraction. The man's done me no ill, except that he's hurt Your bonnie Gibbie. It's Gibbie that has to forgive him and not me. But my man told me not to let him up and how am I to be a wife such as You would have me, O Lord, unless I do as my man tells me! It would ill befit me to let my old man go so far wanting his dinner, all for nothing. What would he think when he came home?

"Of course, Lord, if You'd tell me that would make all the difference, for You're Robert's Master as well as mine and Your will would satisfy him just as well as me. I would fain let Angus go, poor man, but I don't dare. Lord, convert him to the truth. Let him know what hate is, but eh, Lord, I wish You would tell me what to do. Thy will's the beginning and middle and end of all things to me. I'm willing enough to let him go, but he's Robert's prisoner and Gibbie's enemy; he's not *my* prisoner and he's not *my* enemy, and I don't think I have the right. Ill would I like to have a hand in the hanging of him, though he may deserve it, Lord, I don't know. But I'm thinking You didn't make him so well tempered—as my Robert, for instance."

Here her voice ceased, and she fell a-moaning.

Her trouble was echoed in dim pain from Gibbie's soul. Now first he understood the real state of the affair in the purport of the old man's absence; also how he was himself potently concerned in the business: if the offense had been committed against Gibbie, then with Gibbie lay the power, therefore the duty, of forgiveness. Few things were easier to him than to love his enemies, and his merit in obeying the commandment was small indeed. No enemy had as yet done him, in his immediate person, the wrong he could even imagine it hard to forgive. No sooner had Janet ceased than he was on his way back to the cottage; on its floor lay one who had to be waited upon with forgiveness.

Wearied with futile struggles, Angus found himself compelled to abide his fate, and was lying quite still when Gibbie re-entered. The boy thought he was asleep, but on the contrary he was watching his every motion, full of dread. Gibbie went hopping upon one foot to the hole in the wall where Janet kept the only knife she had. It was not there. He glanced around but could not see it.

He hopped up to Angus and examined the knots that tied his hands; they were drawn so tight—in great measure by his own struggles—and so difficult to reach from their position that he saw it would take him a long time to undo them. Angus thought, with fresh horror, he was examining them to make sure they would hold, and was so absorbed in watching his movements that he even forgot to curse, which was the only thing left him.

Gibbie looked around again for a moment, then darted upon the tongs—there was no poker—and thrust them into the fire, caught up the asthmatic old bellows, and began to blow the peats. Angus saw the first action, heard the second, and a hideous dismay clutched his very heart; the savage fool was about to take his revenge in pinches with the red-hot tongs! Manhood held him silent until he saw him take the implement of torture from the fire, glowing, not red but white hot, when he uttered such a terrific yell, that Gibbie dropped the tongs—happily not the hot ends—on his own bare foot, but caught them up again instantly, and made a great hop to Angus: if Janet had heard that yell and came in, all would be spoiled. But the faithless keeper began to struggle so fiercely, writhing with every contortion, and kicking with every inch left possible to him, that Gibbie hardly dared attempt anything for dread of burning him. With a sudden thought Gibbie sprang to the door and locked it. Angus, hearing the bolt, was the more convinced that his purpose was cruel, and struggled and yelled, with his eyes fixed on the glowing tongs, now fast cooling in Gibbie's hand.

In the meantime Janet, in her perplexity, had, quite forgetful of the poor cow's necessities, abandoned Crummie, and wandered down the path as far as the shoulder her husband must cross ascending from the other side; thither, a great rock intervening, so little of Angus' cries reached, that she heard nothing through the deafness of her absorbing appeal for direction to her shepherd, the Master of Men.

Gibbie thrust the tongs again into the fire, and while blowing it, bethought him that it might give Angus confidence if he removed the chain from his neck. He laid down the bellows and did so. But to Angus the action seemed only preparatory to taking him by the throat with the horrible implement. In his agony and wild endeavor to frustrate the supposed intent, he struggled harder than ever. But now Gibbie was undoing the rope fastened round the chest. This Angus did not perceive, and when it came suddenly loose in the midst of one of his fierce straining contortions, the result was that he threw his body right over his head, and lay on his face for a moment confused. Gibbie saw his advantage. He snatched his clumsy tool out of the fire, seated himself on the corresponding part of Angus' person, and seizing with the tongs the rope between his feet, held on to both, in spite of his heaves and kicks.

In the few moments that passed while Gibbie burned through a round of the rope, Angus imagined a considerable number of pangs; but when Gibbie rose and hopped away, he discovered that his feet were at liberty, and scrambled up, his head dizzy, and his body reeling. Such was then the sunshine of delight in Gibbie's countenance that even Angus stared at him for a moment. But Gibbie still had the tongs, and Angus' hands were still tied. He held them out to him. Gibbie pounced upon the knots with hands and teeth. They occupied him some little time, during which Angus was almost compelled to take better cognizance of the face of the savage; and dull as he was to the good things of human nature, he was yet in a measure subdued by what he there looked upon, while he could scarcely mistake the hearty ministration of his teeth and nails! The moment his hands were free, Gibbie looked up at him with a smile, and Angus did not even box his ears. Holding by the wall, Gibbie limped to the door and opened it.

With a nod meant for thanks, the gamekeeper stepped out, took up his gun from where it leaned against the wall, and hurried away down the hill. A moment sooner and he would have met Janet; but she had just entered the byre again to milk poor Crummie.

When she came into the cottage, she stared with astonishment to see no Angus on the floor. Gibbie, who had lain down again in much pain, made signs that he had let him go; whereupon such a look of relief came over her countenance that he was filled with fresh gladness and was, if possible, more satisfied still with what he had done.

It was late before Robert returned—alone, weary, and disappointed. The magistrate was from home; he had waited for him as long as he dared; but at length, both because of his wife's unpleasant position, and the danger to himself if he longer delayed his journey across the mountain, seeing it threatened a storm and there was no moon, he set out. That he too was relieved to find no Angus there, he did not attempt to conceal.

The next day he went to see him, and told him that, to please Gibbie, he had consented to say nothing more about the affair. Angus could not help being sullen, but he judged it wise to behave as well as he could, kept his temper therefore, and said he was sorry he had been so hasty, but that Robert had punished him pretty well, for it would be weeks before he recovered from the blow on the head he had given him. So they parted on tolerable terms, and there was no further persecution of Gibbie from that quarter.

It was some time before he was able to be out again, but no hour spent with Janet was lost.

That winter the old people were greatly tried with rheumatism; for not only were the frosts severe, but there was much rain between. Their children did all in their power to minister to their wants, and Gibbie was nurse as well as shepherd. Gibbie still occupied his heather bed on the floor, and it was part of his business as nurse to keep up a good fire on the hearth; peats, happily, were plentiful.

For weeks he had been picking out tunes on his Panpipe; also, he had lately discovered that, although he could not articulate, he could produce tones, and had taught himself to imitate the pipes. Now, to his delight, he found that the noises he made were recognized as song by his father and mother. From that time he was often heard crooning to himself.

9: *The Meeting on the Mountain*

CHANGE WAS taking place in other ways upon the foot as well as the high side of Glashgar. Business affairs had gone well for the laird and he had added to his land another small farm. The purchase gave him particular pleasure, because the farm not only marched with his home grounds, but filled up a great notch in the map of the property between Glashruach and the Mains, with which also it marched. It was good land, and he let it at once, on his own terms, to Mr. Duff. However, in the spring, business took a turn for the worse and he was obliged to leave his daughter and go to London to look after his investments.

Ginevra was still a silent, simple, unconsciously retiring, and therewith dignified girl, in whom childhood and womanhood had begun to interchange hues, as it were with the play of colors in a dove's neck. At one moment Ginevra would draw herself up with involuntary recoil from doubtful approach; the next, Ginny would burst out in a merry laugh at something in which only a child could have perceived the mirth-causing element; then again the woman would seem suddenly to re-enter and rebuke the child, for the sparkle would fade from her eyes, and she would look solemn, and even a little sad. The people about the place loved her, but from the stillness on the general surface of her behavior, the faraway feeling she gave them, and the impossibility of divining how she was thinking except she chose to unbosom herself, they were all a little afraid of her as well.

Nicie Grant had, earlier in the winter, been engaged by the housekeeper at Glashruach chiefly to wait upon Miss Galbraith. She was the youngest of Janet's girls, about four years older than Donal, not clever, but as sweet as honest, and full of divine service. Always ready to think others better than herself, the moment she saw the still face of Ginevra, she took her for a little saint and accepted her as a queen, whose will to her should be law. Ginevra, on her part, was taken with the healthy hue and honest eyes of the girl, and neither felt any dislike to her touching her hair, nor lost her temper when she was awkward and pulled it. Before the winter was over, the bond between them was strong.

One principal duty required of Nicie was to accompany her mistress every fine day to the manse, a mile and a half from Glashruach. For some time Ginevra had been under the care of Miss Machar, the daughter of the parish clergyman, an old gentleman of sober aspirations, to whom the last century was the Augustan age of English literature. He was genial, gentle, and a lover of his race. Partly that the living was a poor one, and her father old and infirm, Miss Machar, herself middle-aged, had undertaken the instruction of the little heiress. What lessons she taught her, she taught her well.

One morning they found, on reaching the manse, that the minister was very unwell, and that in consequence Miss Machar could not attend to Ginevra; they turned, therefore, to walk home again. Now the manse, upon another root of Glashgar, was nearer than Glashruach to Nicie's home, and many a time as she went and came, did she lift longing eyes to the ridge that hid it from her view. This morning, Ginevra observed that, every other moment, Nicie was looking up the side of the mountain, as if she saw something unusual upon it—occasionally, indeed, when the winding of the road turned their backs to it, stopping and turning around to gaze.

"What is the matter with you, Nicie?" she asked. "What are you looking at up there?"

"I'm wondering what my mother will be doing," answered Nicie. "She's up there."

"Up there!" exclaimed Ginny, and, turning, stared at the mountain too, expecting to perceive Nicie's mother somewhere upon the face of it.

"No, no, missie! You can't see her," said the girl; "she's not in sight. She's over beyond there. But if we were up where you see two or three sheep against the sky, we could see the wee hoose where she and my father bide."

"How I *should* like to see your father and mother, Nicie!" exclaimed Ginevra.

"Well, I'm sure they would be right glad to see yourself, missie, any time that you'd like to go and see them."

"Why shouldn't we go now, Nicie? It's not a dangerous place, is it?"

"No, missie. Glashgar's as quiet and well behaved a hill as any in all the country," answered Nicie, laughing. "She's poor like my family and hasn't muckle to spare, but the sheep get a few nibbles upon her, here and there; and my mother manages to keep a cow, and get plenty of milk for her tea."

"Come, then, Nicie. We have plenty of time. Nobody wants either you or me, and we shall get home before any one misses us."

Nicie was glad enough to consent; they turned at once to the hill, and began climbing. But Nicie did not know this part of it nearly so well as that which lay between Glashruach and the cottage, and after they had climbed some distance, often stopping and turning to look down on the valley below, the prospect of which, with its streams and river, kept still widening and changing as they ascended, they arrived at a place where the path grew very doubtful, and she could not tell in which of two directions they ought to go.

"I'll take this way, and you take that, Nicie," said Ginevra, "and if I find there is no path my way, I will come back to yours; and if you find there is no path your way, you will come back to mine."

It was a childish proposal, and one to which Nicie should not have consented, but she was little more than a child herself. Advancing a short distance in doubt, and the path reappearing quite plainly, she sat down, expecting her little mistress to return directly. No thought of anxiety crossed her mind; how should one, in broad sunlight, on a mountainside, in the first of summer, and with the long day before them? So, there sitting in peace, Nicie fell into a maidenly reverie, and so there Nicie sat for a long time, half-dreaming in the great light, without once really thinking about anything.

All at once she came to herself: some latent fear had exploded in her heart: yes! what could have become of her little mistress? She jumped to her feet, and shouted "Missie! Missie Galbraith! Ginny!" but no answer came back. The mountain was as still as at midnight. She ran to the spot where they had parted, and along the other path; it was plainer than that where she had been so idly forgetting herself. She hurried on, wildly calling as she ran.

In the meantime Ginevra, having found the path indubitable, and imagining it led straight to the door of Nicie's mother's cottage, and that Nicie would be after her in a moment, thinking also to have a bit of fun with her, set off dancing and running so fast, that by the time Nicie came to herself, she was a good mile from her. What a delight it was to be thus alone upon the grand mountain, with the earth banished so far below, and the great rocky heap climbing and leading and climbing up and up toward the sky!

Ginny was not in the way of thinking much about God. But there was in her soul a large wilderness ready for the voice that should come crying to prepare the way of the King.

The path was after all a mere sheeptrack, and led her at length into a lonely hollow in the hillside, with a swampy peat bog at the bottom of it. She stopped. The place looked unpleasant, reminding her of how she always felt when she came unexpectedly upon Angus MacPholp. She would go no farther alone; she would wait till Nicie overtook her. As she thought thus, a lonehearted bird uttered a single, wailing cry, strange to her ear. The cry remained solitary, unanswered, and then first suddenly she felt that there was nobody there but herself, and the feeling had in it a pang of uneasiness. She turned and went slowly back to the edge of the hollow.

In her haste and anxiety, however, Nicie had struck into another sheeptrack, and was now higher on the hill; so that Ginny could see no living thing nearer than in the valley below; far down there she saw upon the road, so distant that it seemed motionless, a cart with a man in it, drawn by a white horse. Never in her life before had she felt that she was alone. She had often felt lonely, but she had always known where to find the bodily presence of somebody. Now she might cry and scream the whole day, and nobody answer! Her heart swelled into her throat, then sank away, leaving a wide hollow.

She sat down on a stone, where she could see the path she had come a long way back. At last she began to cry. All at once a verse she had heard the Sunday before at church seemed to come of itself into her head: "Call upon Me in the time of trouble and I will answer thee." So thinking, she began to pray.

"O God, help me home again," cried Ginevra and stood up in her great loneliness to return.

The same instant she spied, seated upon a stone, a little way off, but close to her path, the beast-boy. There could be no mistake. He was just as she had heard him described by the children at the gamekeeper's cottage. That was his hair sticking all out from his head, though the sun in it made it look like a crown of gold or a shining mist. Those were his bare arms. Worst of all, he was playing upon a curious kind of whistling thing, making dreadfully sweet music to entice her nearer that he might catch her and tear her to pieces! But the horrid creature's music should not have any power over her! She would rather run down to the black water, glooming in those holes, and be drowned, than the beast-boy should have her to eat!

Most girls would have screamed, but such was not Ginny's natural mode of meeting a difficulty. With fear, she was far more likely to choke than to cry out. So she sat down again and stared at him. Perhaps he would go away when he found he could not entice her. He did not move, but kept playing on his curious instrument. Perhaps, by returning into the hollow, she could make a circuit, and so pass him, lower down the hill. She rose at once and ran.

Now Gibbie had seen her long before she saw him, but, from experience, was afraid of frightening her. He had therefore drawn gradually near, and sat as if unaware of her presence. Treating her as he would a bird with which he wanted to make better acquaintance, he would have her get accustomed to the look of him before he made advances. But when he saw her run in the direction of the swamp, knowing what a dangerous place it was, he was terrified, sprung to his feet, and darted off to get between her and the danger.

She heard him coming like the wind at her back, and made straight for the swamp. But as she approached the place, there he was, on the edge of a great hole half full of water, as if he had been sitting there for an hour!

She turned again and ran toward the descent of the mountain. But there Gibbie feared a certain precipitous spot; so Ginevra had not run far before again she saw him right in her way. She threw herself on the ground in despair and hid her face. Fearfully expectant, she lay breathless. But nothing came. Still she lay, and still nothing came. But she dared not look up. She lay and lay, weary and still, with the terror slowly ebbing away out of her.

At length to her ears came a strange sweet voice of singing—such a sound as she had never heard before. It seemed to come from far away; what if it should be an angel God was sending, in answer to her prayer! He would, of course, want some time to come, and certainly no harm had happened to her yet. The sound grew and grew, and came nearer and nearer. But although it was song, she could distinguish no vowel-melody in it, nothing but a tone-melody, a crooning, as it were, ever upon one vowel in a minor key. It came quite near at length, and yet even then had something of the faraway sound left in it. It was like the wind of a summer night inside a great church bell in a deserted tower. It came close and ceased suddenly, as if, like a lark, the angel ceased to sing the moment he lighted. She opened her eyes and looked up.

Over her stood the beast-boy, gazing down upon her! Could it really be the beast-boy? If so, then he was fascinating her, to devour her the more easily, as she had read of snakes doing to birds; but she could not believe it. Still, she could not take her eyes off him—that was certain. But no marvel! From under a great crown of reddish gold looked out two eyes of heaven's own blue, and through the eyes looked out something that dwells behind the sky and every blue thing.

She lay motionless, flat on the ground, her face turned sideways upon her hands, and her eyes fixed on the heavenly vision. Then a curious feeling began to wake in her of having seen him before—somewhere, ever so long ago—and that sight of him as well as this had to do with misery—with something that made a stain that would not come out. Yes—it was the very face, only larger, and still sweeter, of the little naked child whom Angus had so cruelly lashed! That was ages ago, but she had not forgotten and never could forget either the child's back, or the lovely innocent white face that he turned around upon her. If it was indeed he, perhaps he would remember her. In any case, she was now certain he would not hurt her.

While she looked at him thus, Gibbie's face grew grave; seldom was his grave when fronting the face of a fellow creature, but now he too was remembering and trying to recollect; as through a dream of sickness and pain he saw a face like the one before him, yet not the same.

Ginevra recollected first, and a sweet slow diffident smile crept like a dawn up from the depth of her underworld to the sky of her face but settled in her eyes and made two stars of them. Then rose the very sun himself in Gibbie's and flashed a full response of daylight. From brow to chin his face was radiant.

Timidly yet trustingly Ginevra took one hand from under her cheek and stretched it up to him. He clasped it gently. She moved, and he helped her to rise.

"I've lost Nicie," she said.

Gibbie nodded, but did not look concerned.

"Nicie is my maid," said Ginevra.

Gibbie nodded several times. He knew who Nicie was rather better than her mistress.

"I left her away back there, a long, long time ago, and she has never come to me," she said.

Gibbie gave a shrill loud whistle that startled her. In a few seconds, from somewhere unseen, a dog came bounding to him over stones and heather. How he spoke to the dog, or what he told him to do, she had not an idea; but the next instant Oscar was rushing along the path she had come and was presently out of sight. So full of life was Gibbie, so quick and decided was his every motion, so full of expression his every glance and smile, that she had not yet begun to wonder he had not spoken; indeed she was hardly yet aware of the fact.

Gibbie took her hand and led her toward the path she had left; she yielded without a movement of question. But he did not lead her far in that direction; he turned to the left up the mountain. It grew wilder as they ascended. But the air was so thin and invigorating, the changes so curious and interesting, as now they skirted the edge of a precipitous rock, now scrambled up the steepest of paths by the help of the heather that nearly closed over it, and the reaction of relief from the terror she had suffered so exciting that she never for a moment felt tired. Then they went down the side of a little burn—a good stream, whose dance and song delighted her; it was the same, as she learned afterward, whose song under her window she listened to every night in bed, trying in vain to make out the melted tune. Ever after she knew this, it seemed, as she listened, to come straight from the mountain to her window, with news of the stars and the heather and the sheep.

They crossed the burn and climbed the opposite bank. Then Gibbie pointed, and there was the cottage, and there was Nicie coming up the path to it, with Oscar bounding before her! The dog was merry, but Nicie was weeping bitterly. They were a good way off, with another larger burn between; but Gibbie whistled, and Oscar came flying to him. Nicie looked up, gave a cry, and like a sheep to her lost lamb came running.

"Oh, missie!" she said, breathless, as she reached the opposite bank of the burn, "what made you run away?"

"There *was* a road, Nicie, and I thought you would come after me."

"I was a muckle goose, missie; but eh! I'm glad I have got you. Come along and see my mother."

"Yes, Nicie. We'll tell her all about it. You see, I haven't got a mother to tell, so I will tell yours."

From that hour Nicie's mother was a mother to Ginny as well.

"Another of his lambs to feed!" Janet said to herself.

Never before had Ginny spent such a happy day, drunk such milk as Crummie's, or eaten such cakes as Janet's. She saw no more of Gibbie; the moment she was safe, he and Oscar were off again to the sheep, for Robert was busy cutting peats that day, and Gibbie was in sole charge. Eager to know about him, Ginevra gathered all that Janet could tell of his story, and in return told the little she had seen of it, which was the one dreadful point.

"Is he a good boy, Mistress Grant?" she asked.

"The best boy ever I knew—better than my own Donal, and he was the best before him," answered Janet.

Ginny gave a little sigh.

"When did you see Donal?" asked Janet of Nicie.

"Not this long time—not since I was here last," answered Nicie.

"I was thinking," returned her mother, "you should be able to see him now from the back of the muckle hoose; for he was telling me he was with the nowt in the meadow upon the Lorrie bank."

"Oh, is he there?" said Nicie. "I'll maybe get a sight of him if I don't get a word. He came once to the kitchen door to see me, but Mistress MacFarlane would not let him in. She would have no loons coming about the place, she said. I said that he was my brother and she said that was nothing to her. I told her that all my brothers were well known to be douce lads, but she told me to hold my tongue. I could have given her a box on the ear, I was that angry with her."

"She'll be sorry for it someday," said Janet, with a quiet smile; "and what a body's sure to be sorry for, you may as well forgive them at once."

"How do you know, Mother, that she'll be sorry for it?" asked Nicie, not very willing to forgive Mistress MacFarlane.

" 'Cause the Master says that we'll have to pay the uttermost farthing. There's nobody will be let off. We must all do right to our neighbors."

When Ginevra went home that night, it was with a good many new things to think about.

10: *The Meeting in the Meadow*

IT WAS high time that Donal Grant should be promoted a step in the ranks of labor, but Donal was not ambitious, at least in that direction. He was more and more in love with books and learning and the music of thought and word; and he knew well that no one doing a man's work upon a farm could have much time left for study—certainly not a quarter of what the herdboy could command. Therefore, with his parents' approval, he continued to fill the humbler office, and receive the scantier wages belonging to it.

The day following their adventure on Glashgar, in the afternoon, Nicie being in the grounds with her little mistress, proposed that they should look whether they could see her brother down in the meadow of which her mother had spoken. Ginevra willingly agreed, and they took their way through the shrubbery to a certain tall hedge which divided the grounds from a little grove of larches on the slope of a steep bank descending to the Lorrie, on the other side of which lay the meadow. It was a hawthorn hedge, very old, and near the ground very thin, so that they easily found a place to creep through. But they were no better on the other side, for the larches hid the meadow. They went down through them, therefore, to the bank of the little river—the largest tributary of the Daur from the roots of Glashgar.

"There he is!" cried Nicie.

"I see him," responded Ginny, "with his cows all about the meadow."

Donal sat a little way from the river, reading.

"He's aye at his book!" said Nicie.

"I wonder what book it is," said Ginny.

"That would be hard to say," answered Nicie. "Donal reads a hantle of books."

"Do you think it's Latin, Nicie?"

"Ow! I daresay. But no; it can't be Latin—for, look! he's laughing, and he couldn't do that if it were Latin. I'm thinking it'll be a story; there's a heap of them printed now, they tell me. Or it may be a song. I heard my mother once say she was some feared Donal might have taken to making songs himself; not that there was any harm in that, she said, but it was just some trifling like, and they look for better from Donal, with all his book learning, and his Euclid."

"What's Euclid, Nicie?"

"You may well ask, missie! but I find it hard to tell you. It's a curious name for a book, and makes me think of nothing but when the lid of your eye itches, and as to what lies between the two covers, I know no more than the man in the moon."

"I should like to ask Donal what book he has got," said Ginny.

"I'll call to him, and you can ask," said Nicie. "Donal! Donal!"

Donal looked up, and seeing his sister, came running to the bank of the stream.

"Can't you come over, Donal?" said Nicie. "Here's Miss Galbraith wants to ask you a question."

Donal was across in a moment, for here the water was nowhere over a foot or two in depth.

"Oh, Donal! you've wet your feet!" cried Ginevra.

Donal laughed.

"What harm will that do me, mem?"

"None, I hope," said Ginny; "but it might, you know."

"I might have been drowned," said Donal.

"Nicie," said Ginny, with dignity, "your brother is laughing at me."

"No, no, mem," said Donal, apologetically. "I was only so glad to see you and Nicie that I forgot my manners."

"Then," returned Ginny, quite satisfied, "would you mind telling me what book you were reading?"

"It's a book of ballads," answered Donal. "I'll read one of them to you, if you like, mem."

"I should like very much," responded Ginny. "I've read all my own books till I'm tired of them, and I don't like Papa's books. And, do you know, Donal, I am very tired of the Bible too."

"That's a pity, mem," replied Donal, shaking his head sadly and wishing she could hear his mother's reading of the book.

A pause naturally followed, which Ginny broke.

"I don't think you told me the *name* of the book you were reading, Donal," she said.

"If you'll sit down a minute, mem," returned Donal, "here's a bonnie gowany spot—I'll read a bit to you and see if you like it before I tell you the name of it."

She dropped at once on the little gowany bed, gathered her frock about her ankles, and said, "Sit down, Nicie. It's so kind of Donal to read something to us! I wonder what it's going to be."

Donal read the ballad of "Kemp Owen."

"I think—I think—I don't think I understand it," said Ginevra. "It is very dreadful, and—and—I don't know what to think. Tell me about it, Donal. Do *you* know what it means, Nicie?"

"No, I don't, missie," answered Nicie.

Donal proceeded at once to an exposition.

"What a good, kind, brave knight!" said Ginevra.

"But it's not true, you know, missie," said Nicie, anxious that she should not be misled. "It's nothing but Donal's nonsense."

"Nonsense here, nonsense there!" said Donal, "I see a heap of sense in it. But nonsense or not, Nicie, it's none of *my* nonsense; I wish it were. It's hundreds of years old, that ballad, I'll warrant."

"It's *beautiful,*" said Ginevra, with decision and dignity. "I hope he married the lady, and they lived happy ever after."

"I don't know, mem. The man that made the ballad, I daresay, thought him well paid if the bonnie lady said *thank you* to him."

Here, unhappily, Donal had to rush through the burn without leave-taking, for Hornie was attempting a trespass; and the two girls, thinking it was time to go home, rose, and climbed to the house at their leisure.

The rest of the day Ginevra talked of little else than the brave knight, saying now and then what a nice boy that Donal of Nicie's was. Nor was more than the gentlest hint necessary to make Nicie remark, the next morning, that perhaps, if they went down again to the Lorrie, Donal might come and bring the book. But when they reached the bank and looked across, they saw him occupied with Gibbie. They had their heads close together over a slate, upon which now the one, now the other, seemed to be drawing. This went on and on, and they never looked up. Ginny would have gone home and come again in the afternoon, but Nicie instantly called Donal.

He sprang to his feet and came to them, followed by Gibbie. Donal crossed the burn, but Gibbie remained on the other side, and when presently Donal took his book of ballads from his pocket, and the little company seated themselves, Gibbie stood with his back to them, and his eyes on the nowt. That morning they were not interrupted.

Donal read to them for a whole hour, concerning which reading, and Ginevra's reception of it, Nicie declared she could not see why they cared so much about old ballads. "They're not half so bonnie as the Bible, Donal," she said.

After this, Ginevra went frequently with Nicie to see her mother, and learned much of the best from her. Often, also, they went down to the Lorrie and had an interview with Donal, which was longer or shorter as Gibbie was there or not to release him.

Ginny's life was now far happier than it had ever been. New channels of thought and feeling were opened, new questions were started, new interests awakened; so that, instead of losing by Miss Machar's continued inability to teach her, she was learning far more than she could give her, learning it, too, with the pleasure which invariably accompanies true learning.

Donal felt from the first the charm of her society; and she by no means received without giving, for his mental development was greatly expedited thereby. Few weeks passed before he was her humble squire, devoted to her with all the chivalry of a youth for a girl whom he supposes as much his superior in kind as she is in worldly position; his sole advantage, in his own judgment, and that which alone procured him the privilege of her society, being that he was older and therefore knew a little more.

So potent and genial was her influence on his imagination, that, without once thinking of her as their object, he now first found himself capable of making verses—such as they were;

and one day, with his book before him, he ventured to repeat, as if he read them from the book, some verses about a burn running on to the sea, a wind blowing clean and clear, and the sun shining strong and fine; beneath the verses was the thought that if the man who wrote them were a burn, the wind, or the sun, he, too, would run and rejoice and shine. The verses halted a little, no doubt, in rhythm; neither were they perfectly rimed, but for a beginning they had promise.

Gibbie, who had thrown himself down on the other bank, and lay listening, at once detected the change in the tone of his utterance, and concluded that Donal was not reading them and that they were his own. Hardly had Donal ended, when Gibbie's pipes began from the opposite side of the water, and, true to time and cadence and feeling, followed with just the one air to suit the song—from which Donal, to his no small comfort, understood that one at least of his company had received his lilt. But Ginevra had not received it, and being therefore of her own mind, and not of the song's, was critical.

"That one is nonsense, Donal," she said. "Isn't it now? How could a man be a burn, or a wind, or the sun? But poets *are* silly. Papa says so."

In his mind Donal did not know which way to look; physically, he regarded the ground. Happily at that very moment Hornie caused a diversion, and Gibbie understood what Donal was feeling too well to make even a pretense of going after her. Donal was in no haste to return to his audience. To have his first poem thus rejected was killing. He called himself a fool and resolved never to read another poem to a girl as long as he lived. By the time he had again walked through the burn, however, he was calm and comparatively wise, and knew what to say.

"Do you hear yon burn after you go to bed, mem?" he asked Ginevra, as he climbed the bank, pointing a little lower down the stream to the mountain brook which there joined it.

"Always," she answered. "It runs right under my window."

"What kind of a din does it make?" he asked again.

"It is different at different times," she answered. "It sings and chatters in summer, and growls and cries and grumbles in winter, or after rain up in Glashgar."

"Do you think the burn is any happier in the summer, mem?"

"No, Donal; the burn has no life in it, therefore can't be happier one time than another."

"Well, mem, when you're lying listening to the burn, did you never imagine yourself running with it down to the sea?"

"No, Donal; I always fancy myself going up to the mountain where it comes from, and running about wild there in the wind, when all the time I know I'm safe and warm in bed."

"Well, maybe that's better yet—I wouldn't say," answered Donal, "but just tonight, for a change like, turn and go down with it, in your thoughts, I mean. Lie still and listen till the sound runs away with you and you forget about yourself and think you're the burn, running, running through this and through that, through stones and birks and bracken, through heather and plowed land and corn, and weeds and gardens, singing and changing your tune accordingly till you end up in the muckle roaring sea. Then the first night that the wind is up, do the same, mem, with the wind. Get up on the back of it as if it was your muckle horse and ride him to the death. After that, mem, I'm thinking you won't be so ready to find fault with the laddie who made yon small song."

"Are you vexed with me, Donal? I'm *so* sorry!" said Ginevra, taking the earnestness of his tone for displeasure.

"No, no, mem. You're over good and over bonnie," answered Donal, "to be a vex to anybody; but it would be a vex to hear such a creature as you speaking like one of the fools of the world who believes nothing but what comes in at the holes in their heads."

Ginevra was silent. She could not quite understand Donal,

but she felt she must be wrong somehow; and of this she was the more convinced when she saw the beautiful eyes of Gibbie fixed in admiration, and brimful of love, upon Donal.

The way Donal kept his vow never to read another poem of his own to a girl was to proceed that very night to make another for the express purpose, as he lay awake in the darkness.

When by degrees it dawned upon Ginevra that Donal was the maker of the verses he read, she grew half afraid of him, and began to regard him with big eyes. She could not help trying to think how he did the thing; and as she felt no possibility of making verses herself, it remained a mystery and an astonishment, causing a great respect for the poet to mingle with the kindness she felt toward Nicie's brother.

11: *Gain of a Year*

BY DEGREES Gibbie had come to be well known about the Mains and Glashruach, and the tales about the beast-loon were dying out from Daurside. Jean Mavor was a special friend to him; for she knew now well enough who had been her brownie and made him welcome as often as he showed himself with Donal. Fergus was sometimes at home, sometimes away; but he was now quite a fine gentleman and only condescendingly cognizant of the existence of Donal Grant. All he said to him when he came home was that he ought to be something more than herd by this time. Donal smiled and said nothing. He had just finished a little song that pleased him and could afford to be patronized.

In the autumn, Mr. Galbraith returned to Glashrauch, but did not remain long. He was kinder than usual to Ginevra and told her she must keep up her studies by herself as well as she could. Ginevra never said anything about Donal or Gibbie, or her friendship for Nicie. He had himself to blame altogether; he had made it impossible for her to talk to him. But it was well he remained in ignorance, and so did not put a stop to the best education she could at this time of her life have been having.

It was interrupted, however, by the arrival of the winter—a wild time in that region, fierce storm alternating with the calm of death. After howling nights, in which it seemed as if all the poltergeists of the universe must be out on a disembodied lark, the mountains stood there in the morning solemn still, each with his white turban of snow unrumpled on his head, in the profoundest silence of blue air, as if he had never in his life passed a more thoughtful, peaceful time than the very last night of all. The cottage on Glashgar was for months inaccessible. More than once the Daur was frozen thick; for weeks every beast was an absolute prisoner to the byre, and for months was fed with straw and turnips and potatoes and oilcake. Then was the time for stories; and often in the long dark, while yet it was hours too early for bed, would Ginevra go with Nicie to the kitchen to get one of the other servants to tell her an old tale. Not a glimpse did Ginevra get all this time of Donal or of Gibbie.

At last, like one of its own flowers in its own bosom, the spring began again to wake in God's thought of His world; and the snow, like all other deaths, had to melt and run, leaving room for hope; then the summer woke smiling, as if she knew she had been asleep; and the two youths and the two maidens met yet again on Lorrie bank, with the brown water falling over the stones, the gold nuggets of the broom hanging over the water, and the young larchwood scenting the air all up the brae side between them and the house, which the tall hedge hid from their view. The four were a year older, a year nearer trouble, and a year nearer getting out of it. Ginevra was more of a woman, Donal more of a poet, Nicie as nice and much the same, and Gibbie, if possible, more a foundling of the universe than ever. The mountain was a grand nursery for him, and the result, both physical and spiritual, corresponded.

Janet, who, better than anyone else, knew what was in the mind of the boy, revered him as much as he revered her;

the first impression he made upon her had never worn off—had only changed its color a little. More even than a knowledge of the truth is a readiness to receive it; and Janet saw from the first that Gibbie's ignorance at its worst was but room vacant for the truth; when it came it found neither bolt nor bar on door or window, but had immediate entrance. The secret of this power of reception was that to see a truth and to do it was one and the same thing with Gibbie. To know and not do would have seemed to him an impossibility.

This unity of vision and action was the main cause also of a certain daring simplicity in the exercise of the imagination. He did not do the less well for his sheep, that he fancied they knew when Jesus Christ was on the mountain, and always at such times both fed better and were more frolicsome. He thought Oscar knew it also, and interpreted a certain look of the dog by the supposition that he had caught a sign of the bodily presence of his Maker. The direction in which his imagination ran forward was always that in which his reason pointed; and so long as Gibbie's fancies were bud blooms upon his obedience, his imagination could not be otherwise than in harmony with his reason.

In the summer, Mr. Galbraith, all unannounced, reappeared at Glashruach, but so changed that, startled at the sight of him, Ginevra stopped midway in her advance to greet him. The long thin man was now haggard and worn; he looked sourer too, and more suspicious. He was annoyed that his daughter should recognize an alteration in him, and, turning away, leaned his head on the hand whose arm was already supported by the mantelpiece, and took no further notice of her presence.

Ginevra knew from experience that the sight of tears would enrage him, and with all her might repressed those she felt beginning to rise. She went up to him timidly, and took the hand that hung by his side. He did not repel her, but he left it hanging lifeless, and returned with it no pressure upon hers.

"Is anything the matter, Papa?" she asked with trembling voice.

"I am not aware that I have been in the habit of communicating with you on the subject of my affairs," he answered.

"Oh, Papa! I was frightened to see you looking so ill."

"Such a remark upon my personal appearance is but a poor recognition of my labors for your benefit, I venture to think, Jenny," he said.

He was at the moment contemplating, as a necessity, the sale of every foot of the property her mother had brought him. Nothing less would serve to keep up his credit and gain time to disguise more than one failing scheme. Everything had of late been going so badly that he had lost a good deal of his confidence and self-satisfaction; but he had gained no humility instead. He was a proud man, whose pride was always catching cold from his heart. The servants found more change in him than Ginevra did. Now he found fault with everyone, so that even Joseph dared hardly open his mouth, and said he must give warning.

The day after his arrival, having spent the morning with Angus walking over certain fields, he scolded Ginevra severely on his return because she had not had lunch, but had waited for him; whereas a little reflection might have shown him she dared not take it without him. Naturally, therefore, she could not now eat, because of a certain sensation in her throat. The instant he saw she was not eating, he ordered her out of the room; he would have no such airs in his family! By the end of the week such a sense of estrangement possessed Ginevra that she would turn on the stair and run up again, if she heard her father's voice below.

In this evil mood he received from someone a hint concerning the relations between his daughter and his tenant's herdboy. He was overwhelmed with a righteous disgust. He did himself the justice of making himself certain before he took measures; but he never thought of doing them the justice of acquainting himself first with the nature of the intercourse they held.

He watched and waited, and more than once pretended to go from home; at last one morning, from the lárchwood, he saw the unnatural girl seated with her maid on the bank of the river, the cowherd reading to them, and on the other side the dumb idiot lying listening. He was almost beside himself. In a loud voice of bare command he called to her to come to him. With a glance of terror at Nicie she rose, and they went up through the larches together.

A verbal torrent of wrath, wounded dignity, disgust, and contempt was poured upon Ginevra. Nicie was dismissed on the spot. Not another night would he endure her in the house, after her abominable breach of confidence! She had to depart without even a good-by from Ginevra and went home weeping, in great dread of what her mother would say.

"Lassie," said Janet, when she heard her story, "if anything is to blame it's myself; for you let me know that you went with your bonnie missie to have a bit of talk with Donal and I could see nothing wrong in that. But the folk of this world have other ways of judging and I must find out what lesson of the serpent's wisdom is in this for me. You're welcome home, my bonnie lass. You know I keep the wee closet ready for any of you that might come unexpectedly."

Nicie, however, had not long to occupy the closet, for those of her breed were in demand in the country.

12: *The Storm*

EVER SINCE he became a dweller in the air of Glashgar, Gibbie had been in the habit, as often as he saw reason to expect a thunderstorm, and his duties would permit, of ascending the mountain, and there on the crest of the granite peak, awaiting the arrival of the tumult.

Toward the evening of a wondrously fine day in the beginning of August, it began to rain. All the next day the slopes and stairs of Glashgar were alternately glowing in the sunshine, and swept with heavy showers, driven slanting in strong gusts of wind from the northwest. How often he was wet through and dried again that day, Gibbie could not have told. He wore so little that either took but a few moments, and he was always ready for a change. The wind and the rain together were cold, but that only served to let the sunshine deeper into him when it returned.

In the afternoon there was less sun, more rain, and more wind; and at last the sun seemed to give it up; the wind grew to a hurricane, and the rain strove with it which should inhabit the space. The whole upper region was like a huge mortar, in which the wind was the pestle, and, with innumerable gyres, vainly ground at the rain.

Gibbie drove his sheep to the refuge of a pen on the lower slope of a valley that ran at right angles to the wind, where they were sheltered by a rock behind, forming one side of the enclosure, and dikes of loose stones, forming the others at a height there was no tradition of any flood having reached. He then went home and having told Robert what he had done, and had his supper, set out in the early-failing light to ascend the mountain. A great thunderstorm was at hand and was calling him. It was almost dark before he reached the top, but he knew the surface of Glashgar nearly as well as the floor of the cottage. Just as he had fought his way to the crest of the peak in the face of one of the fiercest of the blasts abroad that night, a sudden rush of fire made the heavens like the smoke-filled vault of an oven, and at once the thunder followed, in a succession of single sharp explosions without any roll between. The mountain shook with the windy shocks, but the first of the thunderstorm was the worst, and it soon passed. The wind and the rain continued, and the darkness was filled with the rush of the water everywhere wildly tearing down the sides of the mountain. Thus heaven and earth held communication in torrents all the night. To the ears and heart of Gibbie their noises were a mass of broken music.

It required some care to find his way down through the darkness and the waters to the cottage, but as he was neither in fear nor in haste, he was in little danger, and his hands and feet could pick out the path where his eyes were useless. When at length he reached his bed, it was not for a long time to sleep, but to lie awake and listen to the raging of the wind all about and above and below the cottage and the rushing of the streams down past it on every side.

He awoke and in his ears was the sound of many waters. It was morning. He rose and, dressing hastily, opened the door. The wind fiercely invaded the cottage, thick charged with waterdrops, and stepping out he shut the door in haste, lest it should blow upon the old people in bed and awaken them. He could not see far on any side for the rain that fell, and the mist and steam that rose, upon which the wind seemed to have no power; but wherever he did see, there water was running down. Up the mountain he went. By the time he reached the top, it was as light as it was all the day.

That moment Glashgar gave a great heave under him, then rocked and shook from side to side a little, and settled down so still and steady, that motion and the mountain seemed again two ideas that never could be present together in any mind. The next instant came an explosion, followed by a frightful roaring and hurling, as of mingled water and stones; and on the side of the mountain beneath him he saw what, through the mist, looked like a cloud of smoke or dust rising to a height. He darted toward it. As he drew nearer, the cloud seemed to condense, and presently he saw plainly enough that it was a great column of water shooting up and out from the face of the mountain. Already it had scattered masses of gravel on all sides, and down the hill a river was shooting in sheer cataract, raving and tearing, and carrying stones and rocks with it like foam.

Suddenly Gibbie, in the midst of his astonishment and awful delight, noted the path of the new stream, and from his knowledge of the face of the mountain, perceived that its course was direct for the cottage. Down the hill he shot after it, as if it were a wild beast that his fault had freed from its cage.

The torrent had already worn for itself a channel; what earth there was, it had swept clean away to the rock, and the loose stones it had thrown up aside or hurled with it in its headlong course. But as Gibbie bounded along, following it with a speed almost equal to its own, he was checked in the midst of his hearty haste by the sight, a few yards away, of another like terror—another torrent issuing from the side of the hill and rushing to swell the valley stream. Another and another he saw, with growing wonder, as he ran. Two of them joined the one he was following, and he had to cross them as he could; the others he saw near and farther off. Now and then a huge boulder, loosened from its bed, would go rolling, leaping, bounding down the hill before him, and just in time he escaped one that came springing after him as if it were a living thing. And still the wind was raging, and the rain tumbling to the earth, rather in sheets than in streams.

Gibbie at length forsook the bank of the new torrent to take the nearest way home and soon reached the point whence first, returning in that direction, he always looked to see the cottage. For a moment he was utterly bewildered: no cottage was to be seen. From the top of the rock against which it was built shot the whole mass of the water he had been pursuing, now dark with stones and gravel, now gray with foam, or glassy in the lurid light.

When he came nearer, to his amazement there stood the little house unharmed, the very center of the cataract! For a few yards on the top of the rock, the torrent had a nearly horizontal channel, along which it rushed with unabated speed to the edge, and thence shot clean over the cottage, dropping only a dribble of rain on the roof from the underside of its half arch. The garden ground was gone, swept clean from the bare rock, which made a fine smooth shoot for the water a long distance in front. He darted through the drizzle and spray, reached the door, and lifted the latch. The same moment he heard Janet's voice in joyful greeting.

"Now, now! come along, laddie," she said. "Who would have thought we would have to leave the mountain to escape the water? We're but waiting for you to go. Come, Robert, we'll be away down the hill."

She stood in the middle of the room in her best gown, as if she had been going to church, her Bible, a good-sized octavo, under her arm, with a white handkerchief folded around it, and her umbrella in her hand.

"He that believeth shall not make haste," she said, "but he

must not tempt the Lord, either. Drink that milk, Gibbie, and put a bannock in your pocket, and come away."

Robert rose from the edge of the bed, staff in hand, ready too. He also was in his Sunday clothes. Oscar, who could make no change of attire, but was always ready, and had been standing looking up in his face for the last ten minutes, wagged his tail when he saw him rise and got out of his way. On the table were the remains of their breakfast of oatcake and milk. The water kept coming in splashes down the chimney, the hillocks of the floor were slimy, and in the hollows little lakes were gathering; the lowest film of the torrent water ran down the rock behind, and making its way between rock and roof, threatened soon to render the place uninhabitable.

"Why laden yourself with the umbrella?" said Robert. "You'll get it drenched."

"Oh, I'll just take it," replied Janet, with a laugh in acknowledgment of her husband's fun; "it'll keep the rain from blinding me."

"That's if you're able to keep it up against the wind. I'm thinking, though, you're taking it to keep the book dry!"

Janet smiled and made no denial.

"Now, Gibbie," she said, "you go and loose Crummie. But you'll have to lead her."

"Where do you think of going?" asked Robert, who, satisfied as usual with whatever might be in his wife's mind, had not till this moment thought of asking her where she meant to take refuge.

"Oh, we'll just make for the Mains, if you're agreeable, Robert," she answered. "It's there we belong to, and weather like this nobody would refuse shelter to a beggar, not to say Mistress Jean to her own folk."

With that she led the way to the door and opened it.

"His voice was like the sound of many waters," she said to herself softly, as the liquid thunder of the torrent came in the louder.

Gibbie shot around the corner to the byre, whence through all the roar, every now and then they had heard the cavernous mooing of Crummie, piteous and low. He found a stream a foot deep running between her fore- and hindlegs, and did not wonder that she wanted to be on the move. Speedily he loosened her, and fastening the chain-tether to her halter, led her out. She was terrified at sight of the falling water, and they had some trouble in getting her through behind it, but presently after, she was making the descent as carefully and successfully as any of them.

It was a heavy undertaking for the two old folk to walk all the way to the Mains, and in such a state of the elements. Janet was half-troubled that her mountain, and her foundation on the rock, should have failed her; but consoled herself that they were but shadows of heavenly things and figures of the true; and that a mountain or a rock was in itself no more to be trusted than a horse or a prince or the legs of a man. Robert plodded on in contented silence, and Gibbie was in great glee, singing after his fashion all the way, though now and then half-choked by the fierceness of the wind around some corner of rock, filled with raindrops that stung like hailstones.

By and by Janet stopped and began looking about her. This naturally seemed to her husband rather odd in the circumstances.

"What are you after, Janet?" he said, shouting through the wind from a few yards off, by no means sorry to stand for a moment, although any recovering of his breath seemed almost hopeless in such a tempest.

"I want to lay my umbrella in safety," answered Janet, "if I could but perceive a suitable spot. You were right, Robert, it's more wealth than I can get the good of."

"Hoots! fling it from you, then, lass," he returned. "Is this a day to be thinking of worldly gear?"

"What for not, Robert?" she rejoined. "Any day's as good as another for thinking about anything the right way."

"What!" retorted Robert, "when we have taken our lives in our hands, and can no more than hope we may carry them through safe!"

"What's that that you call our lives, Robert? The Master never made muckle of the saving of such like them. It seems to me they're nothing but a kind of worldly gear themselves."

"And yet," argued Robert, "you'll take thought about an old umbrella? Where's your consistency, lass?"

"If I were troubled about my life," said Janet, "I could ill spare thought for an old umbrella. But they both trouble me so little that I may just as well look after them both. No," she continued, looking about her, "I must just do my duty by the old umbrella."

So saying, she walked to the lee side of a rock and laid the umbrella close under it, then a few large stones upon it to keep it down.

They reached at length the valley road. When they approached the bridge by which they must cross the Lorrie, their worst trouble lay before them. For the road was flooded for a long way on both sides of the bridge. There was therefore a good deal of wading to be done; but the road was an embankment, there was little current, and in safety at last they ascended the rising ground on which the farm building stood. When they reached the yard, they sent Gibbie to find shelter for Crummie, and themselves went up to the house.

"The Lord preserve us!" cried Jean Mavor, with uplifted hands, when she saw them enter the kitchen.

"He'll do that, mem," returned Janet, with a smile.

"But what *can* He do? If you've been driven out of the hills what's to become of houses in the meadows? I'd like to know that."

"The water's not up to your door yet," remarked Janet.

"God forbid!" retorted Jean. "But, eh, you're wet!"

"*Wet's* not the word," said Robert, trying to laugh, but

failing from sheer exhaustion, and the beginnings of an asthmatic attack.

The farmer, hearing their voices, came into the kitchen.

"Hoot, Rob!" he said roughly as he entered, "I thought you had more sense! What's brought you here at such a time?" As he spoke he held out his snuffbox to the old man.

"Fell necessity, sir," answered Robert, taking a good pinch.

"Necessity!" retorted the farmer. "Were you out of meal?"

"Out of dry meal, I don't doubt, by this time, sir," replied Robert.

"Hoots! It's just clean ridiculous! You should have known better at your age, Rob. You should have thought twice, man."

" 'Deed, sir," answered Robert, quietly finishing his pinch of snuff, "there was small need, and less time to think, with Glashgar bursten, and the water coming over the top of the bit hoosie as if it were a muckle overshot wheel and not a place to bide in. You don't think Janet and me would be two such old fools as to put on our Sunday clothes to swim in, if we thought to see things as we left them when we went back!"

"Haith! if the water was running over the top of your hoose, man, it was time to flit. It's perfectly ridiculous!"

The old people went to change their clothes for some Jean had provided, and in the meantime she made up her fire and prepared some breakfast for them.

"And where's your dummie?" she asked as they re-entered the kitchen.

"He had poor Crummie to look after," answered Janet; "but he might have been in by this time."

"He'll be with Donal in the byre, no doubt," said Jean; "he's aye some shy of coming in wanting an invitation." She went to the door, and called with a loud voice across the yard, through the wind and the clashing torrents, "Donal, send Dummie in to his breakfast."

"He's gone back to his sheep," cried Donal in reply.

"Preserve us!—the creature will be lost!" said Jean.

"Less likely than any man about the place," bawled Donal, half-angry with his mistress for calling his friend "dummie." "Gibbie knows better what he's about than any two that thinks him a fool because he can't let out such stuff and nonsense as they can't keep in."

Jean went back to the kitchen, only half-reassured concerning her brownie, and far from contented with his absence. But she was glad to find that neither Janet nor Robert appeared alarmed at the news.

"I wish the creature had had some breakfast," she said.

"He has a bannock in his pocket," answered Janet.

"Hoots!" returned Jean.

When they had eaten their breakfast, Robert took his pipe to the barn, saying there was not much danger of fire that day; Janet washed up the dishes and sat down to her book; and Jean went out and in, attending to many things.

Meantime the rain fell, the wind blew, the water rose. Little could be done beyond feeding the animals, threshing a little corn in the barn, and twisting straw ropes for the thatch of the ricks of the coming harvest. Already not a few of last year's ricks, from farther up the country, were floating past the Mains, down the Daur to the sea. The sight was a dreadful one to farmers' eyes. From the Mains, to right and left beyond the rising ground on which the farm buildings stood, everywhere as far as the bases of the hills, instead of fields, was water, yellow brown, here in still expanse or slow progress, there sweeping along in fierce current. The quieter parts of it were dotted with trees, divided by hedge, shaded with ears of corn; upon the swifter parts floated objects of all kinds.

Mr. Duff went wandering restlessly from one spot to another, finding nothing to do. In the gloaming, which fell the sooner that a rain blanket miles thick wrapped the earth up from the sun, he came across from the barn, and, entering the kitchen, dropped, weary with hopelessness, on a chair.

"Hold your tongue, Janet. I'm not saying there's anything wrong; I'm saying nothing but the sore truth, that I can't see the what for of this. I can't see the good of it to anybody. The land is just melting away into the sea!"

Janet sat silent, knitting hard at a stocking she had got hold of that Jean had begun for her brother. She knew argument concerning the uses of adversity was vain with a man who knew of no life but that which consisted in eating and drinking, sleeping and rising, working and getting on in the world.

From being nearly in the center of its own land, the farmsteading of the Mains was at a considerable distance from any other; but there were two or three cottages upon the land, and as the evening drew on, another aged pair, who lived in one only a few hundred yards from the house, made their appearance, and were soon followed by the wife of the foreman with her children, who lived farther off. Quickly the night closed in, and Gibbie had not come. Robert was growing very uneasy; Janet kept comforting and reassuring him.

"There's one thing," said the old man; "Oscar's with him."

"Ay," responded Janet, unwilling, in the hearing of others, to say a word that might seem to savor of rebuke to her husband, yet pained that he should go to the dog for comfort. "Ay; he's a well-made animal, Oscar! There's been a lot of sheep-care put into him."

"Oscar's not with him," said Donal. "The dog came to me in the byre looking for Gibbie."

Robert gave a great sigh but said nothing.

Janet did not sleep a wink that night: she had so many to pray for. Not Gibbie only, but every one of her family was in perils of waters, all being employed along the valley of the Daur. It was not, she said, confessing to her husband her sleeplessness, that she was afraid. She was only "keeping them company, and holding the gate open," she said. She never said she *prayed;* she *held the gate open.*

The dawn appeared—but the farm had vanished. Not even heads of growing corn were anywhere more to be seen. The loss would be severe, and John Duff's heart sank within him. The sheep which had been in the mown cloverfield that sloped to the burn were now all in the cornyard, and the water was there with them. If the rise did not soon cease, every rick would be afloat.

"Take your breakfast, John," said his sister.

"Let them take that hungers," he answered.

"Take, or you'll not have the wit to save," said Jean.

Thereupon he fell to, and ate, if not with appetite, then with a will that was wondrous.

The flood still grew, and still the rain poured, and Gibbie did not come. Indeed no one any longer expected him, whatever might have become of him. Soon after breakfast, a strange woman came to the door. Jean, who opened it to her knock, stood and stared speechless. It was a gray-haired woman, with a more disreputable look than her weather-flouted condition would account for.

"Grand weather for the ducks!" she said.

"Where do *you* come from?" returned Jean, who did not relish the freedom of her address.

"From over by," she answered.

"And how got you here?"

"Upon my two legs."

Jean looked this way and that over the watery waste, and again stared at the woman in growing bewilderment.

"Your legs must be longer than they look then, woman," said Jean, glancing at the lower part of the stranger's person.

The woman only laughed—a laugh without any laughter in it.

"What's your will, now that you *are* here?" continued Jean, with severity. "You did not come to the Mains to tell them there what kind of weather it is!"

"I came where I could get in," answered the woman.

"Woman," said Jean, "Mr. Duff doesn't like tramps."

"Tramps here, tramps there!" exclaimed the woman, starting into high displeasure. "I would have you know I'm an honest woman and no tramp!"

"You shouldn't look as like one then," said Jean coolly. "But come in, and I'll say nothing as long as you behave."

The woman followed her, took the seat pointed out to her by the fire, and sullenly ate, without a word of thanks, the cakes and milk handed her. On the other side of the fire sat Janet, knitting away busily, with a look of ease and leisure. She said nothing, but now and then cast a kindly glance out of her gray eyes at the woman; there was an air of the lost sheep about the stranger, which, in whomsoever she might see it, always drew her affection. "She must be one of those the Master came to call," she said to herself. But she was careful to suggest no approach, for she knew the sheep that has left the flock has grown wild and is more suspicious and easily startled than one in the midst of its brethren.

With the first of the light, some of the men on the farm had set out to look for Gibbie, well knowing it would be a hard matter to touch Glashgar. About nine they returned, having found it impossible. One of them, caught in a current, and swept into a hole, had barely escaped with his life. But they were unanimous that the dummie was better off in any cave on Glashgar than he would be in the best bedroom at the Mains, if things went on as they threatened.

Robert had kept on going to the barn and back again to the kitchen, all the morning, consumed with anxiety about the son of his old age; but the barn began to be flooded, and he had to limit his prayer-walk to the space between the door of the house and the chair where Janet sat—knitting busily and praying with countenance untroubled, amid the rush of the seaward torrents, the mad howling and screeching of the wind, and the lowing of the imprisoned cattle.

"O Lord," she said in her great trusting heart, "if my bonnie man is drowning in the waters, or dying of cold on the hill-side, hold his hand. Don't be far from him, O Lord; don't let him be afraid."

Robert seemed at length to have ceased his caged wandering. For a quarter of an hour he had been sitting with his face buried in his hands. Janet rose, went softly to him, and said in a whisper—

"Is Gibbie worse off, Robert, in this water upon Glashgar than the disciples in the boat upon yon loch of Galilee, and the Master not come to them? Robert, my own man! don't make the Master say to you, *O ye of little faith! Wherefore did you doubt?* Take heart, man; the Master would not have His men be cowards."

"You're right, Janet, you're aye right," answered Robert, and rose.

She followed him into the passage.

"Where are you going, Robert?" she said.

"I wish I could tell you," he answered. "I'm just hungering to be by myself. I wish I had never left Glashgar. There's aye room there. Or if I could run out among the ricks, but there's none of them left. I want to go to the Lord, but I mustn't wet Willie Mackay's clothes."

"It's a sore pity," said Janet, "that the menfolk don't learn to knit stockings, or do something or other with their hands. Many's the time my stocking has been 'most as good as a closet to me, though I could not go into it. But what matters that! A prayer in the heart is sure to find the road out. The heart's the last place that can hold one in. A praying heart has no roof to it."

She turned and left him. Comforted by her words, he followed her back into the kitchen and sat down beside her.

"Gibbie will be here mayhap when least you look for him," said Janet.

Neither of them caught the wild eager gleam that lighted the face of the strange woman at those last words of Janet. She looked up at her with the sharpest of glances, but the same instant compelled her countenance to resume its former expression of fierce indifference, and under that became watchful of everything said and done.

Still the rain fell and the wind blew; the torrents came tearing down from the hills and shot madly into the rivers; the rivers ran into the valleys, and deepened the lakes that filled them. On every side of the Mains, from the foot of Glashgar to Gormdhu, all was one yellow and red sea, with roaring currents and vortexes numberless. It burrowed holes, it opened long-deserted channels and watercourses; here it deposited inches of rich mold, there yards of sand and gravel; here it was carrying away fertile ground, leaving behind only bare rock or shingle where the corn had been waving; there it was scooping out the bed of a new lake.

Houses were torn to pieces, and their contents, as from broken boxes, sent wandering on the brown waste, through the gray air, to the discolored sea. Haymows were buried to the very top in sand; others went sailing bodily down the mighty stream—some of them followed or surrounded, like big ducks, by a great brood of ricks for their ducklings. Huge trees went past as if shot down an alpine slide, cottages and bridges of stone giving way before them. Wooden mills, thatched roofs, great mill wheels, went dipping and swaying and hobbling down. From the upper windows of the Mains, looking toward the chief current, they saw a drift of everything belonging to farms and dwelling houses that would float. Chairs and tables, chests, carts, saddles, chests of drawers, tubs of linen, beds and blankets, workbenches, harrows, girnels, planes, cheeses, churns, spinning wheels, cradles, iron pots, wheelbarrows—all these and many other things hurried past as they gazed. Everybody was looking, and for a time all had been silent.

"Lord save us!" cried Mr. Duff with a great start and ran for his telescope.

A fourpost bed came rocking down the river, now shooting straight for a short distance, now slowly wheeling, now shivering, struck by some swifter thing, now whirling giddily around in some vortex. The soaked curtains were flacking and flying in the great wind—and—yes, the telescope revealed it!—there was a figure in it! A cry burst from them all; but on swept the strange boat, bound for the world beyond the flood, and none could stay its course.

The water was now in the stable and cowhouses and barn. A few minutes more and it would be creeping into the kitchen. The Daur and its tributary, the Lorrie, were about to merge their last difference on the floor of Jean's parlor. Worst of all, a rapid current had set in across the farther end of the stable, which no one had as yet observed.

Jean bustled about her work as usual, accepting no help from any of her guests. Janet had got so far with the strange woman as to call her by her name, Mistress Croale; but Jean refused to address her in any way but as "the tramp wife."

"There's one thing, Mother," Donal said, entering the kitchen, covered with mud, a rabbit in one hand and a large salmon in the other, "we're no like to starve, with salmon in the hedges, and rabbits in the trees!"

His master questioned him with no little incredulity. It was easy to believe in salmon anywhere, but rabbits in trees!

"I caught it in the branches of a larch," Donal answered, "easy enough, for it couldn't run far and was more frightened of the water than of me; but for the salmon, haith, I was over and over with it in the water, after I gripped it, before I could call it my own."

Donal was still being cross-questioned by his master when the strange woman spoke.

"I doubt," she said, addressing no one in particular, "the gable of the stable will stand more than another half-hour."

"It must fall then," said the farmer.

"Hoots!" said the woman, "don't speak that way, sir. You might at the least give the poor beasts a chance."

"How would you do that?" said Jean. "If you loosed them they would but take to the water with fear and drown the sooner."

"No, no, Jean," interposed the farmer, "they would take care of themselves to the last, and aye hold to the dryest, just as you would yourself."

"Allowing," said the stranger, "I would rather drown swimming than tied by the head. But, you have where to put them. What kind of floors up the stair, sir?"

"Oh, good enough floors," answered the farmer. "It's the walls, woman, not the floors we have to be concerned about in this weather."

"If the joists are strong and well set into the walls, why shouldn't you take the horses up the stair to your bedrooms? It'll be all to the good of the walls, for the weight of the beasts will be upon them to hold them down, and the whole hoose against the water. And if I were you, I would put the best of the cows and the nowt into the parlor and the kitchen here."

Mr. Duff broke into a strange laughter.

"Would you not take up the carpets first, woman?" he said.

"I would," she answered; "that goes without saying—if there was time; but I tell you there's none; and you'll buy two or three carpets for the price of one horse."

"Haith! the woman's in the right," he cried, suddenly waking up to the sense of the proposal, and shot from the house.

All the women, Jean making no exception to any help now, rushed to carry the beds and blankets to the garret.

Just as Mr. Duff entered the stable from the nearer end, the opposite gable fell out with a great splash, letting in the wide level vision of turbidly raging waters, fading into the obscurity of the wind-driven rain. While he stared aghast, a great tree struck the wall like a battering ram, so that the stable shook. The horses, which had been for some time moving uneasily, were now quite scared. There was not a moment to be lost.

Duff shouted for his men; one or two came running; and in less than a minute more, those in the house heard the iron-shod feet splashing and stamping through the water, as, one after another, the horses were brought across the yard to the door of the house. Mr. Duff led by the halter his favorite Snowball, who was a good deal excited, plunging and rearing so that it was all he could do to hold him. He had ordered the men to take the others first, thinking he would follow more quietly. But the moment Snowball heard the first thundering of hoofs on the stairs, he went out of his senses with terror, broke from his master, and went plunging back to the stable. Duff darted after him, but was only in time to see him rush from the farther end into the swift current, where he was at once out of his depth, and was instantly caught and hurried, rolling over and over, from his master's sight. He ran back into the house and up the highest window. From that he caught sight of him a long way down, swimming. Once or twice he saw him turned heels over head—only to get his neck up again presently and swim as well as before.

With troubled heart he strained his sight after him as long as he could distinguish his lessening head, but it got among some wreck, and unable to tell anymore whether he saw it or not, he returned to his men with his eyes full of tears.

13: *Rescue*

As soon as Gibbie had found a stall for Crummie, and thrown a great dinner before her, he turned and sped back the way he had come; there was no time to lose if he would have the bridge to cross the Lorrie by; and his was indeed the last foot that ever touched it. Guiding himself by well-known points yet salient, for he knew the country perhaps better than any man born and bred in it, he made straight for Glashgar, itself hid in the rain.

Now wading, now swimming, now walking along the top of a wall, now caught and baffled in a hedge, Gibbie held stoutly on. Again and again he got into a current, and was swept from his direction, but he soon made his leeway good, and at length, clear of the level water and with only the torrents to mind, seated himself on a stone under a rock a little way up the mountain. There he drew from his pocket the puttylike mass to which the water had reduced the cakes with which it was filled, and ate it gladly, eying from his shelter the slanting lines of the rain and the rushing sea from which he had just emerged. So lost was the land beneath the water that he had to think to be certain under which of the roofs, looking like so many foundered Noah's arks, he had left his father and mother. Ah!

yonder were cattle!—a score of heads, listlessly drifting down, all the swim out of them, their long horns, like bits of dry branches, knocking together! There was a pig, and there another! And, alas! yonder floated half-a-dozen helpless sponges of sheep!

At sight of these last he started to his feet and set off up the hill. It was not so hard a struggle as to cross the water, but he had still to get to the other side of several torrents far more dangerous than any current he had been in. Again and again he had to ascend a long distance before he found a possible place to cross at; but he reached the fold at last.

It was in a little valley opening on that where lay the tarn. Swollen to a lake, the waters of it were now at the very gate of the pen. For a moment he regretted he had not brought Oscar, but the next he saw that not much could with any help have been done for the sheep, beyond what they could, if at liberty, do for themselves. Left where they were they would probably be drowned; if not they would be starved; but if he let them go, they would keep out of the water, and find for themselves what food and shelter were to be had. He opened the gate, drove them out, and a little way up the hill, and left them.

By this time it was about two o'clock, and Gibbie was very hungry. He turned toward the cottage. Great was his pleasure when, after another long struggle, he perceived that not only was it there, but the torrent gone.

He swept out the water that lay on the floor, took the driest peats he could find, succeeded with the tinderbox and sulfur match at the first attempt, lighted a large fire, and made himself some water brose. His hunger appeased, he sat resting in Robert's chair, gradually drying; and falling asleep, slept for an hour or so. When he woke, he took his New Testament from the crap o' the wa', and began to read. He read until he came to these words: "Hereby perceive we the love of God, because He laid down His life for us, and we ought to lay down our lives for the brethren."

"What learned him that?" said Gibbie to himself; Janet had taught him to search the teaching of the apostles for what the Master had taught them. He thought and thought, and at last remembered, "This is my commandment, that ye love one another as I have loved you."

"And here am I," said Gibbie to himself, "sitting here in idleseat, with my fire, and my food, and my Bible, and all the world beneath Glashgar lying in a flood! I can't lay down my life to save their souls; I must save for them what I can—it may be but a hen or a calf. I must do the works of him who sent me—he's aye saving men."

The Bible was back in its place and Gibbie out of the door the same moment. He had not an idea what he was going to do. All he yet understood was that he must go down the hill, to be where things might have to be done—and that before the darkness fell. He must go where there were people. As he went his heart was full of joy, as if he had already achieved some deliverance. His first definitely directive thought was that his nearest neighbors were likely enough to be in trouble—"the folk at the muckle hoose." He would go thither straight.

Glashruach stood on one of the roots of Glashgar, where the mountain settles down into the valley of the Daur. Immediately outside its principal gate ran the Glashburn; on the other side of the house, within the grounds, ran a smaller hill stream. Both these fell into the Lorrie. Straight from the mountain, between the two streams, Gibbie approached the house through larches and pines raving and roaring in the wind. When he reached a certain point whence the approach from the gate was visible, he started, stopped, and stared. He rubbed his eyes.

No; he was not asleep and dreaming by the cottage fire; the wind was about him, and the firs were howling and hissing;

there was the cloudy mountain, with the Glashburn, fifty times its usual size, darting like brown lightning from it; but where was the iron gate with its two stone pillars, crested with wolfs' heads? where was the bridge? where were the wall and the graveled road to the house? Bridge and gate and wall were gone utterly. The burn had swallowed them, and now, foaming with madness, was roaring along a great way within the grounds, and rapidly drawing nearer to the house, tearing to pieces and devouring all that defended it. There! what a mouthful of the shrubbery it gobbled up! Slowly, graciously, the tall trees bowed their heads and sank into the torrent, but the moment they touched it, shot away like arrows.

Rousing himself from his bewildered amazement, he darted down the hill. If the other burn was behaving in like fashion, then indeed the fate of the house was sealed.

The laird was away and Ginevra sat alone in her room, while Mistress MacFarlane, the housekeeper, and Angus MacPholp, the gamekeeper sat in the kitchen. They were well aware of the storm, but they had not yet the smallest suspicion of the damage it was doing.

Ginevra, tiring of the book she had been trying to read, wandered listlessly to the window and stood there gazing out on the wild confusion—the burn roaring below, the trees opposite ready to be torn to pieces by the wind, and the valley beneath covered with stormy water. The tumult was so loud that she did not hear a gentle knock at her door: as she turned away, weary of everything, she saw it softly open—and there to her astonishment stood Gibbie.

"You mustn't come here, Gibbie," she said, advancing. "Go down to the kitchen, to Mistress MacFarlane. She will see to what you want."

Gibbie made eager signs to her to go with him. She concluded that he wanted her to accompany him to the kitchen and speak for him; but she shook her head and went back to the window. She thought, as she approached it, there seemed a lull in the storm, but the moment she looked out, she gave a cry of astonishment, and stood staring. Gibbie had followed her as softly as swiftly, and looking out also, saw good cause indeed for her astonishment—the channel of the raging burn was all but dry!

Instantly he understood what it meant. In his impotence to persuade, he caught the girl in his arms, and rushed with her from the room. She had faith enough in him by this time not to struggle or scream. He shot down the stair with her, and out of the front door. The moment they issued, and she saw the Glashburn raving along through the lawn, with little more than the breadth of the drive between it and the house, she saw the necessity of escape, though she did not perceive half the dire necessity for haste. Every few moments, a great gush would dash out twelve or fifteen yards over the gravel and sink again, carrying many feet of the bank with it, and widening by so much the raging channel.

"Put me down, Gibbie," she said; "I will run as fast as you like."

He obeyed at once.

"Oh!" she cried, "Mistress MacFarlane! I wonder if she knows. Run and knock at the kitchen window."

Gibbie darted off, gave three loud hurried taps on the window, came flying back, took Ginevra's hand in his, drew her on till she was at her full speed, turned sharp to the left around the corner of the house, and shot down to the empty channel of the burn. As they crossed it, even to the inexperienced eyes of the girl it was plain what had caused the phenomenon. A short distance up the stream, the whole facing of its lofty right bank had slipped down into its channel. Not a tree, not a shrub, not a bed of moss was to be seen; all was bare wet rock. A confused heap of mold, with branches and roots sticking out of it in all directions, lay at its foot, closing the view upward. The other side of the heap was beaten by the raging burn. They could hear, though they could not see it. Any moment the barrier might give way, and the water resume its course. They made haste, therefore, to climb the opposite bank.

The wind nearly swept them from their place; but they clung to the great stones and saw the airy torrent, as if emulating that below it, fill itself with branches and leaves and lumps of foam. Then first Ginevra became fully aware of the danger in which the house was and from which Gibbie had rescued her.

"But where's Mistress MacFarlane?" she said. "Oh, Gibbie! we mustn't leave her."

He replied by pointing down to the bed of the stream; there were she and Angus crossing. Ginevra was satisfied when she saw the gamekeeper with her, and they set out, as fast as they could go, ascending the mountain, Gibbie eager to have her in warmth and safety before it was dark.

It was an undertaking hard for any girl, especially such for one unaccustomed to exertion. But the excitement of battling with the storm, the joy of adventure, and the pleasure of feeling her own strength, sustained her well for a long time; and in such wind and rain, the absence of bonnet and cloak was an advantage, so long as exertion kept her warm. She never lost her courage, and Gibbie, though he could not hearten her with words, was so ready with smile and laugh, was so cheerful—even merry, so fearless, so free from doubt and anxiety, while doing everything he could think of to lessen her toil and pain, that she hardly felt in his silence any lack.

Once inside the cottage, Ginevra threw herself into Robert's chair, and laughed, and cried, and laughed again. Gibbie blew up the peats, made a good fire, and put on water to boil; then opened Janet's drawers, and having signified to his companion to take what she could find, went to the cowhouse, threw himself on a heap of wet straw, worn out, and had enough to do to keep himself from falling asleep. A little rested, he rose and re-entered the cottage, when a merry laugh from both of them went ringing out into the storm—the little lady was dressed in Janet's workday garments and making porridge. She looked very funny. Gibbie found plenty of milk in the dairy under the rock, and they ate their supper together in gladness. Then Gibbie prepared the bed in the little closet for his guest and she slept as if she had not slept for a week.

Gibbie woke with the first of the dawn. The rain still fell—descending in spoonfuls rather than drops; the wind kept shaping itself into long hopeless howls, rising to shrill yells that went drifting away over the land; and then the howling rose again. There must be more for Gibbie to do! He must go again to the foot of the mountain and see if there was anybody to help.

Ginevra awoke, rose, made herself as tidy as she could, and left her closet. Gibbie was not in the cottage. She blew up the fire, and, finding the pot ready beside it, with clean water, set it on to boil. Gibbie did not come. The water boiled. She took it off, but being hungry, put it on again. Several times she took it off and put it on again. Gibbie never came. She made herself some porridge at last. Everything necessary was upon the table, and as she poured it into the wooden dish for the purpose, she took notice of a slate beside it, with something written upon it. The words were, "I will cum back as soon as I cann."

She was alone, then! It was dreadful; but she was too hungry to think about it. She ate her porridge and then began to cry. It was very unkind of Gibbie to leave her, she said to herself. But then he was a sort of angel, and doubtless had to go and help somebody else. There was a little pile of books on the table, which he must have left for her. She began examining them, and soon found something to interest her, so that an hour or two passed quickly. But Gibbie did not return, and the day went wearily.

The noises were terrible. She seemed to inhabit noise. Through the general roar of wind and water and rain every now and then came a sharper sound, like a report or crack, followed by a strange low thunder, as it seemed. They were the noises of stones carried down by the streams, grinding against each other, and dashed stone against stone; and of rocks falling and rolling, and bounding against their fast-rooted neighbors. When it began to grow dark, her misery seemed more than she could bear; but then, happily, she grew sleepy, and slept the darkness away.

With the new light came new promise and fresh hope. It no longer rained so fiercely; the wind had fallen and the streams did not run so furious a race down the sides of the mountain. She ran to the burn, got some water to wash herself and put on her own clothes, which were now quite dry. Then she got herself some breakfast and after that tried to say her prayers.

Gibbie sped down the hill through a worse rain than ever. Going down his own side of the Glashburn, the nearest path to the valley, the gamekeeper's cottage was the first dwelling on his way.

It had been with great difficulty that the gamekeeper reached it with the housekeeper the night before. All night he watched, peering out ever again into the darkness. When the morning came, there was the Glashburn meeting the Lorrie in his garden. But the cottage was well built and fit to stand a good siege. In a few minutes they were isolated, with the current of the Glashburn on one side, and that of the Lorrie in front. When he saw the water come in at front and back doors at once, Angus ordered his family up the stair.

As Gibbie approached the cottage, he heard Mistress MacPholp screaming and soon saw that the gamekeeper was in the water, trying to rescue a young dog of which he was fond. Strong swimmer as he was, the current bore Angus toward a large elder tree in whose branches he was soon caught fast.

Gibbie quickly saw that hope of rescue lay on getting a line from the house to Angus. So he caught hold of the eaves and scrambled onto the roof. But Mistress MacPholp, thinking he was bent on mischief, would not let him enter. She struck at him from the attic window, crying, "You shall not come in here, and my man drowning yonder! Go to him, you coward!"

Never had poor Gibbie so much missed the use of speech. On the slope of the roof he could do little to force an entrance, therefore threw himself off it to seek another, and betook himself to the windows below. Through that of Angus' room, he caught sight of a floating anchor cask. It was the very thing!—and there on the walls hung a quantity of nets and cordage! But how to get in? It was a sash window, and of course swollen with the wet, therefore not to be opened; and there was not a square in it large enough to let him through. He swam to the other side and crept softly onto the roof, and over the ridge. But a broken slate betrayed him. The woman saw him, rushed to the fireplace, caught up the poker, and darted back to defend the window.

"You shall not come in here, I tell you," she screeched, "and my man caught helpless in a tree!"

Gibbie advanced. She made a blow at him with the poker. He caught it, wrenched it from her grasp and threw himself from the roof. The next moment they heard the poker at work, smashing the window.

"He'll be in and murdering us all!" cried the mother, and ran to the stair, while the children screamed and danced with terror.

But the water was far too deep for her. She returned to the attic, barricaded the door, and went again to the window to watch her drowning husband.

Gibbie was inside in a moment, and seizing the cask, proceeded to attach to it a strong line. He broke a bit from a fishing rod, secured the line around the middle of it with a notch, put the stick through the bunghole in the bilge, and corked up the hole with a net float. He then joined strong lines together until he thought he had length enough, secured the last end to a bar of the grate, and knocked out both sashes of the window with an ax.

Satisfied at length, he floated out his barrel, and followed with the line in his hand, to aid its direction if necessary. It struck the tree. With a yell of joy Angus laid hold of it, and hauling the line taut, and feeling it secure, committed himself at once to the water, holding by the barrel, and swimming with his legs, while Gibbie, away to the side with a hold of the rope, was swimming his hardest to draw him out of the current. But a weary man was Angus when at length he reached the house. It was all he could do to get himself in at the window and crawl up the stair. At the top of it he fell benumbed on the floor.

Gibbie resumed his journey to the Mains, taking advantage of the current as he swam with it. When he was about halfway, a whole fleet of ricks bore down upon him. He boarded one and scrambled to the top of it. From its peak he surveyed the wild scene. All was running water. Not a human being was visible, and but a few house roofs. Here and there were the tops of trees, showing like low bushes. Nothing was uplifted except the mountains. He drew near the Mains. All the ricks in the yard were bobbing about, as if amusing themselves with a slow *contredanse;* but they were as yet kept in by the barn and a huge old hedge of hawthorn.

What was that cry from far away? Surely it was that of a horse in danger! It brought a lusty equine response from the farm. Where could horses be with such a depth of water about the place? Then began a great lowing of cattle. But again came the cry of the horse from afar, and Gibbie, this time recognizing the voice as Snowball's, forgot the rest. He stood up on the very top of the rick and sent his keen glance around on all sides. The cry came again and again, so that he was satisfied in what direction he must look. The rain had abated a little, but the air was so thick with vapor that he could not tell whether it was really an object he seemed to see, white against the brown water, far away to the left, or a fancy of his excited hope; it *might* be Snowball on the turnpike road, which thereabout ran along the top of a high embankment. He tumbled from the rick and swam vigorously for what might be the horse.

It took him a weary hour—in so many currents was he caught, one after the other, all straining to carry him far below the object he wanted to reach; an object it plainly was before he had got halfway across, and by and by as plainly it was Snowball. When at length he scrambled on the embankment beside him, the poor, shivering, perishing creature gave a low neigh of delight; he did not know Gibbie, but he was a human being. He was quite cowed and submissive, and Gibbie at once set about his rescue. Encouraged by the hand upon his head, the horse followed, and they made for the Mains. It was a long journey, and Gibbie had not breath enough to sing to Snowball, but he made what noise he could, and they got slowly along.

New arrivals were constantly reaching the Mains; one such was a woman on a raft, with her four little children seated around her, holding the skirt of her gown above her head and out between her hands for a sail. She had made the raft herself, by tying some bars of a paling together and crossing them with what other bits of wood she could find. Nobody knew her. She had come down the Lorrie. John Duff was so struck with admiration of her invention, daring, and success, that he vowed he would keep the brander as long as it would stick together; and as it could not be taken into the house, he secured it with a rope to one of the windows.

The strangers were mostly in Fergus' bedroom; the horses were all in their owner's; and the cattle were in the remaining rooms. Bursts of talk among the women were followed by fits of silence; who could tell how long the flood might last—or indeed whether the house might not be undermined before morning, or be struck by one of those big things of which so many floated by, and give way with one terrible crash! Mr. Duff, while preserving a tolerably calm exterior, was nearly at his wit's end. He would stand for half an hour together, with his hands in his pockets, looking motionless out of a window, murmuring now and then to himself, "This is clean ridiculous!" But when anything had to be done he was active enough. Mistress Croale sat in a corner, very quiet, and looking not a little cowed. There was altogether more water than she liked. Now and then she lifted her lurid black eyes to Janet, who stood at one of the windows, knitting away at her master's stocking and casting many a calm glance at the brown waters and the strange drift that covered them.

"If only Gibbie were here!" she crooned now and again. A hand was laid on her arm. She looked up. The black eyes were close to hers and the glow that was in them gave the lie to the tone of indifference with which Mistress Croale spoke.

"You have more than once made mention of someone connected with you by the name of Gibbie," she said.

"Ay," answered Janet, sending for the serpent to aid the dove; "and what may be your will with him?"

"Ow, nothing," returned Mistress Croale. "I knew one by the same name long ago, but he was lost sight of."

"There's Gibbies here and Gibbies there," remarked Janet, probing her.

"Well I wat!" she answered peevishly, "but there's not many wee Sir Gibbies, or the world wouldn't be as it is."

Janet was arrested in her turn: could the fierce, repellent woman be the mother of her gracious Gibbie? Could she be, and look so lost? But the loss of him had lost her perhaps. Anyhow God was his Father, whoever was the mother of him.

"How came you to lose your bairn, woman?" she asked.

But Mistress Croale was careful also, and had her reasons.

"He ran from the bloody hand," she said enigmatically.

Janet recalled how Gibbie came to her, scored by the hand of cruelty.

"How came he by the bonnie nickname?" she asked at length.

"Nickname!" retorted Mistress Croale fiercely; "I think I hear you! His own name and title by law and right, as sure's ever there was a King James that first put his hand to the making of baronets! It was often that I heard Sir George, the father of him, tell the same."

She ceased abruptly, annoyed with herself, as it seemed, for having said so much.

"You wouldn't be my lady yourself, would you, mem?" suggested Janet in her gentlest voice.

Mistress Croale made her no answer.

"Is it long since you lost him?" asked Janet, after a bootless pause.

"Ay," she answered, gruffly and discourteously, in a tone intended to quench interrogation.

But Janet persisted.

"Would you know him again if you saw him?"

"Know him? I would know him if he had grown a grandfather. Know him, quoth she! Whoever knew him as I did, bairn that he was, and wouldn't know him if he were dead and an angel made of him!—But well I wat, it's little difference that would make!"

She rose in her excitement, and going to the other window, stood gazing vacantly out upon the rushing sea. To Janet it was plain she knew more about Gibbie than she was inclined to tell, and it gave her a momentary sting of apprehension.

"What was there about him you knew so well?" she asked in a tone of indifference, as if speaking only through the meshes of her work.

"I'll know those who ask before I tell," she replied sullenly. But the next instant she screamed aloud, "Lord God Almighty! yon's *him!* yon's himself!" and, stretching out her arms, dashed a hand through a pane, letting in an eddying swirl of wind and water, while the blood streamed unheeded from her wrist.

The same moment Jean entered the room. She heard both the cry and the sound of breaking glass.

"Care what set the beggar wife!" she exclaimed.

Mistress Croale took no heed. She stood now staring from the window, still as a statue except for the panting motion of her sides. At the other window stood Janet, gazing also, with blessed face. For there, like a triton on a seahorse, came Gibbie through the water on Snowball, swimming wearily.

He caught sight of Janet at the window, and straightway his countenance was radiant with smiles. Mistress Croale gave a shuddering sigh, drew back from her window, and betook herself again to her dark corner. Jean went to Janet's window, and there beheld the triumphal approach of her brownie, saving from the waters the lost and lamented Snowball. She shouted to her brother.

"John! John! here's your Snowball; here's your Snowball."

John ran to her call, and, beside himself with joy when he saw his favorite come swimming along, threw the window wide.

"Lord preserve us!" cried Mr. Duff, recognizing the rider at last, "it's Rob Grant's innocent! Who would have thought it?"

"The Lord's babes and sucklings are often very capable," remarked Janet to herself.

"Take him round to the door."—"Where did you find him?" —"You'll best get him in at the window upon the stair."—

"He'll be very hungry."—"You'll be some wet, I'm thinking!" —"Come on up the stair, and tell us all about it."

When they arrived at the door, they found a difficulty waiting them; the water was now so high that Snowball's head rose above the lintel; and, though all animals can swim, they do not all know how to dive. A tumult of suggestions immediately broke out. But Donal had already thrown himself from a window with a rope, and swum to Gibbie's assistance; the two understood each other, and heeding nothing the rest were saying, held their own communications.

In a minute the rope was fastened around Snowball's body, and the end of it drawn between his forelegs and through the ring of his head stall, when Donal swam with it to his mother who stood on the stairs, with the request that, as soon as she saw Snowball's head under the water, she would pull with all her might and draw him in at the door. Donal then swam back and threw his arms around Snowball's neck from below, while the same moment Gibbie cast his whole weight of it from above; the horse was over head and ears in an instant, and through the door in another. With snorting nostrils and blazing eyes his head rose in the passage, and in terror he struck out for the stair. As he scrambled heavily up from the water, his master and Robert seized him, and with much petting and patting and gentling, though there was little enough difficulty in managing him now, conducted him into the bedroom to the rest of the horses. There he was welcomed by his companions and immediately began devouring the hay upon his master's bedstead. Gibbie came close behind him, was seized by Janet at the top of the stair, embraced like one come alive from the grave, and led, all dripping as he was, into the room where the women were.

The farmer looked back from the door as he was leaving the room; Gibbie was performing a wild circular dance of which Janet was the center, throwing his limbs about like the toy the children call a jumping Jack, which ended suddenly in a motionless ecstasy upon one leg. Having regarded for a moment the rescuer of Snowball with astonishment, John Duff turned away. It did not occur to him that it was the joy of having saved that caused Gibbie's merriment thus to overflow.

When Gibbie told Janet that he had been home, and had found the cottage uninjured and out of danger, she grew very sober in the midst of her gladness. "Eh!" she said to herself, "if only I had been praying instead of running away, I would have been there when He turned the water aside! I would have seen the miracle! O my Master! what think You of me now?"

For all the excitement Mistress Croale had shown at first view of Gibbie, she sat still in her dusky corner, made no movement toward him, nor did anything to attract his attention, only kept her eyes fixed upon him; and Janet in her mingled joy and pain forgot her altogether. When at length it recurred to Janet that she was in the room, she cast a somewhat anxious glance toward the place she had occupied all day. It was empty; and Janet was perplexed to think how she had gone unseen.

At suppertime Mistress Croale was missing altogether. Nobody could with certainty say when he had last seen her. The house was searched from top to bottom, and the conclusion arrived at was that she must have fallen from some window and been drowned. Examining certain of the windows to know whether she might not have left some sign of such an exit, the farmer discovered that the brander was gone.

"Losh!" cried the orra man, with a face bewildered to shapelessness, like that of an old moon rising in a fog, "yon'll be her I saw an hour ago, far down the water!"

"You muckle gowk!" said his master, "how could she go so far without going to the bottom?"

"Upon the brander, sir," answered the orra man. "I took her for a muckle dog upon a door. The wife must be a witch!"

John Duff stared at the man with his mouth open, and for half a minute all were dumb. The thing was incredible, yet hardly to be controverted. The woman was gone, the raft was gone, and something strange that might be the two together had been observed about the time, as near as they could judge, when she ceased to be observed in the house.

Mr. Duff said the luck changed with the return of Snowball; his sister said, with the departure of the beggar wife. Before dark the rain had ceased, and it became evident that the water had not risen for the last half-hour. In two hours more it had sunk a quarter of an inch. The water continued to fall rapidly and almost as soon as it was morning, the people at the Mains could begin doing a little toward restoration.

In the afternoon, Gibbie with Robert and Janet set out to go home. It was a long journey. They saw much misery on their way, and it was night before they arrived at the cottage. They found it warm and clean and tidy; Ginevra had, like a true lady, swept the house that gave her shelter. It was heavenly bliss to her to hear their approaching footsteps; and before she left them she had thoroughly learned that the poorest place where the atmosphere is love is more homely, and by consequence more heavenly, than the most beautiful even, where law and order are elements supreme.

"Eh, if I had only had faith and stayed!" said Janet to herself as she entered; and to the day of her death she never ceased to bemoan her too hasty desertion of the wee hoose upon the muckle rock.

As to the strange woman's evident knowledge concerning Gibbie, Janet could do nothing but wait—fearing rather than hoping; but she had got so far above time and chance that nothing really troubled her, and she could wait quietly.

14: *The Mickle Hoose and the Muckle Hoose*

GIBBIE MIGHT have forgotten the city during the intervening years, but it was not to forget him entirely. Reverend Clement Sclater went about gathering all the information he could about the boy's family and history, and discovered that Gibbie had one remaining relative, a distant cousin on his mother's side by the name of William Withrop. Mr. Sclater then approached Mr. Withrop, who was a member of a shipbuilding firm in Greenock. But, though Mr. Withrop had no family of his own, he had not the slightest interest in any heir of the Galbraiths.

One morning, some three years later, as Mr. Sclater sat at breakfast reading the paper, his eye fell upon a paragraph which said that William Withrop, of the shipbuilding firm of the same name, had died leaving no will but a large estate. Mr. Sclater left the table quickly and went to consult with his lawyer.

From his lawyer he would have gone at once to Mistress Croale, but he had not an idea where she might even be heard of. For some years now she had made her living, one poor enough, by hawking small household necessities; and not infrequently where she appeared, the housewives bought of her because her eyes and her nose and an undefined sense of evil in her presence made them shrink from the danger of offending her.

On her next return to the Daurfoot, as the part of the city was called where now she was most at home, she heard the astounding and welcome news that Gibbie had fallen heir to a large property, and that the reward of one hundred pounds had been proclaimed by tuck of drum to anyone giving such information as should lead to the discovery of Sir Gilbert Galbraith, commonly known as "wee Sir Gibbie." A description of him was added, and the stray was so "kenspeckle" that Mistress Croale saw the necessity of haste to any hope of advantage. She had nothing to guide her beyond the fact of Sir George's habit of referring to the property on Daurside and the assurance that with the said habit Gibbie must have been as familiar as herself.

With this initiative, as she must begin somewhere, and could prosecute her business anywhere, she filled her basket and set out at once for Daurside. There, after a good deal of wandering hither and thither, and a search whose fruitlessness she probably owed to too great caution, she made the desired discovery unexpectedly and marvelously.

The morning after the flood, Janet felt herself in duty bound to make inquiry concerning those interested in Miss Galbraith. She made, therefore, the best of her way with Gibbie to the "Muckle Hoose," but, as the latter expected, found it a ruin in a wilderness. Acres of trees and shrubbery had disappeared, and a hollow waste of sand and gravel was in their place. What was left of the house stood on the edge of a red gravelly precipice of fifty feet in height, at whose foot lay the stones of the kitchen wing, in which had been the room whence Gibbie carried Ginevra. The newer part of the house was gone from its very roots; the ancient portion stood grim, desolated, marred, and defiant as of old. Not a sign of life was about the place; the very birds had fled.

"My dear missie," said Janet, when they got home, "you must write to your father, or he'll be out of his wits about you."

Ginevra wrote therefore to the duke's, and to the laird's usual address in London as well; but he was on his way from the one place to the other, and received neither letter.

Now came to the girl a few such days of delight, of freedom, of life, as she had never even dreamed of. She roamed Glashgar with Gibbie, the gentlest, kindest, most interesting of companions. Wherever his sheep went, she went too, and to many places besides—some of them such strange, wild, terrible places, as would have terrified her without him. How he startled her once by darting off a rock like a sea gull, straight, head foremost, into the Deid-Pot! She screamed with horror, but he had done it only to amuse her; for, after what seemed to her a fearful time, he came smiling up out of the terrible darkness. What a brave, beautiful boy he was! He never hurt anything, and nothing ever seemed to hurt him. And what a number of things he knew! He showed her things on the mountain, things in the sky, things in the pools and streams wherever they went. He did better than tell her about them; he made her see them, and then the things themselves told her. She was not always certain she saw just what he wanted her to see, but she always saw something that made her glad with knowledge.

He had a New Testament Janet had given him, which he carried in his pocket, and when she joined him, for he was always out with his sheep hours before she was up, she would generally find him seated on a stone, or lying in the heather, with the little book in his hand, looking solemn and sweet. But the moment he saw her, he would spring merrily up to welcome her.

On the fourth day, the rain, which had been coming and going, finally cleared off, the sun was again glorious, and the farmers began to hope a little for the drying and ripening of some portion of their crops. Then first Ginevra asked Gibbie to take her down to Glashruach; she wanted to see the ruin they had described to her. When she came near, and notions changed into visible facts, she neither wept nor wailed. So utterly altered was the look of everything, that had she come upon it unexpectedly, she would not have recognized either place or house.

They went up to a door. She seemed never to have seen it; but when they entered, she knew it as one from the hall into a passage, which, with what it led to being gone, the inner had become an outer door. A quantity of sand was heaped up in the hall, and the wainscot was wet and swelled and bulging. They went into the dining room. The thick carpet was sodden—spongy like a bed of moss after heavy rains; the paper hung loose from the walls; and everything lay where the water, after floating it about, had let it drop as it ebbed.

She ascended the old stone stairs which led to her father's rooms above, went into his study, and walked toward the window to look across to where once had been her own chamber. But as she approached it, there, behind the curtain, she saw her father, motionless, looking out. She turned pale, and stood. Even at such a time, had she known he was in the house, she would not have dared set her foot in that room.

Gibbie, who had followed and entered behind her, perceived her hesitation, saw and recognized the back of the laird, knew that she was afraid of her father, and stood also awaiting he knew not what.

Becoming aware of a presence, the laird half turned, and seeing Gibbie, imagined he had entered in a prowling way, supposing the place deserted. With stately offense he asked him what he wanted here and waved his dismissal. Then first he saw another, standing whitefaced, with eyes fixed upon him. He turned pale also and stood staring at her; for one instant of unreasoning weakness, he imagined he saw a ghost.

It was but one moment but it might have been more, had not Ginevra walked slowly up to him, saying in a trembling voice, as if she expected the blame of all that had happened, "I couldn't help it, Papa."

He took her in his arms and kissed her. She clung to him, trembling now with pleasure as well as apprehension. But the end came yet sooner than she feared. For, when the father rose erect from her embrace, and was again the laird, there, to his amazement, still stood the odd-looking, outlandish intruder, smiling with the most impertinent interest!

"Go away, boy. You have nothing to do here," said the laird.

"Oh, Papa!" cried Ginevra, clasping her hands, "that's Gibbie! He saved my life. I should have been drowned but for him."

"I am much obliged to him," the laird said haughtily; "but there is no occasion for him to wait."

At this point his sluggish mind began to recall something: why, this was the very boy he had seen in the meadow with Ginevra! He turned fiercely upon him. "Leave the house instantly," he said, "or I will knock you down."

"Oh, Papa!" moaned Ginevra wildly—"don't speak so to Gibbie. He is a good boy. It was he that Angus whipped so cruelly—long ago: I have never been able to forget it."

"If he does not get out of this house directly," he cried, "I will have him whipped again. Angus!"

He shouted the name, and its echo came back in a wild tone, altogether strange to Ginevra. Involuntarily she uttered a cry of terror and distress. Gibbie was at her side instantly, putting out his hand to comfort her. She was just laying hers on his arm when her father seized him and dashed him to the other side of the room. He went staggering backward, vainly trying to recover himself, and fell, his head striking against the wall. The same instant Angus entered and approached his master.

Gibbie had recovered and risen. He saw now that he could be of no service to Ginevra, and that his presence only made things worse for her. But he saw also that she was unhappy about him, and that must not be. He broke into such a merry laugh—and it had need to be merry, for it had to do the work of many words of reassurance—that she could scarcely refrain from a half-hysterical response as he walked from the room. The moment he was out of the house, he began to sing; and for many minutes, as he walked up the gulf hollowed by the Glashburn, Ginevra could hear the strange, other-world voice, and knew it was meant to hold communion with her and comfort her.

"What do you know of that fellow, Angus!" asked his master.

"He's the very devil himself, sir," muttered Angus.

"You will see that he is sent off the property at once—and for good, Angus," said the laird. "His insolence is insufferable. The scoundrel!"

On the pretext of following Gibbie, Angus was only too glad to leave the room.

"So, Jenny!" Mr. Galbraith said, with his loose lips pulled out straight, "that is the sort of companion you choose when left to yourself!—a low, beggarly, insolent scamp!—scarcely the equal of the brutes he has the charge of!"

"They're sheep, Papa!" pleaded Ginevra, in a wail that rose almost to a scream.

"I do believe the girl is an idiot!" said her father, and turned from her contemptuously.

"I think I am, Papa," she sobbed. "Don't mind me. Let me go away and I will never trouble you any more." She would go to the mountain, she thought, and be a shepherdess with Gibbie.

Her father took her roughly by the arm, pushed her into a closet, locked the door, went and had his luncheon, and in the afternoon, having borrowed Snowball, took her just as she was, drove to meet the mail coach, and in the middle of the night was set down with her at the principal hotel in the city, whence the next morning he set out early to find a school where he might leave her and his responsibility with her.

When Gibbie knew himself beyond the hearing of Ginevra, his song died away, and he went home sad. The gentle girl had stepped at once from the day into the dark, and he was troubled for her.

When he reached home, he found Janet in serious talk with a stranger. The tears were in her eyes, and had been running down her cheeks, but she was calm and dignified as usual.

"Here he comes!" she said as he entered. "The will of the Lord be done—now and forever more! I'm at His bidding. And so is Gibbie."

It was Mr. Sclater. The witch had sailed her brander well.

15: *The City Again*

ONE BRIGHT afternoon, toward the close of the autumn, the sun shining straight down one of the wide clean stony streets of the city, with a warmth which he had not been able to impart to the air, a company of schoolgirls, two and two in long file, mostly with innocent, and rather uninteresting faces, was walking in orderly manner, a female grenadier at its head, along the pavement. Among the faces was one very different from the rest, a countenance almost solemn and a little sad, of still, regular features, in the eyes of which by loving eyes might have been read uneasy thought patiently carried, and the lack of some essential to conscious well-being. The other girls were looking on this side and that, eager to catch sight of anything to trouble the monotony of the daily walk; but the eyes of this one were cast down, except when occasionally lifted in answer to words of the schoolmistress by whose side she was walking.

Suddenly came a rush, a confusion, a fluttering of the doves, a gentle shriek from several of the girls, a general sense of question and no answer; but, as their ruffled nerves composed themselves a little, there was the vision of the schoolmistress poking the point of her parasol at the heedless face, radiant with smiles, that of an odd-looking lad who had got hold of one of the daintily gloved hands of her companion, laid a hand which, considered conventionally, was not that of a gentleman, upon her shoulder, and stood, without a word, gazing in rapturous delight.

"Go away, boy! What do you mean by such impertinence?" cried the outraged Miss Kimble, changing her thrust, and poking in his chest the parasol with which she had found it impossible actually to assail his smiling countenance.

Her companion stood quite still and was now looking in the lad's face with roseate cheeks and tear-filled eyes, apparently forgetting to draw her hand from his, or to move her shoulder from under his caress. The next moment, up, with hasty yet dignified step, came the familiar form of their own minister, the Reverend Clement Sclater, who, with reproof in his countenance, which was red with annoyance and haste, laid his hands on the lad's shoulders to draw him from the prey on which he had pounced.

"Remember, you are not on a hillside, but in a respectable street," said the reverend gentleman.

The youth turned his head over his shoulder, not otherwise changing his attitude, and looked at him with some bewilderment. Then, not he, but the young lady spoke.

"Gibbie and I are old friends," she said, and reaching up laid her free hand in turn on his shoulder as if to protect him.

Gibbie had darted from his companion's side some hundred yards off. The cap which Mr. Sclater had insisted on his wearing had fallen as he ran, and he had never missed it; his hair stood out on all sides of his head, and the sun behind him shone in it like a glory, just as when first he appeared to Ginevra in the peat moss, like an angel standing over her.

"Miss Galbraith!" said Miss Kimble, "I am astonished at you! What an example to the school! I never knew you misbehave yourself before! Take your hand from this—this—very strange looking person's shoulder directly."

Ginevra obeyed, but Gibbie stood as before.

"Remove your hand, boy, instantly," cried Miss Kimble, growing more and more angry, and began knocking the hand on the girl's shoulder with her parasol, which apparently Gibbie took for a joke, for he laughed aloud.

"Pray do not alarm yourself, ma'am," said Mr. Sclater, slowly recovering his breath; "this young—gentleman is Sir Gilbert Galbraith, my ward. Sir Gilbert, this lady is Miss Kimble."

Gibbie smiled.

"Oh!" said the lady, who had ceased her battery and stood bewildered and embarrassed.

Ginevra's eyes too had filled with wonder; she cast them down, and a strange smile began to play about her sweet strong mouth. All at once she was in the middle of a fairy tale, and had not a notion what was coming next. Her dumb shepherd boy a baronet!—and, more wonderful still, a Galbraith! She must be dreaming in the wide street! The last she had seen of him was as he was driven from the house by her father, when he had just saved her life. That was but a few weeks ago, and here he was, called Sir Gilbert Galbraith! It was a delicious bit of wonderment.

"Oh!" said Miss Kimble a second time, recovering herself a little, "I see! A relative, Miss Galbraith! I did not understand. That of course sets everything right—at least—even then—the open street, you know! *You* will understand, Mr. Sclater—I beg your pardon, Sir Gilbert. I hope I did not hurt you with my parasol!"

Gibbie again laughed aloud.

"Thank you," said Miss Kimble confused and annoyed with herself for being so, especially before her girls. "I should be sorry to have hurt you. Going to college, I presume, Sir Gilbert?"

Gibbie looked at Mr. Sclater.

"He is going to study with me for a while first," answered the minister.

"I am glad to hear it. He could not do better," said Miss Kimble. "Come, girls."

And with friendly farewells, she moved on, her train after her, thinking to herself what a boor the young fellow was.

Mr. Sclater had behaved judiciously and taken gentle pains to satisfy the old couple that they must part with Gibbie. One of the neighboring clergy knew Mr. Sclater well, and with him paid the old people a visit, to help them dismiss any lingering doubt that he was the boy's guardian legally appointed. To their own common sense indeed it became plain that, except some such story was true, there would be nothing to induce him to come after Gibbie or desire to take charge of the outcast; but they did not feel thoroughly satisfied until Mr. Sclater brought Fergus Duff to the cottage, to testify to him as being what he pretended. It was a sore trial, but among the griefs of losing him, no fear of his forgetting them was included.

Mr. Sclater's main difficulty was with Gibbie himself. At first he laughed at the absurdity of his going away from his father and mother and the sheep. They told him he was Sir Gilbert Galbraith. He answered on his slate, as well as by signs which Janet, at least, understood perfectly that he had told them so, and had been so all the time, "And what differ dos that mak?" he added. Mr. Sclater told him he was—or would be, at least, he took care to add, when he came of age—a rich man as well as a baronet.

"Writch men," wrote Gibbie, "do as they like, and I shall bide."

Mr. Sclater told him it was only poor boys who could do as they pleased, for the law looked after boys like him so that, when it came into their hands, they might be capable of using their money properly. Almost persuaded at length that he had no choice, that he could no longer be his own master until he was one and twenty, he turned and looked at Janet, his eyes brimful of tears. She gave him a little nod. He rose and went out, climbed the crest of Glashgar, and did not return to the cottage till midnight.

In the morning appeared on his countenance signs of unusual resolve. Amid the many thoughts he had had the night before had come the question—what he would do with the money when he had it? First of all, what he *could* do for Janet and Robert and every one of their family; and naturally enough to a Scotch boy, the first thing that occurred to him was to give Donal money to go to college like Fergus Duff. In that he knew he made no mistake. It was not so easy to think of things for the rest, but that was safe.

Before he went to bed, he got his slate, and wrote as follows: "My dear minister, if you will teak Donal too, and lett him go to the kolledge, I will go with you as seens you like; butt if you will not, I will runn away."

When Mr. Sclater, who had a bed at the gamekeeper's, appeared the next morning, anxious to conclude the business and get things in motion for their departure, Gibbie handed him the slate the moment he entered the cottage, and while he read, stood watching him.

Now Mr. Sclater was a prudent man, and always looked ahead, therefore apparently took a long time to read Gibbie's very clear, although unscholarly communication; before answering it, he must settle the probability of what Mrs. Sclater would think of the proposal to take *two* savages into her house together, where also doubtless the presence of this Donal would greatly interfere with the process of making a gentleman of Gibbie. Unable to satisfy himself, he raised his head at length, unconsciously shaking it as he did so. That instant Gibbie was out of the house. Mr. Sclater, perceiving the blunder he had made, hurried after him, but he was already out of sight. Returning in some dismay, he handed the slate to Janet, who, with sad, resigned countenance, was baking. She rubbed the oatmeal dough from her hands, took the slate, and read with a smile.

"You mustn't take Gibbie for a young colt, Master Sclater, and think to break him in," she said, after a thoughtful pause, "or you'll have to learn your mistake. There's not enough of himself in him for you to get a grip on him by that handle. He aye knows what he would have, and he'll aye get it, as sure as it'll aye be right. As for Donal, Donal's my own, and I shall say nothing. Sit you down, sir; you'll not see Gibbie the day again."

"Is there no means of getting at him, my good woman?" said Mr. Sclater, miserable at the prospect of a day utterly wasted.

"I could give you sight of him, I daresay, but what better would you be for that? If you had all the lawyers of Edinburgh at your back, you wouldn't touch Gibbie upon Glashgar."

"But you could persuade him, I am sure, Mistress Grant. You have only to call him in your own way, and he will come at once."

"What would you have me persuade him to, sir? To anything that's right, Gibbie wants no persuading; and for this that's between you, the laddies are just like brothers, and I have no right to interfere with what the one would do for the other, the thing seeming to me reason enough."

"What sort of lad is this son of yours? The boy seems much attached to him!"

"He's a laddie that's been given over to his book since ever I taught him to read myself," Janet answered. "But he'll be here the night, I'm thinking, to see the last of poor Gibbie, and you can judge for yourself."

It required but a brief examination of Donal to satisfy Mr.

Sclater that he was more than prepared for the university. As to Donal's going to Mr. Sclater's house, Janet soon relieved him.

"No, no, sir," she said; "it would be to learn ways that wouldn't be fitting a poor lad like him."

"It would be much safer for him," said Mr. Sclater, but incidentally.

"If I couldn't trust my Donal to his own company and the hunger for better, I would begin to doubt who made the world," said his mother; and Donal's face flushed with pleasure at her confidence. "No, he must get a garret roomie somewhere in the town, and there keep to his book; and you'll let Gibbie go and see him when he can be spared. There must be many a decent woman that would be pleased to take him in."

When they met Miss Kimble and her "young ladies," they were on their way from the coach office to the minister's house in Daur Street. Gibbie was in a dream of mingled past and future delights, when his conductor stopped at a large and important-looking house, with a flight of granite steps up to the door. Gibbie had never been inside such a house in his life, but when they entered, he was not much impressed. He did look with a little surprise, but it was down, not up: he felt his feet walking soft, and wondered for a moment that there should be a field of grass in a house. Then he gave a glance around, thought it was a big place, and followed Mr. Sclater up the stairs with the free mounting step of the Glashgar shepherd.

Forgetful and unconscious, he walked into the drawing room with his bonnet on his head. Mrs. Sclater rose when they entered, and he approached her with a smile of welcome to the house which he carried, always full of guests, in his bosom. He never thought of looking to her to welcome him. She shook hands with him in a doubtful kind of way.

"How do you do, Sir Gilbert?" she said. "Only ladies are allowed to wear their caps in the drawing room, you know," she added, in a tone of courteous rebuke.

What she meant by the drawing room, Gibbie had not an idea. He knew well enough bonnets had to be taken off in house or cottage: he had never done so because he never had worn a bonnet. But it was with a smile of amusement only that he now took it off. He put the cap in his pocket, and catching sight of a footstool by the corner of the chimney piece, was so strongly reminded of his creepie by the cottage hearth, which, big lad as he now was, he had still haunted, that he went at once and seated himself upon it. From this coign of vantage he looked around the room with a gentle curiosity, casting a glance of pleasure every now and then at Mrs. Sclater.

Gibbie had not been educated in the relative grandeur of things of this world, and he regarded the things he now saw just as things, without the smallest notion of any power in them to confer superiority by being possessed. Man was the one sacred thing. Gibbie's unconscious creed was a powerful leveler, but it was a leveler up, not down. His regard, as it wandered around the room, lighting on this color, and that texture, in curtain, or carpet, or worked screen, found interest and pleasure. Amid the mere upholstery of houses and hearts, amid the common life of the common crowd, he was, and had to be, what he had learned to be among the nobility and in the palace of Glashgar.

Mrs. Sclater was a well-bred woman, much the superior of her husband in the small duties and graces of social life. She was about forty, altogether a handsome woman; precise in her personal rules, but not stiff in the manners wherein she embodied them. It would not have been easy to find one who could do more for Gibbie in respect for the social rapports that seemed to await him. Her husband was confident that, if anybody could, his wife would make a gentleman of Sir Gilbert.

She was now seated on a low chair at the other side of the fire, slowly contemplating out of her black eyes the lad on the footstool, whose blue eyes she saw wandering about the room, in a manner neither vague nor unintelligent, but showing more of interest than of either surprise or admiration. Suddenly he turned them full upon her; they met hers, and the light rushed into them like a torrent, breaking forth after its way in a soulful smile.

Gibbie's smiles were all Gibbie had for the small coin of intercourse. In that which now shone on Mrs. Sclater, there was something which no woman could resist. She responded, and from that moment the lady and the shepherd lad were friends.

Now that a real introduction had taken place between them, and in her answering smile Gibbie had met the lady herself, he proceeded, in most natural sequence, without the smallest shyness or suspicion of rudeness, to make himself acquainted with the phenomena presenting her. As he would have gazed upon a rainbow, trying perhaps to distinguish the undistinguishable in the meeting and parting of its colors, he began to examine the lady's face and form, dwelling and contemplating with eyes innocent as any baby's. This lasted; but did not last long before it began to produce in the lady a certain uncertain embarrassment, a something she did not quite understand, therefore could not account for, and did not like. She began to grow restless and feel as if she wanted to let down her veil. She did not feel that the boy was rude; she was not angry with him as with one taking a liberty; yet she did wish he would not look at her like that; and presently she was relieved.

Her hands, which had been lying all the time in her lap, had at length drawn and fixed Gibbie's attention. They were very ladylike hands, and to Gibbie's eyes they were such beautiful things, that, after a moment or two spent in regarding them across the length of the hairy hearthrug, he got up, took his footstool, crossed with it to the other side of the fire, set it down by Mrs. Sclater, and reseated himself. Without moving more than her fine neck, she looked down on him curiously, wondering what would come next, and what did come next was that he laid one of his hands on one of those that lay in the satin lap; then, struck with the contrast between them, burst out laughing. But he neither withdrew his hand nor showed the least shame of the hard, brown, tarry-seamed, strong though rather small prehensile member, with its worn and blackened nails, but let it calmly remain outspread, side by side with the white, shapely, spotless, gracious, and graceful thing, adorned with a half-hoop of fine blue-green turkises, and a limpid activity of many diamonds.

She laughed also and patted the lumpy thing which was also called a hand with short little pecking pats. Still she found his presence discomposing and was glad when Mr. Sclater took Gibbie away to show him his room and instruct him what changes he must make upon his person in preparation for dinner.

Mrs. Sclater's first piece of business the following morning was to take Gibbie to the most fashionable tailor in the city and have him measured for such clothes as she judged suitable for a gentleman's son. Gibbie seemed as much at home with the handsome lady as if she had been his own mother, and walked by her side with a step and air as free as the wind from Glashgar.

Mrs. Sclater soon began to find that even in regard to social externals, she could never have had a readier pupil. He watched her so closely, and with such an appreciation of the difference in things of the kind between her and her husband, that for a short period he was in danger of falling into habits of movement and manipulation too dainty for a man, a fault happily none the less objectionable in the eyes of his instructress, that she, on her own part, carried the feminine a little beyond the limits of the natural. But here also she found him so readily set right, that she imagined she was going to do anything with him she pleased, and was not a little proud of her conquest and the power she had over the young savage. She had yet to discover that Gibbie had his own ideas too, that it was the general noble teachableness and affection of his nature that had brought about so speedy an understanding between them in everything wherein he saw she could show him the better way, but that nowhere else would he feel bound or inclined to follow her injunctions. Much and strongly as he was drawn to her by her ladyhood, and the sense she gave him of refinement and familiarity with the niceties, he had no feeling that she had authority over him.

Mr. Sclater was conscientious in his treatment of him. The very day following that of their arrival, he set to work with him. He had been a tutor, was a good scholar and a sensible teacher, and soon discovered how to make the most of Gibbie's facility in writing. He was already possessed of a little Latin, and after having for some time accustomed him to translate from each language into the other, the minister began to think it might be to advantage to learning in general if at least half the boys and girls at school, and three parts of every Sunday congregation, were as dumb as Sir Gilbert Galbraith. When at length he set him to Greek, he was astonished at the avidity with which he learned it. He had hardly got him over *τύπτω*, when he found him one day so intent upon the Greek Testament, that, exceptionally keen of hearing as he was, he was quite unaware that anyone had entered the room.

To Mrs. Sclater, it was at first rather depressing, and for a time grew more and more painful, to have a live silence by her side. But when she came into rapport with the natural utterance of the boy, his presence grew more like a constant speech, and that which was best in her was not infrequently able to say for the boy what he would have said could he have spoken; the nobler part of her nature was in secret alliance with the thoughts and feelings of Gibbie. But this relationship between them, though perceptible, did not become at all plain to her until after she had established more definite means of communication. Gibbie, for his part, full of the holy simplicities of the cottage, had a good many things to meet which disappointed, perplexed, and shocked him.

16: *The Sclaters Have Their Troubles*

WITHIN A few weeks, Donal came to the city. His mother's last words were strong within him, "Now, remember, you're not a straw dried on its root, but a growing stalk that must look to its grain." Gibbie was waiting to greet Donal at his lodgings. He surprised him by jumping out on him from behind the curtains of the bed and throwing his arms around him.

"Eh, creature! You gave me such a fright!" said Donal. "But, losh! they have made a gentleman of you already!" he added, holding him at arm's length, and regarding him with wonder and admiration.

A notable change had indeed passed upon Gibbie. Mrs. Sclater had had his hair cut; his shirt was of the whitest of linen, his necktie of the richest of black silk, his clothes were of the newest cut and best possible fit, and his boots perfect; the result was altogether even to her satisfaction. In one thing only was she foiled—she could not get him to wear gloves. He had put on a pair, but found them so miserably uncomfortable that, in merry wrath, he pulled them off on the way home, and threw them—"The best kid!" exclaimed Mrs. Sclater

—over the Pearl Bridge. Prudently fearful of overstraining her influence, she yielded for the present and let him go without.

Mr. Sclater also had hitherto exercised prudence in his demands upon Gibbie. The boy had never yet refused to do anything he required of him, had executed entirely the tasks he set him, was more than respectful and always ready; yet somehow Mr. Sclater could never feel that the lad was exactly obeying him. He thought it over, but could not understand it, and did not like it, for he was fond of authority. Gibbie in fact did whatever was required of him from his own delight in meeting the wish expressed, not from any sense of duty or of obligation to obedience.

The boys had a jolly time of it. They made their tea, for which everything was present, and ate as boys know how, Donal enjoying the rarity of the white bread of the city, Gibbie, who had not tasted oatmeal since he came, devouring "Mother's cakes." When they had done, Gibbie, who had learned much since he came, looked about the room till he found a bell-rope, and pulled it, whereupon the oddest-looking old woman entered, and, with friendly chatter, proceeded to remove the tray. Then, they uncorded Donal's kist, discovered the cause of its portentous weight, took out everything, put the provisions in a cupboard, arranged the few books, and then sat down by the fire for "a read" together.

The hours slipped away; it was night; and still they sat and read. It must have been after ten o'clock when they heard footsteps coming through the adjoining room; the door opened swiftly; in walked Mr. Sclater and closed it behind him. His look was angry. Gibbie had absented himself without permission, had stayed away for hours, had not returned even when the hour of worship arrived; and these were sins against the respectability of his house which no minister like Mr. Sclater could pass by.

When first he entered, Gibbie rose with his usual smile of

greeting and got him a chair. But he waved aside the attention with indignant indifference and went on with his reproof. Gibbie on his feet looked the minister straight in the face. His smile of welcome, which had suddenly mingled itself with bewilderment, gradually faded into one of concern, then of pity, and by degrees died away altogether, leaving in its place a look of question. More and more settled his countenance grew, while all the time he never took his eyes off Mr. Sclater's, until its expression at length was that of pitiful unconscious reproof, mingled with sympathetic shame.

The boys remaining absolutely silent, the minister had it all his own way. But before he had begun to draw to a close, across the blinding mists of his fog-breeding wrath he began to be aware of the shining of two heavenly lights, the eyes of the dumb boy fixed upon him. They jarred him a little in his onward course; they shook him as if with a doubt; the feeling undefined slowly grew to a notion, first obscure, then plain; they were eyes of reproof that were fastened upon his! At the first suspicion, his anger flared up more fierce than ever; but it was a flare of a doomed flame; slowly the rebuke told, was telling; the self-satisfied "in-the-rightness" of the man was sinking before the innocent difference of the boy; he began to feel awkward, he hesitated, he ceased; for the moment Gibbie, unconsciously, had conquered; without knowing it, he was the superior of the two, and Mr. Sclater had begun to learn that he could never exercise authority over him.

After a slight pause, the minister spoke again, but with the changed tone of one who has had an apology made to him, whose anger is appeased.

"Donal Grant," he said, "you had better go to bed at once, and get fit for your work tomorrow. I will go with you to call upon the principal. Get your cap, Sir Gilbert, and come. Mrs. Sclater was already very uneasy about you when I left her."

Gibbie took from his pocket the little ivory tablets Mrs.

Sclater had given him, wrote the following words, and handed them to the minister:

"Dear sir, I am going to slepe this night with Donal. The bed is bigg enuf for two. Good night, sir."

For a moment the minister's wrath seethed again, then he thought better. "Then be sure you are home by lesson time," he said. "Donal can come with you. Good night. Mind you don't keep each other awake."

Donal said "Good night, sir," and Gibbie gave him a serious and respectful nod. He left the room, and the boys turned and looked at each other. Donal's countenance expressed an indignant sense of wrong, but Gibbie's revealed a more profound concern. He stood motionless, intent on the receding steps of the minister. The moment the sound of them ceased, he darted soundless after him. Donal, who from Mr. Sclater's reply had understood what Gibbie had written, was astonished, and starting to his feet followed him. By the time he reached the door, Gibbie was past the second lamp, his shadow describing a huge half-circle around him, as he stole from lamp to lamp after the minister, keeping always a lamppost still between them.

When the minister turned a corner, Gibbie made a soundless dart to it, and peeped around, lingered a moment looking, then followed again. On and on went Mr. Sclater, and on and on went Gibbie, careful constantly not to be seen by him; and on and on went Donal, careful to be seen of neither. At last the minister went up the steps of a handsome house, took a key from his pocket, and opened the door. From some impulse or other, as he stepped in, he turned sharp around, and saw Gibbie.

"Come in," he said, in a loud authoritative tone, probably taking the boy's appearance for the effect of repentance and a desire to return to his own bed.

Gibbie lifted his cap, and walked quietly on toward the other end of Daur Street.

Donal dared not follow, for Mr. Sclater stood between, looking out. Presently however the door shut with a great bang, and Donal was after Gibbie like a hound. But Gibbie had turned a corner and was gone from his sight. Donal turned a corner too, but it was a wrong corner. Concluding that Gibbie had turned another corner ahead of him, he ran on and on, in the vanishing hope of catching sight of him again; but he was soon satisfied he had lost him—nor him only but himself as well, for he had not the smallest idea how to return, even as far as the minister's house. He was not tired, but a city is a dreary place at night, even to one who knows his way in it—much drearier to one lost.

"It's as if all the birds had crept into their wee eggs again, and the day was left bare of song!" said the poet to himself as he walked.

Presently he found himself on the shore of the river, and tried to get to the edge of the water; but it was low tide, the lamps did not throw much light so far, the moon was clouded, he got among logs and mud, and regained the street bemired, and beginning to feel weary. He was saying to himself whatever was he to do all the night long, when around a corner a little way off came a woman. It was no use asking counsel of her, however, or of anyone, he thought, so long as he did not know even the name of the street he wanted. The woman drew near. She was rather tall, erect in the back, but bowed in the shoulders, with fierce black eyes, which were all that he could see of her face, for she had a little tartan shawl over her head, which she held together with one hand, while in the other she carried a basket. But those eyes were enough to make him fancy he must have seen her before. They were just passing each other, under a lamp, when she looked hard at him, and stopped.

"Man," she said, "I have set eye upon *your* face before!"

"If that be the case," answered Donal, "you've set eye upon it again."

"Where come you from?" she asked.

"That's what I would like to ask myself," he replied. "But, woman," he went on, "I fancy I have set eye upon your eye before—I can't well say for your face. Where come *you* from?"

"Know you a place they call—Daurside?" she rejoined.

"Daurside's a gey long place," answered Donal; "and this must be about the tail end of it, I'm thinking."

"You're not far wrong there," she returned; "and you have a gey quick tongue in your head for a lad from Daurside."

"I never heard that tongues were cut any shorter there," said Donal; "but I didn't mean you any offense."

"There's none taken, nor like to be," answered the woman. "Know you a place they call Mains o' Glashruach?"

As she spoke she let go her shawl, and it opened from her face like two curtains.

"Lord! it's the witch wife!" cried Donal, retreating a pace in his astonishment.

The woman burst into a great laugh, a hard, unmusical, but not unmirthful laugh.

"Ay!" she said, "was that how the folk would have it about me?"

"It wasn't muckle wonder, after you came wading through water yards deep, and then went down the flood on a brander."

"Well, it was the maddest thing!" she returned, with another laugh which stopped abruptly. "I wouldn't do the like again to save my life. But the Mighty carried me through. And how's wee Sir Gibbie? Come in—I don't know your name—but we're just at the door of my small garret. Come quietly up the stair, and tell me all about it."

"Well, I wouldn't be sorry to rest a bit, for I have lost myself altogether, and I'm some tired," answered Donal. "I but left the Mains yesterday."

"Come in and welcome; and when you're rested, and I'm rid of my basket, I'll soon put you on your way home."

Donal was too tired and too glad to be once more in the company of a human being to pursue further explanation at present. He followed her, as quietly as he could, up the dark stairs. When she struck a light, he saw a little garret-room—better than decently furnished, it seemed to the youth from the hills, though his mother would have thought it far from tidy. When the woman got a candle lighted, she seated herself and began to relate her adventure in quest of Gibbie. Then she told him a great deal about Gibbie and his father.

"And now," remarked Donal, "he'll be thinking about it all over again, as he runs about the town this very minute, looking for me!"

"Don't you trouble yourself about him," said the woman. "He knows the town as well as any rat knows the drains of it. But where do you put up?" she added, "for it's time decent folk was going to their beds."

Donal explained that he knew neither the name of the street nor of the people where he was lodging.

"Tell me this or that—something—anything about the house or the folk, or what they're like, and it may be that I'll know them," she said.

But scarcely had he begun his description of the house when she cried, "Hoot, man! it's at Lucky Murkison's you are, in the Widdiehill. Come away, and I'll take you home in a jiffy."

So saying, she rose, took the candle, showed him down the stairs, and followed.

It was past midnight, and the moon was down, but the street lamps were not yet extinguished, and they walked along without anything to interrupt their conversation.

Before they reached the Widdiehill, Donal, with the open heart of the poet, was full of friendliness to Mistress Croale, and rejoiced in the mischance that had led him to make her acquaintance.

"You know, of course," he happened to say, "that Gibbie's with Master Sclater?"

"Well enough," she answered. "I have seen him too; but

he's a grand gentleman grown, and I wouldn't like to be affronted laying claim to his acquaintance—welcome as he once was to my house!"

"You little know Gibbie," he said, "if you think that way of him! Go you to the minister's door and ask for him! He'll be down the stair like a shot. But indeed, maybe he's come back, and is in my chamber now! You'll come up the stair and see?"

"No, I won't do that," said Mistress Croale.

She pointed out the door to him, but herself stood on the other side of the way till she saw it opened by Mistress Murkison in her nightcap, and heard her make jubilee over his return. Gibbie had come home and gone out again to look for him, she said.

"Well," remarked Donal, "there would be small good in my going to look for him. It would be but the sheep going to look for the shepherd."

"You're right there," said his landlady. "A lost bairn should aye sit down and sit still."

"Well, you go to your bed, mem," returned Donal. "Let me see how your door works, and I'll let him in when he comes."

Gibbie came within an hour, and all was well. They made their communication, of which Donal's was far the more interesting, had their laugh over the affair, and went to bed.

The minister's wrath, when he found he had been followed home by Gibbie who yet would not enter the house, instantly rose in redoubled strength. His anger went on smoldering all night long, and all through his sleep, without a touch of cool assuagement. In the morning he rose with his temper very feverish. During breakfast he was gloomy, but would confess to no inward annoyance. What added to his unrest was that, although he felt insulted, he did not know what precisely the nature of the insult was. The lad whom he so regarded had first with his mere looks lowered him in his own eyes, then showed himself beyond the reach of his reproof by calmly refusing to obey him, and then became unintelligible by following him like a creature over whom surveillance was needful! The more he thought of this last, the more inexplicable it seemed to become, except on the notion of deliberate insult.

Gibbie made his appearance at ten o'clock, and went straight to the study, where at that hour the minister was always awaiting him. He entered with his own smile, bending his head in morning salutation. The minister said, "Good morning," but gruffly, and without raising his eyes. Gibbie seated himself in his usual place, arranged his book and slate, and was ready to commence—when the minister lifted his head, fixed his eyes on him, and said sternly—

"Sir Gilbert, what was your meaning in following me, after refusing to accompany me?"

Gibbie's face flushed; but he took his slate instantly, found his pencil, wrote, and handed the slate to the minister.

"I thought you was drunnk."

Mr. Sclater started to his feet, the hand which held the offending document uplifted, his eyes flaming, his cheeks white with passion, and with the flat of the slate came down a great blow on the top of Gibbie's head. Happily the latter was the harder of the two, and the former broke, flying mostly out of the frame.

It took Gibbie terribly by surprise. Half-stunned, he started to his feet, and for one moment the wild beast which was in him, as it is in everybody, rushed to the front of its cage. It would have gone ill then with the minister had not as sudden a change followed; the very same instant, it was as if an invisible veil, woven of gracious air and odor and dew, had descended upon him; the flame of his wrath went out, quenched utterly; a smile of benignest compassion overspread his countenance; in his offender he saw only a brother.

Mr. Sclater saw no brother before him, for when Gibbie

rose he drew back to better his position, and so doing trod on the edge of a low footstool, stumbled, and fell.

Gibbie darted forward, and jumped over the prostrate minister, who raised his hands to defend himself, and made a blow at him. Gibbie avoided it, laid hold of his arms inside each elbow, clamped them to the floor, kissed him on forehead and cheek, and began to help him up like a child.

Having regained his legs, the minister stood for a moment, confused and half-blinded. The first thing he saw was a drop of blood stealing down Gibbie's forehead. He was shocked at what he had done.

"Go and wash your face," he said, "and come back again directly."

Gibbie put his hand to his face, and feeling something wet, looked, and burst into a merry laugh.

"I am sorry I have hurt you," said the minister, not a little relieved at the sound; "but how dared you write such a—such an insolence? A clergyman never gets drunk."

Gibbie picked up the frame which the minister had dropped in his fall; a piece of the slate was still sticking in one side, and he wrote upon it—

"I will kno better the next time. I thout it was alwais whisky that made people like that. I begg your pardon, sir."

He handed him the fragment, ran to his own room, returned presently, looking all right, and when Mr. Sclater would have attended to his wound, would not let him even look at it, laughing at the idea. Still further relieved to find there was nothing to attract observation to the injury, and yet more ashamed of himself, the minister made haste to the refuge of their work.

From that time, after luncheon, which followed immediately upon lessons, Gibbie went and came as he pleased. Mrs. Sclater begged he would never be out after ten o'clock without having let them know that he meant to stay all night with his friend; not once did he neglect this request, and they soon came to have perfect confidence not only in any individual promise he might make, but in his general punctuality. Mrs. Sclater never came to know anything of his wounded head, and it gave the minister a sharp sting of compunction when he saw that for a fortnight or so Gibbie never took his favorite place at her feet, evidently that she should not look down on his head.

The same evening they had friends to dinner. Already Gibbie was so far civilized, as they called it, that he might have sat at any dining table without attracting the least attention, but that evening he attracted a great deal. For he could scarcely eat his own dinner for watching the needs of those at the table with him, ready to spring from his chair and supply the least lack. This behavior naturally harassed the hostess, and at last, upon one of those occasions, the servants happening to be out of the room, shc called him to her side, and said—

"You were quite right to do that now, Gilbert, but please never do such a thing when the servants are in the room. It confuses them and makes us all uncomfortable."

Gibbie heard with obedient ear, but took the words as containing express permission to wait upon the company in the absence of other ministration. When therefore the servants finally disappeared, as was the custom immediately after placing the dessert, Gibbie got up, and, much to the amusement of the guests, waited on them as quite a matter of course. Around and around the table, deft and noiseless, he went, altogether aware of the pleasure of the thing, not at all of its oddity.

Presently the ladies rose, and when they had left the room, the host asked Gibbie to ring the bell. He obeyed with alacrity, and a servant appeared. She placed the utensils for making and drinking toddy, after Scotch custom, upon the table. A shadow fell upon the soul of Gibbie: for the first time since he ran from the city, he saw the well-known appointments of midnight orgy, associated in his mind with all the horrors from which he had fled. The memory of old nights in the streets, as he watched for his father and then helped him home; of his father's last prayer, drinking and imploring; of his white, motionless face the next morning, came back upon him, as he stood staring at the tumblers and the wineglasses and the steaming kettle.

"What is the girl thinking of!" exclaimed the minister, who had been talking to his next neighbor, when he heard the door close behind the servant. "She has actually forgotten the whisky!—Sir Gilbert," he went on, with a glance at the boy, "as you are so good, will you oblige me by bringing the bottle from the sideboard?"

Gibbie started at the sound of his name, but did not move from the place. After a moment, the minister, who had resumed the conversation, thinking he had not heard him, looked up. There, between the foot of the table and the sideboard, stood Gibbie as if fixed to the floor gazing out of his blue eyes at the minister—those eyes filmy with gathering tears, the smile utterly faded from his countenance.

Imagining some chance remark had hurt the boy's pride, Mr. Sclater spoke again: "It's just behind you, Sir Gilbert—the whisky bottle—that purple one with the silver top."

Gibbie never moved, but his eyes began to run over. A fearful remembrance of the blow he had given him on the head rushed back on Mr. Sclater: could it be the consequence of that? Was the boy paralyzed? He was on the point of hurrying to him, but restrained himself, and rising with deliberation, approached the sideboard. A nearer sight of the boy's face reassured him.

"I beg your pardon, Sir Gilbert," he said. "I thought you would not mind waiting on us as well as on the ladies. It is your own fault, you know. There," he added, pointing to the table; "take your place, and have a little toddy. It won't hurt you."

The eyes of all the guests were by this time fixed on Gibbie. What could be the matter with the curious creature? they wondered. His gentle merriment and quiet delight in waiting upon them had given a pleasant concussion to the spirits of the party, and there now was the boy all at once looking as if he had received a blow or some cutting insult which he did not know how to resent!

Between the agony of refusing to serve and the impossibility of putting his hand to unclean ministration, Gibbie had stood as if spellbound. But the last words of the minister broke the painful charm. He burst into tears, and darting from the room, not a little to his guardian's relief, hurried to his own.

The guests stared bewildered.

"He'll be gone to the ladies," said their host. "He's an odd creature. Mrs. Sclater understands him better than I do. He's more at home with her."

Therewith he proceeded to tell them his history, and whence the interest he had in him, not bringing down his narrative beyond the afternoon of the preceding day.

The next morning, Mrs. Sclater had a talk with Gibbie concerning his whim of waiting at table, telling him he must not do so again; it was not the custom for gentlemen to do the things that servants were paid to do; it was not fair to the servants, and so on—happening to end with an utterance of mild wonder at this fancy for such a peculiarity.

This exclamation Gibbie took for a question, or at least the expression of a desire to understand the reason of the thing. He went to a sidetable, and having stood there a moment or two, returned with a New Testament, in which he pointed out the words: "But I am among you as he that serveth." Giving her just time to read them, he took the book again, and in addition presented the words, "The disciple is not above his master, but everyone that is perfect shall be as his master."

Mrs. Sclater was as much put out as if he had been guilty of another and worse indiscretion. The idea of anybody ordering his common doings, not to say his oddities, by principles drawn from a source far too sacred to be practically regarded, was too preposterous ever to have become even a notion to her. Henceforth, however, it was a mote to trouble her mind's eye, a mote she did not get rid of until it began to turn to a glimmer of light.

17: *Friends Low and High*

ONE OF THE first things that Mr. Sclater did, when he realized that Gibbie had the capacity to be not only a gentleman but a scholar, was to take him to a specialist to have his organs of speech examined. Dr. Skinner was a surgeon in high repute and a professor at the university, but his examination put an end to question and hope together. What the fault was, he did not say; that it could not be remedied he did say.

Gibbie was not in the least disappointed. He had got on very well as yet without speech. It was not like sight or hearing. The only voice he could not hear was his own, and that was just the one he had neither occasion nor desire to hear. As to his friends, those who had known him the longest minded his dumbness the least. But the moment the defect was understood to be irreparable, Mrs. Sclater very wisely proceeded to learn the finger speech; and as she learned it, she taught it to Gibbie.

It was not long before Mistress Croale, haunted by old memories, summoned her courage and found her way to Mr. Sclater's house. The door was opened by a maid who quickly turned to the dining room to announce the fact that a woman wanted to see Sir Gilbert.

Gibbie looked up, put down his spoon, and was rising to go, when the minister, laying his hand on his arm, pressed him gently back to his chair, and Gibbie yielded, waiting.

"What sort of a woman?" he asked the girl.

"A decent-looking workinglike body," she answered. "I could not see her very well, it's so foggy the night about the door."

"Tell her we're at dinner; she may call again in an hour. Or if she likes to leave a message— Stay: tell her to come again tomorrow morning. I wonder who she is," he added, turning, he thought, to Gibbie.

But Gibbie was gone. He had passed behind his chair, and all he saw of him was his back as he followed the girl from the room. In his eagerness he left the door open, and they saw him dart to the visitor, shake hands with her in evident delight, and begin pulling her toward the room.

Now Mistress Croale, though nowise inclined to quail before the minister, would not willingly have intruded herself upon him, especially while he sat at dinner with his lady; but she fancied that Gibbie was taking her where they might have a quiet "news" together, and remained thus mistaken until she stood on the threshold, when, looking up, she started, stopped, made an obedience to the minister, and another to the minister's lady, and stood doubtful, if not a little abashed.

"Not here! my good woman," said Mr. Sclater, rising. "Oh, it's you, Mistress Croale! I will speak to you in the hall."

Mrs. Croale's face flushed, and she drew back a step. But Gibbie still held her, and with a look to Mr. Sclater that should have sent straight to his heart the fact that she was dear to his soul, kept drawing her into the room; he wanted her to take his chair at the table.

"Gilbert, come here," called Mrs. Sclater.

He went to her side, obedient and trusting as a child.

"Really, Gilbert, you must not," she said, rather loud for a whisper. "It won't do to turn things upside down this way. If you are to be a gentleman, and an inmate of *my* house, you must behave like other people. I *cannot* have a woman like that sitting at *my* table. Do you know what sort of a person she is?"

Gibbie's face shone up. He raised his hands. He was already able to talk a little.

"Is she a sinner?" he asked on his fingers.

Mrs. Sclater nodded.

Gibbie wheeled around and sprang back to the hall, whither the minister had ejected Mistress Croale, and where he was now talking to her with an air of confidential condescension. Gibbie threw his arms around her neck and gave her a great hug.

"Sir Gilbert!" Mr. Sclater exclaimed, very angry, "leave Mistress Croale alone, and go back to your dinner immediately. Jane, open the door."

Jane opened the door, Gibbie let her go, and Mrs. Croale went. But on the threshold she turned.

"Well, sir," she said, with a certain sad injury not unmingled with dignity, "you have stepped over my doorsill many's the time, and that with sorer words in your mouth than I ever used to pay you back; and I never said to you go. So first you turn me out of my own house and now you turn me out of yours; and what's left for you but to turn me out of the house of the Lord? And, indeed, sir, you need never wonder that the likes of me don't care about going to hear a preached gospel: we would fain see a practiced one!"

"You shall have a plate of soup, and welcome, Mistress Croale!" said the minister. "Jane, take Mistress Croale to the kitchen with you, and—"

"The devil's tail in your soup!" cried Mistress Croale, drawing herself up suddenly, with a snort of anger. "When turned I beggar? Was it your soup or your grace I sought for, sir? The Lord be between you and me! There's first that will be last, and last that will be first. But the one's not me, and the other's not you, sir."

With that she turned and walked down the steps, holding her head high.

"Really, Sir Gilbert," said the minister, going back into the dining room—but no Gibbie was there!—nobody but his wife, sitting in solitary discomposure at the head of her dinner table. The same instant, he heard a clatter of feet down the steps, and turned quickly into the hall again, where Jane was in the act of shutting the door.

"Sir Gilbert's run out after the woman, sir!" she said.

"Hoot!" grunted the minister, greatly displeased, and went back to his wife.

"Take Sir Gilbert's plate away," said Mrs. Sclater to the servant. "That's his New Testament again!" she went on, when the girl had left the room.

"My dear! my dear! take care," said her husband. He had not much notion of obedience to God, but he had some idea of respect to religion.

"Really, Mr. Sclater," his wife continued, "I had no idea what I was undertaking. But you gave me no choice. The creature is incorrigible. You knew how he had been brought up, and what you had to expect!"

"Brought up!" cried the minister. "You should have seen him about the streets!—with his trousers—"

"*Mister* Sclater! Then you ought to have known better!" said his wife, and laying down her spoon, sat back into the embrace of her chair.

But in reality she was not the least sorry he had undertaken the charge. She could not help loving the boy, and her words were merely the foam of vexation, mingled with not a little jealousy that he had left her and his nice hot dinner to go with the woman.

Nothing further was said until the second course was on the table. Then the lady spoke again—

"You really must, Mr. Sclater, teach him the absurdity of attempting to fit every point of his behavior to—to—words which were of course quite suitable to the time when they were spoken, but which it is impossible to take literally nowadays. Why! You saw him throw his arms round the horrid creature's neck! Well, he had just asked me if she was a sinner. I made no doubt she was. Off with the word goes my gentleman to embrace her!"

Here they laughed together.

Dinner over, they went to a missionary meeting, where the one stood and made a speech and the other sat and listened, while Gibbie was having tea with Mistress Croale.

From that day Gibbie's mind was much exercised as to what he could do for Mistress Croale, and now first he began to wish he had his money. As fast as he learned the finger alphabet he had taught it to Donal, and, as already they had a good many symbols in use between them, so many indeed that Donal would often instead of speaking make use of signs; they had now the means of intercourse almost as free as if they had had between them two tongues instead of one. It was easy therefore for Gibbie to impart to Donal his anxiety concerning her and his strong desire to help her, and doing so, he lamented in a gentle way his present inability. This communication Donal judged it wise to impart in his turn to Mistress Croale.

She was silent for a whole minute by the clock. From the moment when Gibbie forsook his dinner and his grand new friends to go with her, the woman's heart had begun to grow to the boy, and her old memories fed the new crop of affection.

"Well," she replied at length, with no little honesty, "I may not be so ill as he thinks me, for he had aye his poor father before his eyes; but the bairn's right in the main, and we must look to it, and see what can be done; for eh! I would be loath to disappoint the bonnie lad!—my bonnie wee Sir Gibbie. I can't help calling him *wee* Sir Gibbie—all the town called him that, though haith! he'll be a big man someday."

It had come to be the custom that Gibbie should go to Donal every Friday afternoon about four o'clock, and remain with him till the same time on Saturday, which was a holiday with both. One Friday, when the boys were calling on Mysie and having a good time reminiscing with her in the baker's shop, Mrs. Sclater discovered them there. She was put out, to say the least, at the choice of Sir Gilbert's friends, but she was astute enough to see that if he was to make other acquaintances she must make the introductions.

Recalling what her husband had told her of the odd meeting between the boy and a young lady at Miss Kimble's school, also the desire to see her again which Gibbie, on more than one occasion, had shown, she thought whether she could turn the acquaintance to account. She did not much like Miss Kimble, but she knew her very well, and there was no reason why she should not ask her to come and spend the evening, and bring two or three of the elder girls with her: a little familiarity with the looks, manners, and dress of refined girls of his own age would be the best antidote to his taste for low society, from that of baker's daughters downward.

When Mrs. Sclater's invitation arrived, the schoolmistress was aware of no reason why Miss Galbraith should not be one of the girls to go with her, especially as there was her cousin, Sir Gilbert, whom she herself would like to meet again, in the hope of removing the bad impression which, in the discharge of her duty, she feared she must have made upon him.

One day, then, at luncheon, Mrs. Sclater told Gibbie that

some ladies were coming to tea, and they were going to have supper instead of dinner. He must put on his best clothes, she said. He did as she desired, was duly inspected, approved on the whole, and finished off by a few deft fingers at his necktie, and a gentle push or two from the loveliest of hands against his hairthatch, and was seated in the drawing room with Mrs. Sclater when the ladies arrived. Ginevra and he shook hands, she with the sweetest of rose flushes, he with the radiance of delighted surprise. But, a moment after, when Mrs. Sclater and her guests had seated themselves, Gibbie, their only gentleman, for Mr. Sclater had not yet made his appearance, had vanished from the room. Tea was not brought until some time after, when Mr. Sclater came home, and then Mrs. Sclater sent Jane to find Sir Gilbert; but she returned to say he was not in the house. The lady's heart sank, her countenance fell, and all was gloom: her project had miscarried! he was gone! who could tell whither?

Gibbie had, after his first greeting, darted off to tell Donal and summon him to the Sclaters' house. But the news raised such a commotion in Donal's atmosphere, that for a time it was but a huddle of small whirlwinds. His heart was beating like the trample of a trotting horse. He never thought of inquiring whether Gibbie had been commissioned by Mrs. Sclater to invite him, or reflected that his studies were not half over for the night. He went pacing up and down the room and seemed lost to everything. Gibbie shook him at length, and told him, by two signs, that he must put on his Sunday clothes.

Donal's preparations took a long time and before the boys reached the house, tea was over and gone. They had had some music; and Mrs. Sclater was now talking kindly to two of the girls, seated with her upon the sofa. Ginevra was looking at the pictures in an annual. Mr. Sclater was making Miss Kimble agreeable to herself.

When the boys appeared in the doorway, Mrs. Sclater rose and Mr. Sclater stared. To the astonishment of the company, Ginevra rose and almost timidly held out her hand to Donal. He took it in his horny palm, shook it hither and thither sideways, like a leaf in a doubtful air, then held it like a precious thing he was at once afraid of crushing by too tight a grasp, and of dropping from too loose a hold, until Ginevra took charge of it herself again. Gibbie danced about behind him, all but standing on one leg, but, for Mrs. Sclater's sake, restraining himself. Ginevra sat down, and Donal, feeling very large and clumsy, and wanting to "be naught a while," looked about him for a chair, and then first espying Mrs. Sclater, went up to her and said, holding out his hand,

"How are you tonight, mem? I saw not your bonnie face when I came in. A grand house, like this of yours—and I'm sure, mem, it could not be over grand to fit yourself, but it's just some perplexing to plain folk like me, that's been used to more room, and less in it."

"I was sure of it!" remarked Mrs. Sclater to herself. "One of nature's gentlemen!"

"You will soon get accustomed to our town ways, Mr. Grant. But many of the things we gather about us are far more trouble than use," she replied in her sweetest tones and with a gentle pressure of the hand, which went a long way to set him at his ease. "I am glad to see you have friends here," she added.

"Only one, mem. Gibbie and me—"

"Excuse me, Mr. Grant, but would you oblige me—of course with *me* it is of no consequence, but just for habit's sake, would you oblige me by calling Gilbert by his own name —*Sir* Gilbert, please. I wish him to get used to it."

"Your will be it, mem. Well, as I was saying, Sir Gibbie—Sir Gilbert, that is, mem—and myself, we have known Miss

Galbraith this long time, being of the laird's own folk, as I may say."

"Will you take a seat beside her, then," said Mrs. Sclater, and, rising, herself placed a chair for him near Ginevra.

"I thank you, mem," said Donal, as he took the chair; "you're very condescending."

It was not long before Donal was telling stories. Some of the girls tittered, but Ginevra listened with wide-open eyes and Gibbie seemed pulsing light at every pore.

"Well, well, Donal!" broke in the harsh pompous voice of Mr. Sclater, who, unknown to the poet, had been standing behind him almost the whole time. "You have given the ladies quite enough of your romancing. That sort of thing, you know, my man, may do very well round the fire in the farm kitchen, but it's not the sort of thing for a drawing room. Besides, the ladies don't understand your word of mouth; they don't understand such broad Scotch. Come with me, and I'll show you something you would like to see."

He thought Donal was boring his guests, and at the same time preventing Gibbie from having the pleasure in their society for the sake of which they had been invited.

Donal rose, replying, "Think you so, sir? I thought I was in old Scotland still—here as well as upon Glashgar. But maybe my geography book's some old-fashioned. Didn't you understand me, mem?" he added, turning to Ginevra.

"Every word, Donal," she answered.

Donal followed his host, contented.

Gibbie took his place and began to teach Ginevra the finger alphabet. The other girls found him far more amusing than Donal, and then he had such a romantic history! and was a baronet!

In a few minutes Ginevra knew the letters, and presently she and Gibbie were having a little continuous "talk" together, a thing they had never had before. It was so slow, however, as to be rather tiring. It was mainly about Donal. But Mrs. Sclater opened the piano, and made a diversion. She played something brilliant, and then sang an Italian song. Then she asked Miss Kimble to play something, who declined, but said Miss Galbraith should sing—"for once in a way, as a treat. That little Scotch song you sing now and then, my dear," she added.

Ginevra rose timidly, but without hesitation, and going to the piano, sang, to a simple old Scotch air, to which they had been written, some verses. Before she ended, the minister, the late herdboy, and the dumb baronet were grouped crescent-wise behind the music stool.

Three of them knew that the verses were Donal's.

Later, when supper was announced, Donal felt that he had had enough for one evening and was able to encounter his work again. He reflected, also, that his reception had hardly been such as to justify him in partaking of the Sclaters' food, and that his mother's hospitality to Mr. Sclater had not been in expectation of return. As the company went down the stairs to the dining room, Donal came last and alone behind the two whispering schoolgirls. When they passed into the dining room, he spilled out of the house and ran home to his books.

When the ladies took their leave Gibbie walked with them.

18: *Encounters Old and New*

IN OBEDIENCE to the suggestion of his wife, Mr. Sclater did what he could to show Sir Gilbert how mistaken he was in imagining he could fit his actions to the words of our Lord. But in talking thus to Gibbie, the minister but rippled the air. Nothing he said had the slightest effect upon him. The unseen Lord and His reported words were to Gibbie realities, compared with which the very visible Mr. Sclater and his assured utterance were as the merest seemings of a phantom mood. Gibbie had never resolved to keep the words of the Lord—he just kept them; but he knew among the rest the Lord's words about the keeping of His word, and about being ashamed of Him before men, and it was with a pitiful indignation he heard the minister's wisdom drivel past his ears.

The effect of it all upon Gibbie was to send him to his room to his prayers, more eager than ever to keep the commandments of Him Who had said *If ye love me.* Comforted then and strengthened, he came down to go to Donal—not to tell him, for to none but Janet could he have made such a communication.

Donal had not yet begun to read his New Testament in the way Gibbie did, but he thought in the direction of light and freedom and looked toward some goal dimly seen in vague grandeur of betterness.

Gibbie and he seldom talked about Ginevra. She was generally *understood* between them—only referred to upon needful occasion: they had no right to talk about her, anymore than to intrude on her presence unseasonably. Donal went to Mr. Sclater's church because Mr. Sclater required it, in virtue of the position he assumed as his benefactor. Mr. Sclater in the pulpit was a trial to Donal, but it consoled him to be near Gibbie, also that he had found a seat in the opposite gallery, whence he could see Ginevra when her place happened to be not far from the door of one of the school pews.

Mrs. Sclater showed herself sincere, after her kind, to Donal as well as to Gibbie. She had by no means ceased to grow, and already was slowly bettering under the influences of the New Testament in Gibbie, notwithstanding she had removed the letter of it from her public table. She told Gibbie that he must talk to Donal about his dress and his speech. That he was a lad of no common gifts was plain, she said, but were he ever so "talented" he could do little in the world, certainly would never raise himself, so long as he dressed and spoke ridiculously. The wisest and best of men would be utterly disregarded, she said, if he did not look and speak like other people.

Gibbie thought with himself this could hardly hold, for there was John the Baptist; he answered her, however, that Donal could speak very good English if he chose. As to his dress, Donal was poor, Gibbie said, and could not give up wearing any clothes so long as there was any wear in them. "If you had seen me once!" he added, with a merry laugh to finish for his fingers.

Mrs. Sclater spoke to her husband, who said to Gibbie that, if he chose to provide Donal with suitable garments, he would advance him the money.

Gibbie would thereupon have dragged Donal at once to the tailor; but Donal was obstinate.

"No, no," he said; "the clothes is good enough for him that wears them. You do enough for me, Sir Gilbert, already; and though I would be obliged to you as I would to my mother herself, to clothe me if I weren't decent, I won't take your silver to look fine. No, no, I'll wear the clothes out, and we shall do better with the next."

"What will you do when you are a minister?" asked Gibbie on his fingers.

"Me a minister?" echoed Donal. "Me a minister!" he repeated. "Losh, man! if I can save my own soul, it'll be all that I'm fit for. No, no; if I can be a schoolmaster, and help the bairnies to be good, as my mother taught myself, and have time to read, and a few shillings to buy books, I'll be a happy man! I must have books."

"But wouldn't you like to have a wife, Donal, and children, like your father and mother?" spelled Gibbie.

"No, no; no wife for me, Gibbie!" answered the philosopher. "Who would have either a poor schoolmaster or a shepherd? 'Cept it was maybe some lass like my sister Nicie, that wouldn't know Euclid from her stockings, or Burns from a mill dam, or conic sections from the hole in the great pyramid."

"I don't like to hear you talk like that, Donal," said Gibbie. "What do you say to Mother?"

"The Mother's not to be talked about," answered Donal. "She's one by herself, not one like other folk. You wouldn't think worse of the angel Gabriel that he had not just read Homer clean through, would you?"

"If I did," answered Gibbie, "he would only tell me there was time enough for that."

When they met on a Friday evening, and it was fine, they would rove the streets, Gibbie taking Donal to the places he knew so well in his childhood, and enjoying it the more that he could now tell him so much better what he remembered.

He took him to the court in the Widdiehill and showed him the Auld Hoose o' Galbraith, and the place under the stair where his father had worked. The house was occupied still as then by a number of poor people, and the door was never locked, day or night, anymore than when Gibbie used to bring his father home. He took Donal to the garret where they had slept and where his father died. The door stood open, and the place was just as they had left it.

"If I was you, Sir Gilbert," said Donal, who now and then remembered Mrs. Sclater's request—they had come down, and looking at the outside of the house, had espied a half-obliterated stone carving of the Galbraith arms—"If I was you, Sir Gilbert, I would make Master Sclater keep a sharp lookout for the first chance of buying back this house. It would be a great pity if it should go to worse before you get it. Eh! such tales as this house could tell!"

"How am I to do that, Donal? Mr. Sclater would not mind me. The money's not mine yet, you know," said Gibbie.

"The silver *is* yours, Gibbie," answered Donal; "it's yours as the kingdom of heaven is yours; it's only that you can't just lay your hands on it yet. The sooner you let that Master Sclater know that you know what you're about, the better. And believe me, when he comes to understand that you want that house, he'll not be a day before he goes to somebody or other about it."

Donal was right, for within a month the house was bought, and certain necessary repairs commenced.

Mr. Sclater began, as well, to make other purchases for his ward. When he learned that the laird, Thomas Galbraith, was a ruined man, Mr. Sclater, acting through his lawyer and without permitting his name to appear, purchased the whole of the Glashruach property. For the present, however, he kept Sir Gilbert in ignorance of the fact.

Mrs. Sclater continued to invite young ladies to the house for Gibbie's sake; but Gibbie did not much enjoy these gatherings. It began to trouble him a little that he seemed to care less for his kind than before; but it was only a seeming, and the cause of it was this: he was now capable of perceiving facts in nature and character which prevented real contact, and must make advances toward it appear as offensive as they were useless. But he did not love the less that he had to content himself, until the kingdom should come nearer, with loving at a more conscious distance; by loving kindness and truth he continued doing all he could to bring the kingdom whose end is unity.

Hence he had come to restrain his manner—nothing could have constrained his manners, which now from the conventional point of view were irreproachable; but if he did not so often execute a wild dance, or stand upon one leg, the glow in his eyes had deepened, and his response to any advance was as ready and thorough, as frank and sweet as ever; his eagerness was replaced by a stillness from which his eyes took all coldness, and his smile was as the sun breaking out in a gray day of summer and turning all from doves to peacocks. In this matter there was one thing worthy of note common to Donal and him, who had had the same divine teaching from Janet—their manners to all classes were the same, they showed the same respect to the poor, the same ease with the rich.

The little pocket money Mr. Sclater allowed Gibbie was chiefly spent at the shop of a certain secondhand bookseller. The books bought were carried to Donal's room, there to be considered by Gibbie Donal's, and by Donal Gibbie's.

Every Saturday, Donal went to see his father and mother. Janet kept fresh and lively, although age told on her, she said, more rapidly since Gibbie went away.

"But if the Lord lets old age wither me up," she said, "He'll look after the cracks himself."

Six weeks of every summer between Donal's sessions, while the minister and his wife took their holiday, Gibbie spent with Robert and Janet. It was a blessed time for them all. He led then just the life of the former days, with Robert and Oscar and the sheep, and Janet and her cow and the New Testament —only he had a good many more things to think about now, and more ways of thinking about them. With his own hands he built a neat little porch to the cottage door, with close sides and a second door to keep the wind off; Donal and he carried up the timber and the mortar. But although he tried hard to make Janet say what he could do for her more, he could not bring her to reveal any desire that belonged to this world—except, indeed, for two or three trifles for her husband's warmth and convenience.

"The sight of my Lord's face," she said once, when he was pressing her, "is all that I want, Sir Gibbie. For this life it just blecks me to think of anything I would have or would lose. This body of mine's growing some heavylike, I must confess, but I would not have it taken off of me before the time. It would be an ill thing for the seed to be scattered before it is ripe."

They almost always called him "Sir Gibbie," and he never objected, or seemed either annoyed or amused at it; he took it just as the name that was his, the same way as his hair or his hands were his; he had been called wee Sir Gibbie for so long.

By the time Donal's last winter came, Gibbie was ready for college also. Mr. Sclater consented to his lodging with Donal but would have preferred their taking rooms in some part of the town more suitable to the young baronet's position. However, by this time, Gibbie seldom found difficulty in having his way with the minister.

Often on their long walks at night, the youths would come upon some of the sorry specimens of humanity that had been so familiar to Gibbie in his early years. One poor woman, holding a baby to her bosom and stumbling tipsily through the dark streets, brought tears to Gibbie's eyes.

The woman and her child he would have taken to his very heart and could do nothing for them. Love seemed helpless, for money was useless. It set him thinking much, and the result appeared. From that hour the case of the homeless haunted his heart and brain and imagination; and as his natural affections found themselves repelled and chilled in what is called "society," they took refuge more and more with the houseless and hungry and shivering. Through them, also, he now, for the first time, began to find grave and troublous questions mingling with his faith and hope; so that already he began to be rewarded for his love—to the true heart every doubt is a door. What Gibbie discovered found always its first utterance in action.

The youths' concern about the woman led them to talk with Mistress Croale about her.

They did not lay bare to her their perplexities, but they asked her to find out who the woman was, and see if anything could be done for her. They said to themselves she would know the condition of such a woman, and what would be moving in her mind, after the experience she had herself had, better at least than the minister or his lady-wife. Nor were they disappointed. To be thus taken into counsel revived for Mistress Croale the time of her dignity. She undertook the task with hearty good will, and carried it out with some success. Its reaction on herself to her own good was remarkable.

Soon after this, they had another encounter. One day, as they were approaching the gate of Miss Kimble's school, a thin, careworn man, in shabby clothes, came out, and walked along meeting them. Every now and then he bowed his shoulders, as if something invisible had leaped upon them from behind, and as often seemed to throw it off and with effort walk erect. It was the laird. They lifted their caps, but in return he only stared, or rather tried to stare, for his eyes seemed able to fix themselves on nothing.

19: *A Time of Strain*

THE YEARS that had seen Gibbie go up in the world had seen the laird go down. All his enterprises had failed. The best he could now do for his daughter was to purchase a cottage in a suburban street. There she kept house for him.

Ginevra was still the same brown bird as of old—a bird of the twilight, or rather a twilight itself, with a whole night of stars behind it, of whose existence she scarcely knew, having but just started on the voyage of discovery which life is. She had the sweetest, rarest smile—not frequent and flashing like Gibbie's, but stealing up from below, like the shadowy reflection of a greater light, gently deepening, permeating her countenance until it reached her eyes, thence issuing in soft flame. Always, however, as soon as her eyes began to glow duskily, down went their lids, and down dropped her head like the frond of a sensitive plant. Her atmosphere was an embodied stillness; she made a quiet wherever she entered; she was not beautiful, but she was lovely; and her presence at once made a place such as one would desire to be in.

The most pleasant of her thoughts were of necessity those with which the two youths were associated. Several times every winter they had met at the minister's, and every summer she had again and again seen Gibbie with Mrs. Sclater, and once or twice had had a walk with them, and every time, Gibbie had something of Donal's to give her. Twice Gibbie had gone to see her at the school, but the second time she asked him not to come again, as Miss Kimble did not like it. He gave a big stare of wonder, but followed the stare with a swift smile, for he saw she was troubled, and asked no question, but waited for the understanding of all things that must come.

But now, when or where was she ever to see them more? Gibbie was no longer at the minister's, and perhaps she would never be invited to meet them there again. She dared not ask Donal to call; her father would be indignant; and for her father's sake she would not ask Gibbie; it might give him pain; while the thought that he would of a certainty behave so differently to him now that he was well dressed and mannered like a gentleman was almost more unendurable to her than the memory of his past treatment of him.

Mr. and Mrs. Sclater had called upon them the moment they were settled in the cottage; but Mr. Galbraith would see nobody. When the gate bell rang, he always looked out, and if a visitor appeared, withdrew to his bedroom.

One brilliant Saturday morning, the ground hard with an early frost, the filmy ice making fairy caverns and grottoes in the cart ruts, and the air so condensed with cold that every breath, to those who ate and slept well, had the life of two, Mrs. Sclater rang the said bell. Mr. Galbraith, peeping from the window, saw a lady's bonnet and went. She walked in, followed by Gibbie, and would have Ginevra go with them for a long walk. Pleased enough with the proposal, for the outsides of life had been dull as well as painful of late, she went and asked her father.

"Why do you ask me?" returned her father. "My wishes are nothing to anyone now; to you they never were anything."

"I will stay at home, if you wish it, Papa, with pleasure," she replied, as cheerfully as she could after such a reproach.

"By no means. If you do, I shall go and dine at the Red Hart," he answered.

It made her miserable for a while, but she had got so used to his way of breaking a gift as he handed it that she answered only with a sigh. In haste she put on her little brown-ribboned bonnet, took the motheaten muff that had been her mother's, and rejoined Mrs. Sclater and Gibbie, beaming with troubled pleasure. Life in her was strong, and their society soon enabled her to forget, not her father's sadness but his treatment of her.

At the end of the street, they found Donal awaiting them—without greatcoat or muffler, the picture of such health as suffices to its own warmth. Away they walked together westward, then turned southward. Mrs. Sclater and Gibbie led, and Ginevra followed with Donal. And they had not walked far before something of the delight of old times on Glashruach began to revive in the bosom of the too-sober girl. The sun and the bright air were like wine in her veins. Donal had soon made her cheerful, and now and then she answered his talk with even a little flash of merriment. They crossed the bridge, high-hung over the Daur. They then turned eastward to the sea, and came to the top of the rock border of the coast, with its cliffs rent into gullies, eerie places to look down into, ending in caverns into which the waves rushed with bellow and boom.

It was not long before they met Fergus Duff, now become a minister. He asked them to come to his church the following Sunday evening to hear him preach. In the meantime, Fergus saw to it to call on Miss Galbraith and make his respects to her father.

Gibbie and Donal were but two in a great crowd of people at the North Church and when time for dismissal came, they went around to the door by which they thought Ginevra and her father would issue. Fergus joined them, muffled to the ears against the cold of the night. When the two for whom they all waited appeared, Fergus advanced and approached the laird.

"Ah, Mr. Duff!" said Mr. Galbraith; "excuse me, but would you oblige me by giving your arm to my daughter? I see a friend waiting to speak to me. I shall overtake you in a moment."

Fergus murmured his pleasure, and Ginevra and he moved away together. The youths for a moment watched the father. He dawdled—evidently wanted to speak to no one. They then followed the two, walking some yards behind them. Every other moment Fergus would bend his head toward Ginevra; once or twice they saw the little bonnet turn upward in response or question. When the youths reached the street where the cottage stood, they turned the corner after them and walked quickly up to them where they stood at the gate waiting for it to be opened.

"Such a grand night!" said Donal, after the usual greetings. "Sir Gibbie and me are having a walk in the moonlight. Good night, mem. Good night, Fergus."

Therewith the two young men walked on; but before they had gone far, Donal broke down and said, "Gibbie, yon rascal's going to marry the lady-lass! and it drives me mad to think it. If I could but once see and speak to her—once—just once! Lord! what will come of all the gowans upon the Mains and the heather upon Glashgar!"

Gibbie's face had grown white in the moon gleams, and his lips trembled. He put his arm through Donal's and clung to him, and in silence they went home. When they reached Donal's room, Donal entering shut the door behind him and shut out Gibbie. He stood for a moment like one dazed, then suddenly coming to himself, turned away, left the house, and ran straight to Daur Street.

When the minister's door was opened to him, he went to that of the dining room, knowing Mr. and Mrs. Sclater would then be at supper. Happily for his intent, the minister was at the moment having his tumbler of toddy; his wife therefore, when she saw Gibbie, rose, and, meeting him, took him with her to her own little sitting room, where they had a long talk, of which the result appeared the next night in a note from Mrs. Sclater to Gibbie, asking him and Donal to spend the evening of Tuesday with her.

The hospitable crimson room, with its round table set out for a Scotch tea and its fire blazing hugely, received them. And there sat Ginevra by the fire! with her pretty feet on a footstool before it. She received them, as always, with the same simple sincerity that had been hers on the bank of the Lorrie burn. But Gibbie read some trouble in her eyes, for his soul was all touch, and, like a delicate spiritual seismograph, responded at once to the least tremble of a neighboring soul.

When tea was over, Gibbie went to the window, got within the red curtains, and peeped out. Returning presently, he spelled with fingers and signed with hands to Ginevra that it was a glorious night; would she not come for a walk? Ginevra looked to Mrs. Sclater.

"Gibbie wants me to go for a walk," she said.

"Certainly, my dear—if you are well enough to go with him," replied her friend.

"I am always well," answered Ginevra.

"I can't go with you," said Mrs. Sclater, "for I expect my husband every moment; but what occasion is there, with two such knights to protect you?"

Perceiving Gibbie's design, Donal cast him a grateful glance, while Ginevra rose hastily, and ran to put on her outer garments.

When they stood on the pavement, there was the moon, the very cream of light, ladying it in a blue heaven. The steps of the youths rang on the pavements, and Donal's voice seemed to him so loud and clear that he muffled it all in gentler meaning. He spoke low and Ginevra answered him softly. They walked close together, and Gibbie flitted to and fro, now on this side, now on that, now in front of them, now behind.

"How liked you the sermon, mem?" asked Donal.

"Papa thought it a grand sermon," answered Ginevra.

"And yourself?" persisted Donal.

"Papa tells me I am no judge," she replied.

"That's as muckle as to say you didn't like it so well as he did!" returned Donal, in a tone expressing some relief.

"Mr. Duff is very good to my father, Donal," she rejoined, "and I don't like to say anything against his sermon; but all the time I could not help thinking whether your mother would like this and that; for you know, Donal, any good there is in me I have got from her, and from Gibbie—and from you, Donal."

The youth's heart beat with a pleasure that rose to physical pain. Donal remaining silent, Ginevra presently returned him his own question—"How did *you* like the sermon, Donal?"

"Do you want me to say, mem?" he asked.

"I do, Donal," she answered.

"Well, I would just say, in a general way, that I can't think muckle of any sermon that might make a body think more of the preacher than of Him that he comes to preach about. I mean, that I don't see how anybody was to love God or his neighbor a jot the more for hearing yon sermon Sunday night."

"That's just what I was feeling! I am sorry for Mr. Duff, if he has taken to teaching where he does not understand."

They had left the city behind them and were walking a wide-open road, with a great sky above it. On its borders were small fenced fields and a house here and there with a garden. It was a plain-featured, slightly undulating country, with hardly any trees—not at all beautiful, except as every place under the heaven which man has not defiled is beautiful to him who can see what *is* there. But this night the earth was nothing; what was in them and over them was all. Donal felt that, with this essential love and wonder by his side, to be doomed to go on walking to all eternity would be a blissful fate, were the landscape turned to a brickfield, and the sky to persistent gray.

"Will you not take my arm, mem?" he said at length, summoning courage. "I just find myself like a horse with a rein broken, going by myself through the air this way."

Before he had finished the sentence Ginevra had accepted the offer. It was the first time. His arm trembled. He thought it was her hand.

"You're not cold, are you, mem?" he said.

"Not the least," she answered.

A moment more and Donal broke out singing.

"What's that, Donal?" cried Ginevra.

"Oh, nothing," answered Donal. "It was only my heart laughing."

"Say the words," said Ginevra.

"I can't—I don't know them now," replied Donal.

"Oh, Donal! are those lovely words gone—altogether—forever? Shall I *not* hear them again?"

"I'll try to remember them when I go home," he said. "I can't now. I can think of nothing but one thing."

"And what is that, Donal?"

"Yourself," answered Donal.

Ginevra's hand lifted just a half of its weight from Donal's arm, like a bird that had thought of flying, then settled again.

"It is very pleasant to be together once more as in the old time, Donal—though there *are* no daisies and green fields. But what place is that, Donal?"

Instinctively, almost unconsciously, she wanted to turn the conversation. The place she pointed to was an opening immediately on the roadside, through a high bank—narrow and dark, with one side half lighted by the moon. She had often passed it, walking with her schoolfellows, but had never thought of asking what it was. In the shining dusk it looked strange and a little dreadful.

"It's the muckle quarry, mem," answered Donal; "do you not know that? That's where most of the whole town came from. It's an eerie kind of a place to look at in this light. I wonder that you never saw it."

"I have seen the opening there, but never took much notice of it before," said Ginevra.

"Come and I'll let you see it," rejoined Donal. "It's well worth looking into. You wouldn't be afraid to come and see what the moon makes of it, would you, mem?"

"No, Donal. I would not be frightened to go anywhere with you. But—"

"Eh, mem! it makes me right proud to hear you say that. Come away then."

So saying, he turned aside, and led her into the narrow passage, cut through a friable sort of granite. Gibbie, thinking they had gone to have but a peep and return, stood in the road, looking at the clouds and the moon, and crooning to himself. By and by, when he found they did not return, he followed them.

When they reached the end of the cutting, Ginevra started at the sight of the vast gulf, the moon showing the one wall a ghastly gray, and from the other throwing a shadow half across the bottom. But a winding road went down into it, and Donal led her on.

"Are you sure there are no holes—full of water, down there?" she faltered.

"Ay, there's one or two," replied Donal, "but we'll keep out of them."

Ginevra shuddered, but was determined to show no fear. They stepped at last on the level below, covered with granite chips and stones and great blocks. In the middle rose a confused heap of all sorts. To this, and around to the other side of it, Donal led her. There shone the moon on the corner of a pool, the rest of which crept away in blackness under an overhanging mass. She caught his arm with both hands. He told her to look up. Suddenly Donal caught her hand. She looked in his face. It was not the moon that could make it so white.

"Ginevra!" he said, with trembling voice.

"Yes, Donal," she answered.

"You're not angry at me for calling you by your name? I never did it before."

"I always call you Donal," she answered.

"That's natural. You're a grand lady, and I'm nothing but a herd laddie."

"You're a great poet, Donal, and that's much more than being a lady or a gentleman."

"Ay, maybe," answered Donal listlessly, as if he were thinking of something far away; "but it won't make up for the other; they're not upon the same side of the water, like. A poor lad like me dares not lift an eye to a grand lady like you, mem. My time's near over at the college, and I see nothing for it but go home and hire myself. I'll be better working with my hands than with my head when I have no hope left of ever seeing your face again. It's a long time that I have known myself to be wanting you. You're the body, and I'm the shadow. Eh, mem, but you're bonnie! You don't know yourself how bonnie you are, nor what a subversion you make in my heart and my head."

Still she looked him in the eyes, like one bewildered, unable to withdraw her eyes from his.

"Tell me to hold my tongue, mem, and I'll hold it," he said.

Her lips moved, but no sound came.

"I know well," he went on, "you can never look upon me as anything more than a kind of a human bird, that you would keep in a cage, and give seeds and bits of sugar to, and hearken to when he sang. I'll never trouble you again, mem, and whether you grant me my prayer or not, you'll never see me again."

"What is it, Donal?" said Ginevra, half inaudibly, and with

effort; she could scarcely speak for a fluttering in her throat.

"I could beseech you upon my knees," he went on, as if she had not spoken, "to let me kiss your bonnie foot, but that you might grant for bare pity, and that would do me little good; so for once and for all, till maybe after we're all beyond the muckle sea, I beseech as the favor of your sweet soul, to lay upon me, as upon the lips of the soul that sang you the songs you liked so well to hear when you were but a lady-lassie—one solitary kiss. It shall be holy to me as the light; and I swear by the Truth I'll think of it but as you think, and man nor woman nor bairn, not even Gibbie himself, shall know—"

The last word broke the spell upon Ginevra.

"But, Donal," she said, as quietly as when years ago they talked by the Lorrie side, "would it be right?—a secret with you I could not tell to *any*one?—not even if afterwards—"

Donal's face grew so ghastly with utter despair that absolute terror seized her; she turned from him and fled, calling "Gibbie! Gibbie!"

He was not many yards off, approaching the mound as she came from behind it. He ran to meet her. She darted to him like a dove pursued by a hawk, threw herself into his arms, laid her head on his shoulder, and wept. Gibbie held her fast, and with all the ways in his poor power sought to comfort her. She raised her face at length. It was all wet with tears which glistened in the moonlight. Hurriedly Gibbie asked on his fingers—

"Was Donal not good to you?"

"He's *beautiful,*" she sobbed; "but I couldn't, you know, Gibbie, I couldn't. I don't care a straw about position and all that—who would with a poet?—but I couldn't, you know, Gibbie. I couldn't let him think I might have married him—in any case: could I now, Gibbie?"

She laid her head again on his shoulder and sobbed. Gibbie did not well understand her. Donal, where he had thrown himself on a heap of granite chips, heard and understood, felt and knew and resolved all in one. The moon shone, and the clouds went flitting like ice-floe about the sky, now gray in distance, now near the moon and white; and still the two, Ginevra and Gibbie, stood motionless—Gibbie with the tears in his eyes and Ginevra weeping as if her heart would break.

Again Ginevra raised her head.

"Gibbie, you must go and look after poor Donal," she said.

Gibbie went, but Donal was nowhere to be seen. To escape the two he loved so well, and be alone as he felt, he had crept away softly into one of the many recesses of the place. Again and again Gibbie made the noise with which he was accustomed to call him, but he gave back no answer, and they understood that wherever he was he wanted to be left to himself. They climbed again the winding way out of the gulf, and left him the heart of its desolation.

"Take me home, Gibbie," said Ginevra, when they reached the high road.

As they went, not a word more passed between them. Ginevra was as dumb as Gibbie, and Gibbie was sadder than he had ever been in his life—not only for Donal's sake, but because, in his inexperienced heart, he feared that Ginevra would not listen to Donal because she could not—because she had already promised herself to Fergus Duff; and with all his love to his kind, he could not think it well that Fergus should be made happy at such a price. He left her at her own door, and went home, hoping to find Donal there before him.

He was not there. Hour after hour passed, and he did not appear. At eleven o'clock, Gibbie set out to look for him, but with little hope of finding him. He went all the way back to the quarry, thinking it possible he might be waiting there, expecting him to return without Ginevra. The moon was now low, and her light reached but a little way into it, so that the look of the place was quite altered, and the bottom of it almost dark. But Gibbie had no fear. He went down to the spot, almost feeling his way, where they had stood, got upon the heap, and called and whistled many times. But no answer came. Donal was away, he did not himself know where, wandering wherever the feet in his spirit led him. Gibbie went home again, and sat up all night, keeping the kettle boiling, ready to make tea for him the moment he should come in. But even in the morning Donal did not appear.

He might hear of him at the college, Gibbie thought, and went at the usual hour. Sure enough, as he entered the quadrangle, there was Donal going in at the door leading to the moral philosophy classroom. For hours, neglecting his own classes, he watched about the court, but Donal never showed himself. Gibbie concluded he had watched to avoid him, and had gone home by Crown Street, and himself returned the usual and shorter way, sure almost of now finding him in his room. The room was empty, and Mistress Murkison had not seen him.

Donal's final examination, upon which alone his degree now depended, came on the next day; Gibbie watched at a certain corner, and unseen saw him pass—with a face pale but strong, eyes that seemed not to have slept, and lips that looked the inexorable warders of many sighs. After that he did not see him once till the last day of the session arrived. Then in the public room he saw him go up to receive his degree. As they came from the public room, he lay in wait for him once more, but again in vain.

When he reached his lodging, he found a note from Donal waiting him, in which he bade him good-by, said he was gone to his mother, and asked him to pack up his things for him. A sense of loneliness, such as in all his forsaken times he had never felt, overshadowed Gibbie when he read this letter.

20: *Gibbie Comes of Age*

GIBBIE KNEW that in the month of May, according to the registry of his birth in the parish book, he would be of age; he would also be, as he expected, his own master. As to what he would then do, he had thought much and had plans, but no one knew anything of them except Donal—who had forsaken him.

When the day of his majority came, there were no particular rejoicings. Mr. Sclater, believing he alone had acquainted himself with the date, and desiring to avoid giving his ward a feeling of importance, made no allusion to the fact when they met at breakfast.

Gibbie, finding nothing was said, fingered to Mrs. Sclater, "This is my birthday."

"I wish you many happy returns," she answered. "How old are you today?"

"Twenty-one," he answered—by holding up all his fingers twice and then a forefinger.

She looked struck, and glanced at her husband, who thereupon, in his turn, gave utterance to the usual formula of goodwill, and said no more. Seeing he was about to leave the table,

Gibbie, claiming his attention, spelled on his fingers, very slowly, for Mr. Sclater was slow at following this mode of communication—

"If you please, sir, I want to be put in possession of my property as soon as possible."

"All in good time, Sir Gilbert," answered the minister, with a superior smile, for he clung with hard reluctance to the last vestige of his power.

"But what is good time?" spelled Gibbie with a smile, which, none the less that it was of genuine friendliness, indicated there might be difference of opinion on the point.

"Oh! we shall see," returned the minister coolly. "These are not things to be done in a hurry," he added. "We'll see in a few days what Mr. Torrie proposes."

"But I want my money at once," insisted Gibbie. "I have been waiting for it, and now it is time, and why should I wait still?"

"To learn patience, if for no other reason, Sir Gilbert," answered the minister, with a hard laugh, meant to be jocular. "But indeed such affairs cannot be managed in a moment. You will have plenty of time to make a good use of your money, if you should have to wait another year or two."

So saying he rose from the table.

"When will you see Mr. Torrie?" asked Gibbie, rising too, and working his telegraph with greater rapidity than before.

"By and by," answered Mr. Sclater, and walked toward the door. But Gibbie got between him and it.

"Will you go with me to Mr. Torrie today?" he asked.

The minister shook his head. Gibbie withdrew, seeming a little disappointed. Mr. Sclater left the room.

"You don't understand business, Gilbert," said Mrs. Sclater.

Gibbie smiled, got his writing case, and sitting down at the table, wrote as follows—

"Dear Mr. Sclater, As you have never failed in your part,

how can you wish me to fail in mine? I am now the one accountable for this money, which surely has been idle long enough, and if I leave it still unused, I shall be doing wrong, and there are things I have to do with it which ought to be set about immediately. I am sorry to seem importunate, but if by twelve o'clock you have not gone with me to Mr. Torrie, I will go to Messrs. Hope & Waver, who will tell me what I ought to do next, in order to be put in possession. It makes me unhappy to write like this, but I am not a child any longer, and having a man's work to do, I cannot consent to be treated as a child. I will do as I say. I am, dear Mr. Sclater, your affectionate ward, Gilbert Galbraith."

He took the letter to the study, and having given it to Mr. Sclater, withdrew. The minister came down instantly, put the best face on it he could, said that if Sir Gilbert was so eager to take up the burden, he was ready enough to cast it off, and they would go at once to Mr. Torrie.

With the lawyer, Gibbie insisted on understanding everything and that all should be legally arranged as speedily as possible. Mr. Torrie saw that, if he did not make things plain, or gave the least cause for doubt, the youth would most likely apply elsewhere for advice, and therefore took trouble to set the various points, both as to the property and the proceedings necessary, before him in the clearest manner.

"Thank you," said Gibbie, through Mr. Sclater. "Please remember I am more accountable for this money than you and am compelled to understand." Janet's repeated exhortations on the necessity of sending for the serpent to take care of the dove had not been lost upon him.

The lawyer being then quite ready to make him an advance of money, they went with him to the bank, where he wrote his name, and received a checkbook. As they left the bank, he asked the minister whether he would allow him to keep his place in his house, and was almost startled at finding how his manner to him was changed. He assured Sir Gilbert that he hoped he would always regard his house as one home, however many besides he might now choose to have.

So now at last Gibbie was free to set about realizing a long-cherished scheme.

The repairs upon the Auld Hoose o' Galbraith were now nearly finished. In consequence of them, some of the tenants had had to leave, and Gibbie now gave them all notice to quit at their earliest convenience, taking care, however, to see them provided with fresh quarters, toward which he could himself do not a little, for several of the houses in the neighborhood had been bought for him at the same time as the old mansion. As soon as it was empty, he set more men to work, and as its internal arrangements had never been altered, speedily, out of squalid neglect, caused not a little of old stateliness to reappear. He next proceeded to furnish at his leisure certain of the rooms.

By the time he had finished, his usual day for going home had arrived; while Janet lived, the cottage on Glashgar was home. Just as he was leaving, the minister told him that Glashruach was his. Mrs. Sclater was present, and read in his eyes what induced her instantly to make the remark: "How could that man deprive his daughter of the property he had to take her mother's name to get!"

"He had misfortunes," indicated Gibbie, "and could not help it, I suppose."

"Yes indeed!" she returned, "misfortunes so great that they amounted to little less than swindling. I wonder how many he has brought to grief besides himself! If he had Glashruach once more he would begin it all over again."

"Then I'll give it to Ginevra," said Gibbie.

"And let her father coax her out of it, and do another world of mischief with it!" she rejoined.

Gibbie was silent. Mrs. Sclater was right! To give is not always to bless. He must think of some way. With plenty to occupy his powers of devising he set out.

He would gladly have seen Ginevra before he left but had

no chance. He had gone to the North Church every Sunday for a long time now, neither for love of Fergus, nor dislike to Mr. Sclater, but for the sake of seeing his lost friend—had he not lost her when she turned from Donal to Fergus? Did she not forsake him too when she forsook his Donal? His heart would rise into his throat at the thought, but only for a moment; he never pitied himself. Now and then he had from her a sweet sad smile, but no sign that he might go and see her. Whether he was to see Donal when he reached Daurside, he could not tell; he had heard nothing of him since he went; his mother never wrote letters.

"No, no; I can't," she would say. "It would take all the pith out of me to write letters. All that I have to say I send the up-road; it's sure to win home early or late."

Notwithstanding his new power, it was hardly therefore with his usual elation that he took his seat on the coach. But his reception was the same as ever. At his mother's persuasion, Donal, he found, instead of betaking himself again to bodily labors as he had purposed, had accepted a situation as tutor offered him by one of the professors. He had told his mother all his trouble.

"He'll be all the better for it in the end," she said, with a smile of the deepest sympathy, "though, being my own, I can't help being sorry for him. But the Lord was in the earthquake, and the fire, and the wind that rave the rocks, though the prophet couldn't see Him. Donal will come out of this with more room in his heart and more light in his spirit."

Gibbie took his slate from the crap o' the wa' and wrote, "If money could do anything for him, I have plenty now."

"I know your heart, my bairn," replied Janet; "but no; silver's but a dead horse for anything that smacks of salvation. No; the poor fellow must wrestle out of the thicket of dead roses as best he can—sore scratched, no doubt. Eh! it's a fearful and wonderful thing that drawing of heart to heart, and then a great snap, and a start back, and there's miles between them! The Lord alone knows the bottom of it; but I'm thinking there's more in it, and a heap more to come out of it ere all be done, than we have any guess at."

Gibbie told her that Glashruach was his. Then first the extent of his wealth seemed to strike his old mother.

"Eh! you'll be the laird, will you, then? Eh, sirs! To think of this hoose and all being wee Gibbie's! Well, it dings all. The ways of the Lord are to be thought upon! He made David a king, and Gibbie He's made the laird! Blest be His name."

"They tell me the mountain is mine," Gibbie wrote, "your husband shall be laird of Glashgar if he likes."

"No, no," said Janet, with a loving look. "He's over old for that. And what better would Robert be to be laird? We pay no rent as it is, and he has as many sheep to love as he can well know one from the other. I know nothing that he lacks but Gibbie to go with him about the hill. A neighbor's laddie comes and goes, to help him, but, eh, says Robert, he's no Gibbie! But if Glashruach be your own, my bonnie man, you must go down there this very night, and give a look to the burn; for the last time I was there, I thought it was creeping in against the bank some fearsome like for what's left of the old hoose, and the sooner it's looked after maybe the better. Eh, Sir Gibbie, but you should marry the bonnie lady, and take her back to her own hoose."

Gibbie gave a great sigh to think of the girl that loved the hill and the heather and the burns, shut up in the city, and every Sunday going to the great church—with which in Gibbie's mind was associated no sound of glad tidings. To him Glashgar was full of God; the North Church or Mr. Sclater's church—well, he had tried hard, but had not succeeded in discovering temple signs about either.

The next day he sent to the city for an architect; and within a week masons and quarrymen were at work, some on the hill blasting blue boulders and red granite, others roughly shaping the stones, and others laying the foundation of a huge facing and buttressing wall, which was to slope up from the bed of the Glashburn fifty feet to the foot of the castle, there to culminate in a narrow terrace with a parapet. Others again were clearing away what of the ruins stuck to the old house, in order to leave it, as much as might be, in its original form.

There was no space left for rebuilding, neither was there any between the two burns for adding afresh. The channel of the second remained dry, the landslip continuing to choke it, and the stream to fall into the Glashburn. But Gibbie would not consent that the burn Ginevra had loved should sing no more as she had heard it sing. Her chamber was gone and could not be restored, but another chamber should be built for her, beneath whose window it should again run; when she was married to Fergus, and her father could not touch it, the place should be hers. More masons were gathered, and foundations blasted in the steep rock that formed the other bank of the burn. The main point in the building was to be a room for Ginevra. He planned it himself—with a window turret projecting from the wall, making a recess in the room and overhanging the stream.

The turret he carried a story higher than the wall, and in the wall placed a staircase leading to its top, whence, over the roof of the ancient part of the house, might be seen the great Glashgar, and its streams coming down from heaven and singing as they came. Then from the middle of the first stairs in the old house, the wall, a yard and a half thick, having been cut through, a solid stone bridge, with a pointed arch, was to lead across the burn to a like landing in the new house—a close passage with an oriel window on each side looking up and down the stream and a steep roof. And while these works were going on below, two masons, high on the mountain, were adding to the cottage a warm bedroom for Janet and Robert.

The architect was an honest man and kept Gibbie's secret,

so that, although he was constantly about the place, nothing disturbed the general belief that Glashruach had been bought and was being made habitable by a certain magnate of the county adjoining.

One cold afternoon in the end of October, when Mistress Croale was shutting up her shop in the market, Gibbie came walking up the long gallery with the light hill step which he never lost, and startled her with a hand on her shoulder, making signs that she must come with him. She made haste to lock her door, and they walked side by side to the Widdiehill. They turned into the close of the Auld Hoose o' Galbraith.

Gibbie led her up the dark stairs. At the top, on a wide hall-like landing, he opened a door. She drew back with shy amazement. But his smile reassured her, and she stepped in.

It was almost a grand room, rich and somber in color, old-fashioned in its somewhat stately furniture. A glorious fire was blazing and candles were burning. The table was covered with a white cloth and laid for two. Gibbie shut the door, placed a chair for Mistress Croale by the fire, seated himself, took out his tablet, wrote, "Will you be my housekeeper? I will give you one hundred pounds a year," and handed it to her.

"Lord, Sir Gibbie!" she cried, jumping to her feet, "have you lost your wits? How would an old wife like me look in such a place—and in such duds as this? It would make Satan laugh, and that he can but seldom."

Gibbie rose, and taking her by the hand, led her to the door of an adjoining room.

It was a bedroom, as grand as the room they had left, and if Mistress Croale was surprised before, she was astonished now. A fire was burning here too, candles were alight on the dressing table, a hot bath stood ready, on the bed lay a dress of rich black satin, with linen and everything down, or up, to collars, cuffs, mittens, cap, and shoes. All these things Gibbie had bought himself, using the knowledge he had gathered in shopping with Mrs. Sclater, and the advice of her dressmaker, whom he had taken into his confidence, and who had entered heartily into his plan. He made signs to Mistress Croale that everything there was at her service, and left her.

Like one in a dream she yielded to the rush of events, not too much bewildered to dress with care, and neither too old nor too wicked nor too ugly to find pleasure in it. She might have been a born lady just restored to the habits of her youth, to judge by her delight over the ivory brushes and tortoise-shell comb, and great mirror. In an hour or so she made her appearance. She entered the room neither blushing nor smiling, but wiping the tears from her eyes like a too blessed child.

Gibbie was so satisfied with her appearance that, come of age as he was, and vagrant no more, he first danced around her several times with a candle in his hand, much to the danger but nowise to the detriment of her finery, then set it down, and executed his old lavolta of delight, which, as always, he finished by standing on one leg.

Then they sat down to a nice nondescript meal, also of Gibbie's own providing.

When their meal was ended, he went to a bureau, and brought thence a paper, plainly written to this effect—

"I agree to do whatever Sir Gilbert Galbraith may require of me, so long as it shall not be against my conscience."

He handed it to Mistress Croale; she read, and instantly looked about for pen and ink: she dreaded seeming for a moment to hesitate. He brought them to her, she signed, and they shook hands.

He then conducted her all over the house—first to the rooms prepared for his study and bedroom, and next to the room in the garret, which he had left just as it was when his father died in it. Next, on the floor between, he showed her a number of bedrooms, all newly repaired and fresh-painted—with double windows, the inside ones filled with frosted glass. These rooms, he gave her to understand, he wished her to furnish. Going back then to the sitting room, he proceeded to explain his plans, telling her he had furnished the house that he might not any longer be himself such a stranger as to have no place to take a stranger to. Then he got a Bible there was in the room and showed her those words in the book of Exodus—"Also, thou shalt not oppress a stranger; for ye know the heart of a stranger, seeing ye were strangers in the land of Egypt"; and while she thought again, he made her understand that whomsoever he should at any time bring home she was to treat as his guest.

She expressed hearty acquiescence, the more work the better for her! she said. She would tomorrow arrange for giving up her shop and disposing of her stock and the furniture in her garret.

Next, he insisted that she should never utter a word as to the use he intended making of his house; if the thing came out, it would ruin his plans, and he must give them up altogether—and thereupon he took her to the ground floor and showed her a door in communication with a poor little house behind, by which he intended to introduce and dismiss his guests, that they should not know where they had spent the night. Then he made her read to him the hundred and seventh Psalm; after which he left her, saying he would come to the house in a week; until then he should be at Mr. Sclater's.

Left alone in the great house—like one with whom the most beneficent of fairies had been busy, the first thing Mistress Croale did was to go and have a good look at herself—from head to foot. She was satisfied with everything she saw there, except her complexion, and that she resolved should improve. She was almost painfully happy. Out there was the Widdiehill, dark and dismal and cold, through which she had come, sad and shivering, into warmth and splendor and luxury and bliss! Wee Sir Gibbie had made a lady of her!

21: *Face to Face*

WHEN GIBBIE saw Ginevra at the North Church, she looked so sad and white that his heart was very heavy for her. Could it be that she repented? She must have done it to please her father! If she would marry Donal, he would engage to give her Glashruach. She should have Glashruach all the same whatever she did, only it might influence her father. He paced up and down before the cottage once for a whole night, but no good came of that. He went up to the door once, but in the dread of displeasing her, lost his courage and paced the street the whole morning instead, but saw no one come out.

Fergus had gradually become essential to the small remaining happiness of which the laird was capable. He had gained his favor chiefly through the respect and kindly attention he showed him. And, at length, Fergus summoned courage to ask him if he might "pay his addresses" to Miss Galbraith.

The father reflected that if he declined what he could not call an honor, he must lose what was unquestionably a comfort. Slowly he raised himself in his chair, "You have my permission, Mr. Duff."

The young preacher hastened to find Ginevra, but only to meet a refusal, gentle and sorrowful. He pleaded for permission to repeat his request after an interval, but she distinctly refused. Disappointed and annoyed he was, but he sought and fancied he found reasons for her decision which were not unfavorable to himself and continued to visit her father as before, saying to him he had not quite succeeded in drawing from her a favorable answer but hoped to prevail.

The matter of Donal and his verses came up between the laird and the preacher. The laird chided his daughter in her taste for low company; with her passionate defense of Donal, Ginevra also defended Gibbie. This drew fury fast upon censure and the laird insisted that the only amends for her past was to marry according to his wishes; to give up superstition and poetry and herdboys and dumb rascals, and settle down into a respectable matron, a comfort to the gray hairs she was now bringing with sorrow to the grave. Then Ginevra became absolutely silent. He stormed at her for her sullenness, but she persisted in her silence, sorely distressed to find how dead her heart seemed growing under his treatment of her.

Gibbie found everything at the Auld Hoose in complete order for his reception; Mistress Croale had been very diligent, and promised well for a housekeeper—looked well, too, in her black satin and lace, with her complexion, she justly flattered herself, not a little improved. She had a good meal ready for him, with every adjunct in proper style.

Everything went comfortably. Gibbie was so well up in mathematics, thanks to Mr. Sclater, that, doing all requisite for honorable studentship, but having no desire to distinguish himself, he had plenty of time for more important duty. Now that he was by himself, as if old habit had returned in the shape of new passion, he roamed the streets every night. His custom was this: after dinner, which he had when he came from college, about half-past four, he lay down, fell asleep in a moment, as he always did, and slept till half-past six; then he had tea, and after that, studied till ten o'clock, when he took his Greek

Testament. At eleven he went out, seldom finally returning before half-past one, sometimes not for an hour longer—during which time Mistress Croale was in readiness to receive any guest he might bring home.

Some nights, many nights together, he would not meet a single wanderer; occasionally he would meet two or three in the same night. When he found one, he would stand regarding him until he spoke. If the man was drunk he would leave him—such were not those for whom he could now do most. If he was sober, he made him signs of invitation. If he would not go with him, he left him, but kept him in view, and tried him again. If still he would not, he gave him a piece of bread, and left him. If he called, he stopped, and by circuitous ways brought him to the little house at the back. It was purposely quite dark. If the man was too apprehensive to enter, he left him; if he followed, he led him to Mistress Croale. If anything suggested the possibility of helping further, a possibility turning entirely on the person's self, the attempt was set on foot; but in general, after a good breakfast, Gibbie led him through a dark passage into the darkened house and dismissed him from the door by which he had entered.

He never gave money and never sought such guest except in the winter. It was a tolerable beginning, and during the time not a word reached him indicating knowledge of his proceedings, although within a week or two a rumor was rife in the lower parts of the city of a mysterious being who went about doing this and that for poor folk, but, notwithstanding his gifts, was far from canny.

Fergus had now established himself in the manse of the North Church, and thither he invited Mr. and Miss Galbraith to dine with him on a certain evening. Her father's absolute desire compelled Ginevra's assent; she could not, while with him, rebel absolutely. Fergus did his best to make the evening a pleasant one.

It grew late. The dinner had been at a fashionable hour; they had stayed an unfashionable time: it was nearly twelve o'clock when guests and host left the house in company. Fergus went with the laird and Ginevra.

Hearing the pitiful wailing of a child and the cough of a woman as they went along a street bridge, they peeped over the parapet, and saw, upon the stairs leading to the lower street, a woman with a child asleep in her lap, trying to eat a piece of bread, and coughing as if in the last stage of consumption. On the next step below sat a man hushing in his bosom the baby whose cry they had heard. They stood for a moment, the minister pondering whether his profession required of him action, and Ginevra's gaze fixed on the head and shoulders of the foreshortened figure of the man, who vainly as patiently sought to soothe the child by gently rocking it to and fro. But when he began a strange humming song to it, which brought all Glashgar before her eyes, Ginevra knew beyond a doubt that it was Gibbie.

At the sound the child ceased to wail, and presently the woman with difficulty rose, laying a hand for help on Gibbie's shoulder. Then Gibbie rose also, cradling the infant on his left arm and making signs to the mother to place the child on his right. She did so, and turning, went feebly up the stairs. Gibbie followed with the two children, one lying on his arm, the other with his head on his shoulder, both wretched and pining, with gray cheeks and dark hollows under their eyes. From the top of the stairs they went slowly up the street, the poor woman coughing, and Gibbie crooning to the baby, who cried no more, but now and then moaned.

Then Fergus said to the laird, "Did you see that young man, sir? That is the so-called Sir Gilbert Galbraith we were talking of the other night. They say he has come into a good property, but you may judge for yourself whether he seems fit to manage it!"

Ginevra withdrew her hand from his arm.

"Good God, Jenny!" exclaimed the laird, "you do not mean to tell *me* you have ever spoken to a young man like that?"

"I know him very well, Papa," replied Ginevra, collectedly, "that young man, Sir Gilbert Galbraith—"

"Nonsense, girl! there is no such Galbraith. It is the merest of scoffs."

"Many years ago," she recommenced, "when I was a child—Excuse me, Mr. Duff, but it is quite time I told my father what has been weighing upon my mind for so many years."

"Sir Gilbert!" muttered her father contemptuously.

"One day," again she began, "Mr. Fergus Duff brought a ragged little boy to Glashruach—the most innocent and loving of creatures, who had committed no crime but that of doing good in secret. I saw Mr. Duff box his ears on the bridge; and you, Papa, gave him over to that wretch, Angus MacPholp, to whip him—so at least Angus told me, after he had whipped him till he dropped senseless. I can hardly keep from screaming now when I think of it."

"All this, Jenny, is nothing less than cursed folly. Do you mean to tell me you have all these years been cherishing resentment against your own father for the sake of a little thieving rascal, whom it was a good deed to fright from the error of his ways? I have no doubt Angus gave him merely what he deserved."

"You must remember, Miss Galbraith, we did not know he was dumb," said Fergus, humbly.

"If you had had any heart," said Ginevra, "you would have seen in his face that he was a perfect, angelic child. He ran to the mountain without a rag to cover his bleeding body, and would have died of cold and hunger had not the Grants taken him to their hearts and been father and mother to him. After that," she went on, "Angus shot him like a wild beast, when he was quietly herding Robert Grant's sheep. In return Sir

Gilbert saved his life in the flood. And just before the house of Glashruach fell—the part in which my room was, he caught me up, because he could not speak, and carried me out of it; and when I told you that he had saved my life, you ordered him out of the house, and when he was afraid to leave me alone with you, dashed him against the wall, and sent for Angus to whip him again. But I should have liked to see Angus try it *then!*"

"I do remember an insolent fellow taking advantage of the ruinous state the house was in to make his way into my study," said the laird.

"And now," Ginevra continued, "Mr. Duff makes question of his wits because he finds him carrying a poor woman's children, going to get them a bed somewhere! If Mr. Duff had run about the streets when he was a child, like Sir Gilbert, he might not, perhaps, think it so strange he should care about a houseless woman and her brats!"

Therewith Ginevra burst into tears.

"Abominably disagreeable!" muttered the laird. "I always thought she was an idiot! Hold your tongue, Jenny! you will wake the street. All you say may or may not be quite true; but I see nothing in it to prove the lad a fit companion for a young lady."

Ginevra did not answer him—did not speak another word. When Fergus left them at their own door, she neither shook hands with him nor bade him good night.

"Jenny," said her father, the moment he was gone, "if I hear of your once speaking again to that low vagabond, I will turn you out of the house."

To Ginevra's accumulated misery, she carried with her to her room a feeling of contempt for her father, with which she lay struggling in vain half the night.

Although Gibbie had taken no notice of the laird's party, he had recognized each of the three as he came up the stairs, and in Ginevra's face read an appeal for deliverance. It seemed to say, "You help everybody but me! Why do you not come and help me too? Am I to have no pity because I am neither hungry nor cold?" He did not, however, lie awake the most of the night, or indeed a single hour of it, thinking what he should do; long before the poor woman and her children were in bed, he had made up his mind.

As soon as he came home from college the next day and had hastily eaten his dinner, going upon his vague knowledge of law business lately acquired, he bought a stamped paper, wrote upon it, and put it in his pocket; then he took a card and wrote on it, "Sir Gilbert Galbraith, Baronet, of Glashruach," and put that in his pocket also. Thus provided, and having said to Mistress Croale that he should not be home that night—for he expected to set off almost immediately in search of Donal and had bespoken horses—he walked deliberately along Pearl Street out into the suburb, and turning to the right, rang the bell at the garden gate of the laird's cottage.

When the servant came, he gave her his card, and followed her into the house. She carried it into the room where, dinner over, the laird and the preacher were sitting. Giving time, as he judged, and no more, to read the card, Gibbie entered the room: he would not risk a refusal to see him.

It was a small room with a round table. The laird sat sideways to the door; the preacher sat between the table and the fire.

"What the devil does this mean? A vengeance take him!" cried the laird.

His big tumbling eyes had required more time than Gibbie had allowed, so that, when with this exclamation he lifted them from the card, they fell upon the object of his imprecation standing in the middle of the room between him and the open door. The preacher, snug behind the table, scarcely endeavored to conceal the smile with which he took no notice of Sir Gilbert.

The laird rose in the perturbation of mingled anger and unpreparedness.

"Ah!" he said, but it was only a sound, not a word, "to what —may I ask—have I—I have not the honor of your acquaintance, Mr.— Mr.—" Here he looked again at the card he held, fumbled for and opened a double eyeglass, then with deliberation examined the name upon it. "Mr.—ah, I see! Galbraith, you say. To what do I owe the honor of this unexpected visit? Business, I presume, it must be that brings you, seeing I have not the honor of the slightest acquaintance with you?"

He dropped his eyeglass with a clatter against his waistcoat, threw the card into his finger glass, raised his pale eyes, and stared at Sir Gilbert with all the fixedness they were capable of.

Gibbie answered by drawing from the breast pocket of his coat the paper he had written and presenting it like a petition. Mr. Galbraith sneered, and would not have touched it had not his eye caught the stamp, which from old habit at once drew his hand. From similar habit, or perhaps to get it nearer the light, he sat down. The laird read, but not aloud: "I, Gilbert Galbraith, Baronet, hereby promise and undertake to transfer to Miss Galbraith, only daughter of Thomas Galbraith, Esq., on the day when she shall be married to Donal Grant, Master of Arts, the whole of the title deeds of the house and lands of Glashruach, to have and to hold as hers, with absolute power to dispose of the same as she may see fit. Gilbert Galbraith, Old House of Galbraith, Widdiehill, March," etc., etc.

The laird stretched his neck like a turkeycock, and gobbled inarticulately, threw the paper to Fergus, and turning on his chair, glowered at Gibbie. Then suddenly starting to his feet, he cried—

"What do you mean, you rascal, by daring to insult me in my own house?"

"A trick! a most palpable trick! and an exceedingly silly one!" pronounced Fergus, who had now read the paper; "quite as foolish as unjustifiable! Everybody knows Glashruach is the property of Major Culsalmon! Get away with you," he added, addressing Gibbie across the table. "Make haste before worse comes of it. You have been made a fool of."

When Fergus began to speak, the laird turned, and stared at him with lackluster eyes. Gibbie stood shaking his head, smiling, and making eager signs with hands and arms.

"Why don't you speak, you fool?" he cried. "Get out and don't stand making faces there. Be off with you, or I will knock you down."

Gibbie pointed to the paper, which lay before Fergus, and placed a hand first on his lips, then on his heart.

"Damn your mummery!" said the laird, choking with rage. "Go away, or I will break your head."

Fergus at this rose and came around the table to get between them. But the laird caught up a pair of nutcrackers, and threw it at Gibbie. It struck him on the forehead, and the blood spirted from the wound. He staggered backward. Fergus seized the laird's arm and sought to pacify him.

Her father's loud tones had reached Ginevra in her room; she ran down, and that instant entered: Gibbie all but fell into her arms. The moment's support she gave him, and the look of loving terror she cast in his face, restored him; and he was again firm on his feet, pressing her handkerchief to his forehead, when Fergus, leaving the laird, advanced with the pacific intention of getting him safe from the house. Ginevra stepped between them. Her father's rage thereupon broke loose quite, and was madness. He seized hold of her with violence and dragged her from the room. Fergus laid hands upon Gibbie more gently, and half would have forced, half persuaded him to go. A cry came from Ginevra; refusing to be sent to her room before Gibbie was in safety, her father struck her. Gibbie would have darted to her help. Fergus held him fast, but knew nothing of Gibbie's strength, and the next moment found himself on his back upon the table, amid the crash of glasses and china.

Having locked the door, Gibbie sprang to the laird, who was trying to drag his daughter, now hardly resisting, up the first steps of the stairs, took him around the waist from behind, swept him to the other room, and there locked him up also. He then returned to Ginevra where she lay motionless on the stairs, lifted her in his arms, and carried her out of the house, nor stopped until, having reached the farther end of the street, he turned the corner of it into another equally quiet.

Under a dull smoky oil lamp Gibbie stopped. He knew by the tightening of her arms that Ginevra was coming to herself.

"Let me down," she said feebly.

He did so, but kept his arm around her. She gave a deep sigh, and gazed bewildered. When she saw him, she smiled.

"With *you,* Gibbie!" she murmured. "But they will be after us!"

"They shall not touch you," signified Gibbie.

"What was it all about?" she asked.

Gibbie spelled on his fingers, "Because I offered to give you Glashruach, if your father would let you marry Donal."

"Gibbie! how could you?" she cried almost in a scream, and pushing away his arm, turned from him and tried to run, but after two steps, tottered to the lamppost and leaned against it.

"Then come with me and be my sister, Ginevra, and I will take care of you," spelled Gibbie. "I can do nothing to take care of you while I can't get near you."

"Oh, Gibbie! nobody does like that," returned Ginevra, "else I should be so glad!"

"There is no other way then that I know. You won't marry anybody, you see."

"Won't I, Gibbie? What makes you think that?"

"Because of course you would never refuse Donal and marry anybody else; that is not possible."

"Oh! don't tease me, Gibbie."

"Ginevra, you don't mean you would?"

"Yes, Gibbie," she said, "I would. I thought it was understood between us, ever since that day you found me on Glashgar. In my thoughts I have been yours all the time."

She turned her face to the lamppost. But Gibbie made her look.

"You do not mean," he spelled very hurriedly, "that you would marry *me? Me?* I never dreamed of such a thing!"

"You didn't mean it then!" said Ginevra, with a cry—bitter but feeble with despair and ending in a stifled shriek. "What *have* I been saying then! I thought I belonged to you! I thought you meant to take me all the time!" She burst into an agony of sobbing. "Oh me! me! I have been alone all the time, and did not know it!"

She sank on the pavement at the foot of the lamppost, shaken with her sobs. Gibbie was in sad perplexity. Heaven had opened before his gaze; its colors filled his eyes; its sounds filled his ears and heart and brain; but the portress was busy crying and would not open the door. Neither could he get at her to comfort her, for, her eyes being wanted to cry with, his poor signs were of no use. Dumbness is a drawback to the gift of consolation.

It was a calm night early in March, clear overhead, and the heaven full of stars. The first faint thick odor of spring was in the air. A crescent moon hung halfway between the zenith and the horizon, clear as silver in firelight, and peaceful in the consciousness that not much was required of her yet.

Gibbie held one of Ginevra's hands and stroked it. Then he pulled off his coat and laid it softly upon her. She grew a little quieter.

"Take me home, Gibbie," she said, in a gentle voice.

Gibbie put his arms around her and helped her to her feet. She looked at him, and saw a face glorious with bliss. Never, not even on Glashgar, in the skincoat of the beast-boy, had she seen him so like an angel. And in his eyes was that which triumphed, not over dumbness, but over speech. It brought the rose fire rushing into her wan cheecks; she hid her face on his bosom; and, under the dingy red flame of the lamp in the stony street, they held each other, as blessed as if they had been under an orange tree haunted with fireflies. For they knew each the heart of the other, and God is infinite.

How long they stood thus, neither of them knew. The lady would not have spoken if she could, and the youth could not if he would. But the lady shivered, and because she shivered, she would have the youth take his coat. He mocked at cold—made her put her arms in the sleeves and buttoned it around her; both laughed to see how wide it was. Then he took her by the hand and led her away, obedient as when first he found her and her heart upon Glashgar. Like two children, holding each other fast, they hurried along, in dread of pursuit. He brought her to Daur Street, and gave her into Mrs. Sclater's arms. Ginevra told her everything, except that her father had struck her, and Gibbie begged her to keep his wife for him till they could be married. Mrs. Sclater behaved like a mother to them, sent Gibbie away, and Ginevra to a hot bath and to bed.

Gibbie went home as if Pearl Street had been the stairs of Glashgar, and the Auld Hoose a mansion in the heavens. Love had been gathering and ever storing itself in his heart so many years for this brown dove! now at last the rock was smitten, and its treasure rushed forth to her service. In nothing was it changed as it issued, save as the dark, silent, motionless water of the cavern changes into the sparkling, singing, dancing rivulet. Gibbie's was love simple, unselfish, undemanding—not merely asking for no return, but asking for no recognition, requiring not even that its existence should be known. He was a rare one who did not make the common miserable blunder of taking the shadow cast by love—the desire, namely, to be loved—for love itself; his love was a vertical sun, and his own shadow was under his feet.

The man who loves most will love best. Because Gibbie's love was toward everything human, he was able to love Ginevra as Donal was not yet grown able to love her. The fullness of a world of love ways and love thoughts was Gibbie's. In sweet affairs of loving kindness, he was in his own kingdom, and sat upon its throne. And it was this essential love, acknowledging and embracing, as a necessity of its being, everything that could be loved, which now concentrated its rays on the individual's individual.

The sum of happiness in the city, if gathered that night into one wave, could not have reached halfway to the crest of the mighty billow tossing itself heavenward as it rushed along the ocean of Gibbie's spirit.

22: *And They Lived Happily*

THE NEXT morning, the first thing after breakfast, Mr. Sclater, having reflected that Ginevra was under age and they must be careful, resumed for the nonce, with considerable satisfaction, his office of guardian, and holding no previous consultation with Gibbie, walked to the cottage and sought an interview with Mr. Galbraith.

"I have to inform you, Mr. Galbraith," he began, "that Miss Galbraith—"

"Oh!" said the laird, "I beg your pardon; I was not aware it was my daughter you wished to see."

"Miss Galbraith did us the honor to sleep at our house last night," said Mr. Sclater deliberately.

"Why! What! Are you aware of what you are saying, sir?"

"Perfectly; and of what I saw too. A blow looks bad on a lady's face."

"Good heavens! the little hussy dared to say I struck her?"

"She did not say so; but no one could fail to see someone had. If you do not know who did it, I do."

"Send her home instantly, or I will come and fetch her," cried the laird.

"Come and dine with us if you want to see her. For the present she remains where she is. You want her to marry Fergus Duff; she prefers my ward, Gilbert Galbraith, and I shall do my best for them."

"She is under age," said the laird.

"That fault will rectify itself as fast in my house as in yours," returned the minister. "If you invite the publicity of a legal action, I will employ counsel, and wait the result."

"Mr. Sclater, I am shocked, unspeakably shocked, at my daughter's conduct. To leave the shelter of her father's roof, in the middle of the night, and—"

"About seven o'clock in the evening," interjected Mr. Sclater.

"—and take refuge with strangers!" continued the laird.

"By no means strangers, Mr. Galbraith!" said the minister.

"She is an unnatural child. She knows well enough what I think of her, and what reason she has given me so to think."

"When a man happens to be alone in any opinion," remarked the minister, "even if the opinion should be of his own daughter, the probabilities are he is wrong. Everyone but yourself has the deepest regard for Miss Galbraith."

"She has always cultivated strangely objectionable friendships," said the laird.

"For my own part," said the minister, "although I believe she has no dowry, I do not know a lady I should prefer for a wife to my ward."

"Oblige me by informing my daughter that I request her, for the sake of avoiding scandal, to return to her father's house until she is of age."

"And in the meantime you undertake—"

"I undertake nothing," shouted the laird.

"Then I refuse to carry your message. I will be no bearer of that from which, as soon as delivered, I should dissuade."

"Allow me to ask, are you a minister of the gospel, and stir up a child against her own father?"

"I am not here to bandy words with you, Mr. Galbraith. It is nothing to me what you think of me. If you will engage not to urge your choice upon Miss Galbraith, I think it probable she will at once return to you. If not—"

"I will not force her inclinations," said the laird. "She knows my wish, and she ought to know the duty of a daughter."

"I will tell her what you say," answered the minister and took his departure.

When Gibbie heard, he was not at all satisfied with Mr. Sclater's interference to such result. He wished to marry Ginevra at once, in order to take her from under the tyranny of her father. But he was readily convinced it would be better, now things were understood, that she should go back to him, and try once more to gain him. The same day she did go back, and Gibbie took up his quarters at the minister's.

At the end of the month Gibbie went home as usual, telling Ginevra he must be present to superintend what was going on at Glashruach to get the house ready for her, but saying nothing of what he was building there. By the beginning of the winter, they had got the buttress wall finished and the coping on it, also the shell of the new house roofed in, so that the carpenters had been at work all through the frost and snow, and things had made great progress without any hurry; and now, since the first day the weather had permitted, the masons were at work again. The bridge was built, the wall of the old house broken through, the turret carried aloft. All the hollow where the burn had carried away pinewood and shrubbery, gravel drive and lawn, had been planted, mostly with fir trees; and a weir of strong masonry, a little way below the house, kept the water back, so that it rose and spread, and formed a still pool just under the house, reflecting it far beneath.

As soon as Gibbie returned, Ginevra let him know that things were still going badly with her father. They met, consulted, agreed that the best thing was to be married at once, made their preparations, and confident that, if asked, he would refuse his permission, proceeded, for his sake, as if they had had it.

One morning, as he sat at breakfast, Mr. Galbraith received from Mr. Torrie, whom he knew as the agent in the purchase of Glashruach, and whom he supposed to have bought it for Major Culsalmon, a letter, more than respectful, stating that matters had come to light regarding the property which rendered his presence on the spot indispensable for their solution. The present owner, therefore, through Mr. Torrie, begged most respectfully that Mr. Galbraith would sacrifice two days of his valuable time and visit Glashruach. The result, he did not doubt, would be to the advantage of both parties. If Mr. Galbraith would kindly signify to Mr. Torrie his assent, a carriage and four, with postilions, that he might make the journey in all possible comfort, should be at his house the next morning at ten o'clock, if that hour would be convenient.

For weeks the laird had been an unmitigated bore to himself, and the invitation laid hold upon him by the most projecting handle of his being, namely, his self-importance. He wrote at once to signify his gracious assent; and in the evening told his daughter he was going to Glashruach on business and had arranged for Miss Kimble to come and stay with her till his return.

At nine o'clock the schoolmistress came to breakfast, and at ten a traveling carriage with four horses drew up at the door, looking nearly as big as the cottage. With monstrous stateliness, and a fur coat on his arm, the laird descended to his garden gate, and got into the carriage, which instantly dashed away for the western road, restoring Mr. Galbraith to the full consciousness of his inherent grandeur: if he was not exactly laird of Glashruach again, he was something quite as important. His carriage was just out of the street, when a second, also with four horses, drew up at the garden gate.

Out of it stepped Mr. and Mrs. Sclater, then a young gentleman, and Mr. Torrie, the lawyer. They came trooping into the little drawing room, shook hands with Miss Kimble and Ginevra, and sat down, Sir Gilbert beside Ginevra—but nobody spoke.

What could it mean, wondered Miss Kimble. A morning call? It was too early. And four horses to a morning call! A pastoral visitation? Four horses and a lawyer to a pastoral visitation! A business call? There was Mrs. Sclater! and that Sir Gilbert! It must after all be a pastoral visitation, for there was the minister commencing a religious service!—during which however it suddenly revealed itself to the horrified spinster that she was part and parcel of a clandestine wedding! There was Ginevra being married in a brown dress! to that lad, who called himself a baronet! Just as she was recovering her presence of mind, Mr. Sclater pronounced them husband and wife! Bride and bridegroom broke into "a loud smile." The ceremony over, Ginevra glided from the room and returned almost immediately in her little brown bonnet. Sir Gilbert caught up his hat, and Ginevra held out her hand to Miss Kimble. Then at length the abashed and aggrieved lady found words of her own.

"Ginevra!" she cried, "you are never going to leave me alone in the house!—after inviting me to stay with you till your father returned!"

But the minister answered her.

"It was her father who invited you, I believe, not Lady Galbraith," he said; "and you understood perfectly that the invitation was not meant to give her pleasure."

Miss Kimble burst into tears. Ginevra kissed her and said, "Never mind, dear Miss Kimble. You could not help it. The whole thing was arranged. We are going after my father, and we have the best horses."

Mr. Torrie laughed outright. "A new kind of runaway marriage!" he cried. "The happy couple pursuing the obstinate parent with four horses!"

"But after the ceremony!" said Mr. Sclater.

Here the servant ran down the steps with a carpetbag and opened the gate for her mistress. Lady Galbraith got into the carriage; Sir Gilbert followed; there were kissing and tears at the door of it; Mrs. Sclater drew back; the postilions spurred their horses; off went the second carriage faster than the first; and the minister's party walked quietly away, leaving Miss Kimble to declaim to the maid of all work, who cried so that she did not hear a word she said.

Between the second stage and the third, Gibbie and Ginevra came in sight of their father's carriage. Having arranged with the postilions that the two carriages should not change horses at the same places, they easily passed unseen by him, while, thinking of nothing so little as their proximity, he sat in state before the door of a village inn.

Just as Mr. Galbraith was beginning to hope the major had contrived a new approach to the place, the carriage took an unexpected turn, and he found presently they were climbing, by a zigzag road, the height over the Lorrie burn; but the place was no longer his, and to avoid a sense of humiliation, he avoided taking any interest in the change.

A young woman—it was Donal's eldest sister—opened the door to him and showed him up the stair to his old study. There a great fire was burning; but, beyond that, everything, even to the trifles on his writing table, was just as when last he left the house.

"Very considerate!" he said to himself. "I trust the major does not mean to keep me waiting, though. Deuced hard to have to leave a place like this!"

Weary with his journey he fell into a doze, awoke suddenly, and heard the door of the room open. There was Major Culsalmon entering with outstretched hand! and there was a lady —his wife doubtless! But how young the major was! he had imagined him a man in middle age at least! Bless his soul! was he never to get rid of this impostor fellow! it was not the major! it was the rascal calling himself Sir Gilbert Galbraith! And—bless his soul again! there was the minx, Jenny! looking as if the place was her own!

"Jenny!" he said, as the two stood for a moment regarding him, a little doubtfully, but with smiles of welcome, "what is the meaning of this? I did not know Major Culsalmon had invited *you!* And what is this person doing here?"

"Papa," replied Ginevra, with a curious smile, half merry, half tearful, "This person is my husband, Sir Gilbert Galbraith of Glashruach; and you are at home in your own study again."

"Will you never have done masquerading, Jenny?" he returned. "Inform Major Culsalmon that I request to see him immediately."

He turned toward the fire and took up a newspaper. They thought it better to leave him. As he sat, by degrees the truth grew plain to him. But not one other word on the matter did the man utter to the day of his death.

The next day Gibbie provided him with something to do. He had the chest of papers found in the Auld Hoose o' Galbraith carried into his study, and the lawyer found both employment and interest for weeks in deciphering and arranging them. In the course of a fortnight he found himself so much at home in his old quarters, and so much interested in those papers and his books, that when Sir Gilbert informed him Ginevra and he were going back to the city, he pronounced it decidedly the better plan, seeing he was there *himself* to look after affairs.

Back in the city, they settled for the winter in the Auld

Hoose. Gibbie continued at college until spring when he was awarded his degree. Then they returned to Glashruach. For some little time Ginevra was fully occupied in getting her house in order and furnishing the new part of it. When that was done, Sir Gilbert gave an entertainment to his tenants.

Robert and Janet declined the invitation. "We're over old for making merry except in our own hearts," said Janet. "But bide you, my bonnie Sir Gibbie, till we're all up yonder, and then we'll see."

The place of honor was therefore given to Jean Mavor, who was beside herself with joy to see her broonie lord of the land, and be seated beside him in respect and friendship. But her brother said it was "clean ridiculous"; and not to the last would consent to regard the new laird as other than half-witted, insisting that everything was done by his wife, and that the talk on his fingers was a mere pretense.

When the main part of the dinner was over, Sir Gilbert and his lady stood at the head of the table, and, he speaking by signs and she interpreting, made a little speech together. In the course of it Sir Gibbie took occasion to apologize for having once disturbed the peace of the countryside by acting the supposed part of a broonie, and in relating his adventures of the time, accompanied his wife's text with such graphic illustration of gesture, that his audience laughed at the merry tale till the tears ran down their cheeks. Then with a few allusions to his strange childhood, he thanked the God who led him through thorny ways into the very arms of love and peace in the cottage of Robert and Janet Grant, whence, and not from the fortune he had since inherited, came all his peace.

"He desires me to tell you," said Lady Galbraith, "that he was a stranger, and you folk of Daurside took him in, and if ever he can do a kindness to you or yours, he will. He desires me also to say, that you ought not to be left ignorant that you have a poet of your own, born and bred among you—Donal

Grant, the son of Robert and Janet—the friend of Sir Gilbert's heart, and one of the noblest of men. And he begs you to allow me to read you a poem he had from him this very morning. If any of you do not like poetry, he says—I mean Sir Gilbert says—you can go to the kitchen and light your pipes."

She ceased. Not one stirred, and she read the verses.

After the reading, Sir Gilbert and Lady Galbraith withdrew and went toward the new part of the house, where they had their rooms. On the bridge, they lingered to listen to the song of the burn and watch it. Of a lovely lucid brown, transparent as a smoke crystal, it danced under the bridge and as sweetly sang.

"Let us see it from my room, Gibbie," said Ginevra.

They went up, and from the turret window looked down upon the water. They gazed until, like the live germ of the gathered twilight, it was scarce to be distinguished but by abstract motion.

"It's my own burnie," said Ginevra, "and its own old song! I'll warrant it hasn't forgotten a note of it! Eh, Gibbie, you give me everything!"

"If I were a burnie, wouldn't I run!" sang Gibbie, and Ginevra heard the words, though Gibbie could utter only the air he had found for them so long ago.

She threw herself into his arms, and hiding her face on his shoulder, clung silent to her silent husband. Over her bowed head, he gazed into the cool spring night, sparkling with stars and shadowy with mountains. His eyes climbed the stairs of Glashgar to the lonely peak dwelling among the lights of God; and if upon their way up the rocks they met no visible sentinels of heaven, he needed neither ascending stairs nor descending angels, for a better than the angels was with them.

A SHORT GLOSSARY OF SCOTTISH WORDS

bairn——child
besom——broom
birk——birch
bleck——blacken
brae——hillside
brander——raft
broonie——brownie
bunghole——opening
burn——brook
byre——cow barn
cantrip——spell or trick
caup——shallow wooden bowl
cotter——peasant who lives in a cottage on a larger estate
crap o' the wa'——natural shelf running around the cottage
creel——wickerwork basket for fish
creepie——three-legged stool
dulse——seaweed
gey——very
girnels——meal barrel
gowan——daisy
gowany——full of daisies
gowk——simpleton

hantle——a good many
hoose——house
hum'le——hornless
kenspeckle——conspicuous
kist——chest
laird——lord
loch——lake
manse——minister's house
nowt——cattle, ox
orra——extra
rax——strain
rick——stack of grain
rush-pith-wick——kind of candle
sklet-pike——slate pencil
spurtle——stick for stirring porridge
turkis——pincers
water brose-brose——liquid over meal (cereal)